BETZ

To my loving daughter Talessa.
Love, Dad

Vicki Lea Miller

Library of Congress Control Number: 2015912709
ISBN: Hardcover   978-1-5035-9200-1
               Softcover   978-1-5035-9199-8
               eBook   978-1-5035-9198-1

Print information available on the last page.

Rev. date: 11/05/2015

Contents

Acknowledgment

Again, and as always, I want to give thanks and appreciation to my family. If not for them, I would have never done or even wanted to do any of this; I love them all. A very special thank-you goes to my sweet granddaughter, Kalea Bree. You were the first one to see this book and were always there to help me in any way that you could. To my husband Patrick, who has been with me for over twenty years of devoted companionship; together we have worked on many things in our lives, but this is an endeavor that neither of us could ever have seen coming. I love you, and I'm proud of everything we have done in our lives. You have put a lot of hard work into my books as well as coming up with and designing such beautiful book covers. I love you, and I will always love and need all my family.

I want to give a special thank-you to Sharon for being a good friend to me and for all the time and help you have given to me. Thank you so very much for everything.

Chapter 1

The first real home that I purchased for myself was nestled back in the mountains in the pristine countryside of Southern Oregon; it was so pretty with all the tall, green pine trees and bushes. I wanted to have peace and quiet; it looked like I would have that here.

I guess I need to tell you a little bit about myself. My name is Betz Larson, and I'm running from an old life of, well, let's say, pain. The pain of finding out that the man who I thought loved me did not. He was unfaithful to me and broke my heart. So I did what I needed to do: I left. Maybe that's not what everyone would have done, but that was what I felt I had to do at that time. I try not to dwell on my past because it seems to always bring back the pain I felt the day I found my boyfriend in our bed with someone else. I still have a very hard time dealing with his betrayal. Brokenhearted, I quit my nice marketing job and just got in the car and started driving. That was when I saw this pretty home nestled back in the mountains with trees everywhere. It was so wonderful here and so peaceful and that was what I need right now—peace and quiet, just me and my new little dog, Tucker. I couldn't let anything bring me down, not when I've spent so much time and money to get where I'm at now. It would be a new beginning for me, and the rest really didn't matter anyway.

The real estate lady had informed me that the people who lived in the home last had left because they thought that the place was haunted. They had told her that they kept seeing strange-looking little people walking around the area, mostly at night. She also stated that the current owners wanted to sell because they didn't want their children to be frightened. She informed me that the real estate company was obligated to disclose everything about the place to the new buyers before they could sell the home. I didn't know if I should laugh or not, so I just told the real estate lady that I didn't believe in ghosts, and the deal was made. Late one night, not long after I had moved into my new home, after working all day, I went outside to relax with my favorite crystal glass of wine. I was so exhausted that I was having a hard time staying awake; I could hardly keep my eyes open when I saw something in the bushes that looked like a small man. I sat up to get a better look, but it was gone. I just thought, "Wow, I need to stop paying so much attention to what people say or change my brand of wine."

Either way, I wasn't sure what I had seen. I went back into the house and went to bed, but sometime in the middle of the night I heard Tucker making a fuss over something. I didn't get up to check it out because I really didn't think too much of it. The dog wasn't used to the new place yet either, so I thought he was just barking to make noise. I should have been more aware of what was going on around the place because Tucker was watching a strange-looking little man just outside of my bedroom window. The dog knew he wasn't supposed to be there, but what else could he do other than bark to let me know that something was wrong? I didn't even look out of the window, and maybe that was a good thing because I would have been in danger if I had. Over the next few weeks, I thought I saw someone or something from time to time, and when I did, it was always in the middle of the night. I never got a good enough look to be able to tell what the hell it was. And I didn't really know what to feel about seeing something late at night because my mind kept telling me what I thought I saw couldn't be real. I just chalked it up to what the real estate lady had told me and my overactive imagination. Looking back on it now, I should have paid more attention to what was going on around my home because my whole life would soon change in more ways than anyone could ever imagine.

There had been a few rumors around the small town of Brookings, Oregon, that someone or something had been stealing some of the ranchers' livestock. A few of the ranchers had said that they also saw some kind of dark men on their land mostly at night, but none of them had actually seen these strange little men take any of their livestock although they did say they had seen enough to keep most of them on guard over the years. There were some strange things going on in the small town of

Brookings, to say the least. Now, it seemed that one of its newest residents was also starting to feel a little on edge in her new home.

I had a hard life growing up. My father left me and my mother when I was very young; I had to learn how to go through life without a dad around. I would have loved to have my dad around all the time like most of my friends had; I wanted my father to stay, but no one seemed to care about what I wanted. My father did what he wanted to do—he left and never looked back. He never even tried to get a hold of me through the years, and after a while you learn not to care anymore. The pain of my father walking out on both Mom and me was a very hard part of my young life to get over. As a young girl, I started to hate him for hurting Mom and me like that.

It was not easy for my mother to bring me up by herself either, but she stood her ground and did the best she could to raise a little girl on her own. She was very proud of me for going after what I wanted in life. I'm strong with a mind of my own, and I can more than handle myself and go after whatever I want in life. There was no doubt in her mind that I would go far, and whoever was lucky enough to win my heart would be a lucky man in her book. I have always had an enormous amount of respect and love for my mother for being strong enough to take care of me on my own for years. My mother had worked for years to provide me with a good home. She had put me through school so I could have the best start in life and not have to work as hard as she had to without a good education. Sometimes she had to work three jobs and long hours to make ends meet, and there was no way she was going let that happen to her little girl if she could help it. It didn't matter if she had to work four jobs to make sure I had the best start in life; that was what she would do. She did just that for as long as she could until the day the doctors told her she had cancer.

Even knowing that didn't stop her, she kept working until the day she had paid for all my education, and I was safely on my way in life. By then she was much too sick to keep going, but she didn't let me know that she was sick. No, she wanted me to do my best and thought if I was worrying about my mom that would hold me back. So she kept it to herself until almost the day she was put into the hospital, and by then there was nothing that anyone could do. I was beside myself when I watched my mom take her last breath, but at least I knew that she was no longer in pain. So I said my goodbyes and went on with the life that my mother had worked so hard to make sure I could have. I'm grown now, and my mother died years ago. It was a hard time for me, but I know that my mother was proud of her little girl and that I would be fine. I'm strong, and I can stand on my own in life, and now I have just purchased my first home in the beautiful countryside of Southern Oregon.

The property had several acres that are filled with trees, bushes, and one huge red barn that I have no idea what I'm going to do with. As I walked around the big barn, I could see that in the past someone had loved this home, especially with all the work that had gone into it.

The house was old but was built very well; it would stand the test of time.

The home had hardwood floors, high ceilings, and beautiful doors; all were still in good shape because they were made of solid wood. Most of the wood was quarter sawn oak, but there were also some pretty cherry cabinets in the kitchen, and with all the big windows, it had a lot of light coming into the house.

The floors in the large kitchen, though, were of beautiful wood that was much lighter oak than the rest of the floors in the home, so the dark cabinets made a nice contrast. All they really needed was a good sanding and then redo the stain; they will then last for many more years. This home would once again shine with all the warm woodwork.

Walking around the barn one morning, I bent down to pick up a piece of wood when I saw some footprints all around the barn. Now ordinarily that wouldn't have bothered me, but what was strange about these was that they were shoeless footprints, and there were a lot of them. Also, they were kind of small, but not as small as a child's. By now, the hair was starting to stand up on the back of my neck, and a cold chill was running up my back. I stood there looking at what might have been about twenty shoeless footprints all around the barn area. It made me feel very uneasy to think of that many people walking around my place, yet I had not seen any of them. I stood up and wanted to run to the house, but I just stood there looking at the land and up into the trees that were everywhere, but I didn't see anything. All I could see were the trees. I had bought the place because it was outside of a town with no one around; I wanted to be alone, but right now I so wished there was someone to run to. As far as the eye could see there was no one, only those trees, and right now I felt all alone. The thought made a cold chill run up and down my back as I stood there.

What have I gotten myself into with this place? Just maybe I've bitten off more than I can chew. One thing was for sure: I would pay more attention to my little dog when he tried to let me know something is going on around the place from now on. As I started walking back to the house, I had the feeling that someone was watching me; it made me almost run to the house. *And where was Tucker when I needed him anyway?* I thought to myself. I bet he was still in bed nice and warm while I was out here terrified that someone was watching me. Just then, I saw Tucker running to me as I was almost to the backdoor of the house. I was never so glad to see him in my life; inside I let out a moan as I locked the door behind me.

"Well, big guy, let's get something to eat and try to think of what we should do now that we know we are having visitors in the middle of the night. From the looks of the footprints, there are quite a few of them."

It had to be my mind playing tricks on me, I thought, and so I just pushed the thought of the footprints out of my mind over the next few days.

The home I bought has a long gravel driveway that was bordered by a three-rail white fence, with mature weeping willow trees on either side of it that ran all the way up to the house. It was a white two-story house with lots of windows that frame the wonderful yard with a big oak tree in the middle of it. That made it so peaceful out here, which was why I had purchased the place, and there was that big red barn out behind the house with more trees and bushes all over the place. It gave you the warm feel of *Yes, I'm home at last.* But now, with the newfound bare footprints around the barn, I didn't see it as the wonderful dream home I thought I was getting.

Chapter 2

I haven't always wanted to live in a place like this one. Once I had thought I would get married and have a family of my own, but somehow that just didn't work out for me. At first, I was so happy with the life I thought I was going to have, until the day it all came to an end.

The man I was going to marry was never happy with just one woman; I had come home early from work one day and was going to surprise him with a nice meal when he got home. But I was the one to get the surprise because I found him in our bed with another woman.

That was pretty much one of the worst days of my life to say the least and when he tried to explain it to me, well, let's just say I didn't want to hear it. I left that day and never wanted to go back to that way of life or back to a man that couldn't stay faithful to me. No, now I would make this life work for me; I would take care of myself and my dog Tucker. But even as I thought of it, I could feel the pain cut deep into my heart.

I was not going to go through life with the wrong man, which is why I was here in this beautiful place. It has taken a long time for me to get over this, so I was looking forward to making a new life and stop thinking of the old one. But my heart was still hurting and would be for a long time, no matter what I did.

This was home now, and with some work, it would be beautiful again. Now if I could find the handyman I hired to get things working in the house, I'll be happy. Well, that and some food would be nice right now. Tucker started barking as I started for the door of the house to find food for both of us. I had stopped in town and picked up a few days of food for us until I could get back to the store in town again.

Just as I was about to walk into the door, it opened, and there stood the biggest man that I have ever seen. At first I just stood there without saying anything, and when I found my voice I didn't know what to say. He had bright blue eyes, dark hair, and he had a body like someone who worked out in a gym every spare minute he could find.

"Oh, hi, you must be Betty Larson," he said with a big smile on his handsome face. "I'm Jake Loomis. I was just about to leave you a note to let you know that everything is working for you. All you need to do is have the phone turned on, and you'll be all set."

Jake looked like he had something else on his mind as I watched him move from one foot to the other in an uncomfortable way. "I found some food on the counter, so I put the meat and the milk in the refrigerator for you.

I hope you don't mind, I didn't want it to go bad on you. I wasn't sure when you would get here."

"Thank you for taking the time to do that for me, and its Betz, not Betty. It was a joke from dear old Dad. It seems he liked to gamble, and from what my mother has told me he was pretty good at it. From what I've been told, I guess he thought that by giving me the name Betz it would bring him good luck. Anyway, thank you for coming out here so fast and getting everything ready for me."

As Jake stood there looking at her, all he could think of was with her by his side he didn't think he would ever need any other luck in his life. She was beautiful. She was tall and had long dark hair and a body that was made to make every man want her, and he would love to have a very long night with her in his arms.

Why is it that I always bring up that part of me to everyone I talk to? I wondered as I stood there with someone I have never met before. *I really need to work on my bad habit of telling everyone my life story,* I thought to myself.

"Sure thing," he replied. "Well, I guess I better let you have a look around and make yourself at home. You must be tired after the long drive."

"Yes, I am, but there is way too much to do right now to rest. But thanks again, for everything."

Jake kept thinking stop staring at her, but it was hard. She had long black hair, cat-green eyes, and full red lips, with sun-kissed skin. She was tall, slender. All one hundred fourteen pounds of her would have any man's mouthwatering as she walked by; she was just stunning. He had seen beautiful girls before, but there was something about this one that had him taking a very long wishful look. He just let out a very low moan as he walked away, and kept thinking wow . . .

After Jake had left, I thought I would wait outside for the movers; it was a lovely day, and I was still trying to get a feel for the place. Tucker was busy eating his food. I was one to always have one very large bowl of food set out for Tucker in case I ever had to go somewhere and had to leave him for a few days. He had enough food to last for a long time. It made me feel better just knowing he would be all right and of course he had the biggest self-feeding water bottle I could find as well, so he was always set no matter what. But right now he just wanted to eat dog treats as he sat by me while I had a peanut butter and jelly sandwich. I was here in Oregon on my own land waiting for movers to bring the rest of my things so I could start my new life.

It was a wonderful day full of hope for a bright future, and I was feeling good about my new life here. Just as I was walking into the house, I heard the truck coming up the road; it was time to get back to work. The house was very large and had the most beautiful kitchen with oversized windows to look out at all the lovely trees. There was a big barn with a small pasture to the side of it with a three rail-white fence around it. Most of the paint had worn off so I knew I would be painting soon.

I thought about all the things I had wanted to get done around the place right away. But after finding the footprints by the barn, I didn't really want to do a lot of work by the barn anytime soon. No, for now I would keep my work inside the home and front yard in the daytime. I had a lot of things to do over the next few weeks.

Time went by pretty fast because I had so much to do and no one to help me. I never asked anyone to give me a hand with any part of the move. That was how I wanted it: just me and my best friend Tucker, my little dog with a very big attitude. Tucker may not be very large, and he didn't even have a tail, but he thought he was as big as a Great Dane with an attitude even bigger than that. But he was always there for me, and no one else had been in a very long time.

He was a small schnauzer mix. When I found him in a pet store, he was the only puppy in the pen that didn't seem to care if he had to walk over all the other dogs to get to me. He was going home with me, and so he did.

He was so cute: black and white with a little pink tongue that was very busy licking my face all the way home.

He has pretty much been my only friend ever since that day; I wouldn't let anyone else into my heart, at least not right now. It would take me a while longer to get over the hurt of the last love in my life. Tucker had to make up for other males that only seemed to hurt me, and that was a pretty big job for one small dog to get done. But there was one thing for sure: no one would ever love me more than that little dog.

The living room of my new home was big with a nice corner fireplace for those nights when all I wanted to do was read a good book with my evening glass of wine and Tucker by my side, with a bag of dog treats to spoil him with, of course.

It was always late when I finally got to bed at night, and when I did Tucker was always by my side. He was always there when I woke up in the morning with his little pink tongue licking my face. He has been my best friend, and he was someone who I knew really loved me. In the middle of the night, sometimes he would start growling at something. I didn't let him go outside at night after finding the footprints because I was always afraid he would get hurt.

"Okay, big guy, I hear you, but I can't see anything out there. I'm not known as the brave one, so whatever it is, I'm sure it will wait until morning. Anyway, I really feel the need to have my big boy snuggled up tight next to me," I said as I gave the other side of the bed a pat. With one jump, Tucker was by my side for the night. If someone had told me I would be living here in a large home, with land in Oregon, I would have had a big laugh and told them that they were nuts. But I was here, and now it was time to start over, find new things to keep my mind off the bad things that brought me here in the first place. But that was a lot easier said than done.

As the days went by, I was starting to get used to the place. I was happy with my choice. It was a calm place to live, and that was all I ever really wanted: to have a nice home someplace where I can rest when I was there. There didn't seem to be any more new footprints around the place, so I thought maybe I was making too much of the whole thing. After all, they could have been there for a long time, and anyway, why in the world would anyone be here on my land, watching me? It was silly to think about that in the first place. But still in the back of my mind, I couldn't shake the feeling that someone was watching me all the time now no matter how hard I tried to explain it away. The days went by fast, and before I was ready for it, winter was at hand, but it was not a hard winter like I had seen in other places.

Chapter 3

When I was growing up, I saw a lot of snow. I have a few wonderful memories of playing with my father in it and making snowmen with Dad. But that was before my father left both me and my mother, for whatever he thought was better than his wife and little girl.

I never did understand it, and my mother really never did try to talk to me about him, only to say he was gone one day. Now it was just the two of us. I cried a lot back then because I loved my father and missed him. I prayed every night that he would come back home to us. But he never did, and after I got through school, I really didn't care if I ever saw him again. He was just another man who had hurt me, which seemed to be the only kind I know right now. That was why I hated to think of the past because the hurt runs deep.

Here in my new place, the winter was mild: no snow and not cold. There was just a lot of rain, but that seemed to be kind of comforting to me, and it was a nice change for me.

By the time I was finished getting the house and yard done, winter was almost over. I had pretty much put the footprints out of my mind now and had gotten over the feeling that I was being watched. I was happy in my new home and hated the thought of going out to find a job, but that was on my mind pretty much most days now as money was not unlimited. I would need to do something soon even if it was just a nine-to-five at a store in town, but I was hoping to do a little better than that. I had thought about doing some writing, but this didn't seem to be the time for that, and anyway I wasn't sure what I wanted to write about right now. Other than maybe cheating boyfriends, with a small smile starting at the corner of my mouth, I thought, *Okay back to earth*. I knew I would have to come up with something to do, or I would need money soon. It was about time to get a job again; I used to be pretty good in sales, but that seemed to be so long ago, even though in reality it was only a few months ago. But maybe I could find something like that when I go looking for a job.

There were days when I would think of my past. Whenever I did, it would bring back the day that I met Matt. He was very cute and had one of those smiles that made you like him right away. It started off as friends, and it just happened one day. I'm not really sure who made the first move, but it didn't matter. We fell in love, and after a few months, we moved into a pretty place downtown, so we could walk everywhere together.

It was so good at first. I loved coming home to him and fixing meals for him and the lovemaking was great too. But it all came to an end the day I wanted to surprise him with an early dinner and found him with someone else.

I ran out of the apartment and never looked back. One of my friends at work went and got all my things for me, and then I quit my job. Luckily I had some money saved, and that was when I found this place. I was driving, saw it, and bought it; just like that, I was a homeowner in, of all places, Southern Oregon.

I would go into town in a few days and start looking for work. I was exhausted and didn't want to do anything else for the night. All I wanted was to take a few minutes to rest and not think of anything other than what to fix the dog and myself to eat tonight. I went outside just as it was getting dark and sat on my new lawn chair in my front yard with a nice warm throw over my lap. Tucker was already in bed, waiting for me to snuggle up next to him. As tired as I was, the thought of a nice glass of wine won out, so I went outside to rest and have my nightly glass of wine before going to bed. I was feeling good with my wine and not really thinking of anything when I heard something over by one of the rosebushes. As I looked over there, I thought I saw something running across the yard. It looked like a small man; he was dark and had some kind of what looked like fur on. But that couldn't be right—who would have something like that on these days, and what would someone be doing here in my yard? *Okay, you have got to stop doing this to yourself,* I thought. *This is silly, so stop with the thinking that there are people way out here in your yard in the middle of the night with fur on.* What the hell was wrong with my mind? I closed my eyes tightly as if to block out the very thought that I was starting to lose my mind. It had to be the wine I was drinking, playing mind games on me, but the old feelings of fear and the cold chills were starting to crawl up my back once again. I was starting to feel faint and closed my eyes for a few minutes, but it was for more than just a few minutes because I did see someone. But because I was tired and had too much wine, I passed out. As I did, I thought I heard Tucker growling over something, but it seemed to be so far away from me, and I was pretty much out of it by that time.

Chapter 4

When I opened my eyes, I felt so dizzy and couldn't see very well, but I was not in my yard anymore. I was in a dark place. It looked like a cave of some kind, and I was held down by a strange-looking rope. I didn't understand why or who would do this to me. I also had an awful headache. *This has to be a very bad dream*, I thought as I fell in and out of consciousness.

"Where am I? And what do you want from me?" I yelled out as loudly as I could, but no one was there to hear me.

Before I could get an answer from anyone, I passed out again. The next time I woke up, I was in a big bed; it was warm, and as hard as I tried, I couldn't stay awake for very long. I didn't understand what was going on with me; it was not like me to sleep so long like this.

But as I drifted off this time, I thought I heard someone talking, but it seemed to be so far away, almost like it was coming from a tunnel. *What a crazy dream*, I thought, as

I drifted off to sleep again. At least I felt warm in the big bed. I smiled to myself; it was just a dream.

Kyle was talking to his father about why they had to bring this woman here when he didn't really think she saw any of them in the trees.

"We should have left her there! Why do we have her here? What are we going to do with her?" Kyle's father was the clan lord in their world, and this world was a secret from the rest of the world. No one was sure how the clan got started, but it had been here for many years now. The clan was pretty large in size: there were about fifty of them now, and the clan was still growing every year with the birth of new babies. Kyle himself had asked his father once as a child where they came from. His father only told him that he really didn't know, only that, a long time ago, there was a man from the upper world that had found the clan, and the clan had made him one of them. He went on to say that he was very wise and showed them how to do things that made their life here better.

"How come we go to the upper world sometimes and get things to bring back here, and who are the strange-looking ones there?"

"We call them upper world people, and they don't know who we are or that we even live here. We have to keep it that way so that all of us stay safe in our world, son. Do you understand?" Kyle nodded that he did, but really he never did understand any of it.

Orlando brought Kyle out of his thoughts as he brought him back to what was going on today in the clan as he said.

"I never thought she saw any of us either, but some of the men did, and so they acted in the only way they thought they could. So that's why she's here."

"Son, I really think you hurt her. I tried to tell you to go easy, but you never seem to hear me anymore," Orlando stated.

"I tried to tell you that you hit her too hard, didn't I?" Orlando asked.

"Okay, so I might have. I never meant to hit her that hard, but the men were going after her, and they would have hurt her a lot more than I did. I had to get to her before they did—who knows how bad it would have been if I let them get to her first. I'm sure she'll be all right."

"I hope you're right. I'm not so sure of that right now. She seems to be pretty much out of it if you ask me. But you're right about the men they might have gone so far as to kill her if not for you getting to her first."

"It was never my intention to hurt her, and I hope she'll be all right. But don't blame me for what happens when she does wake up. Cal is already making trouble with the rest of the clan. He doesn't want this woman here, and you know as well as I do he will get the whole clan worked up into a fighting mode before the night is over with. Right now, he has a real reason to get them going. The clan will get worked up over this woman being here and want to kill her because she's not of the clan. So please tell me, what are we going to do to keep her safe from the rest of the clan?"

"I'm not sure what to do, but I'll take care of it. And yes, I know that Cal is a real ass. He has a real reason for it now with her here, but I'm the clan lord here, and they will do what I say over whatever he has to say." But even as he said it, he knew that the clan was ready to listen to whatever Cal had to say with this woman here now.

Orlando knew it would take a lot of explaining to get the clan to settle down. But he was sure they would when he was done explaining to all of them that this woman was not a threat to their way of life. And he would also let Cal know he was on very shaky ground. He really needed to stop stirring up shit over every little thing to get the whole clan upset all the time. The last thing Orlando needed was his whole clan in a killing mood over this young woman when she didn't do anything to any one of them to deserve to be put to death.

Cal had better stop stirring up shit if he wanted to stay in this clan; he had better live by the rules of the clan lord, and that was Orlando. It was always hard to stop Cal from getting the whole clan going, and usually it was over nothing. That never seemed to matter to him; just as long as he was the center of attention he was happy. Orlando didn't have a problem with anyone else in the clan but Cal, and he really didn't like Cal at all. But he was still one of the clan, so he had put up with a lot of his shit for years now. He knew that one day he would push him too far, and Orlando would beat the shit out of him. Maybe that was what the guy really needed.

Kyle was a big man; he was good-looking with dark hair, deep green eyes, and he was also tall with a hard body like someone who lifted weights. But life was hard here, and hunting and hauling game back to the caves to get the clan through the winter was much better than any weights as far as keeping someone in good shape. And everyone here had to walk or run for miles to get to where they wanted to be. So it was a good workout every time they went on a hunting trip for the clan and carried game back to the clan's cave.

Kyle had a very big heart, and he didn't like to see this woman hurt like this. There was something about her that he liked a lot, even though he had no idea why. He was sorry that he was the one who had hurt her; he didn't mean to hit her that hard. He wasn't sure if she did see the clan the night that they brought her back here to the caves. But no one was sure that she hadn't either; maybe all of them had overreacted. It was too late to do anything now but wait and hope she would be all right.

She was so small and had a pretty face. He ran his trembling hand slowly over her face just to feel the touch of her skin; it was warm and soft, and it made him feel better. Just to know that she was still breathing, he had to believe she would be all right. He knew that he was starting to have the wrong feelings for this strange woman. He also knew that he had to stop these feelings right now because this was forbidden here; no one could mate with an outsider, it was a rule that could not be broken in this clan. But rule or not, he had to be close to her, and when she was asleep like this, he just wanted to watch her and take care of her. He had been brushing her dark hair away from her pretty face with his hand when his father came into the cave and saw him.

"What do you think you're doing, son? You know that we should not touch her. She is not like us, she is from the other world, and we can't be a part of it. That is one rule we cannot break here, so don't do something that you will regret. And I won't be able to fix either, son. Don't think that because I'm the clan lord here that I can change the rules. Even I can't stop the clan from banishing you from here if you try to be with this woman. You'll be an outcast."

"I know, Father. I'm just so taken by her, she seems so still lying there, and I just wanted to touch her face to make sure she was all right, that's all. I feel responsible for her, I'm the one who hit her, and now she can't seem to wake up because of me, so it's not easy for me to see her like this. I just feel that I have to take care of her and make sure she's going to be all right. Can't you see that?" Kyle put his face in his big hands as he bent his head down and closed his eyes so his father wouldn't see just how much she already meant to him.

As the days went by, Kyle could not stop thinking of her, and he knew that it was not a good thing for him to do. She was not of his world, and nothing good could ever come of his feelings for an upper world woman. But he could not stop thinking of her. What was he doing falling for an upper world woman when he knew the clan would not let him be with her? They might even kill her if he was ever to try to be with her, and he could be killed as well. It didn't matter that his father was the lord of the clan. But he had no idea how to stop thinking of her; he was pretty sure that his feelings for this woman would keep growing, and he could not be with her. But that didn't stop him from wanting her.

It was a full day before I came to again, and this time I was so dizzy that I was not sure if I could stand up or not. But I was going to try anyway. As I put my feet on the floor, I could feel dirt under them so I now knew I was not on a floor—I was on sand. It was hard to stay on my feet because I was still very unsteady. But I was strong and wanted to find out what was going on. Why I was here in a dark room of some kind? The room was like a cave; the walls were also dirt. I felt like I was dreaming or in some kind of a terrible nightmare.

Why was I here? None of it made any sense to me; the last thing I remembered was sitting on my chair in my front yard. Now I was in this dark room that looked like some kind of cave; I wanted to scream until someone woke me up. If only I were asleep . . .

The room was large and had what to me looked like cutouts for holding things. I could see there was a small bowl or what kind of looked like a bowl, in one of the cutouts made in the wall. As I walked around the room, I knew it was too soon to be up. I could feel it getting darker in the room as I tried to stay on my feet.

It wasn't working, I was going to pass out, I wanted to cry out, but I didn't think I could. I went down hard and was out like a light again, but this time I felt the strong arms of someone carrying me to the bed again.

I felt safe in these arms, and I wanted to stay in them, but I couldn't stay awake. I was in a dark place now and was not sure if I could wake up again, it was so dark here, and I didn't know how to get back.

Kyle had just come into the room when he saw the woman start to fall, and he caught her in his arms before she hit the floor. She was so small and so very pretty he could feel his manhood start to wake up just from holding her like this. He already wanted her much more than he had ever wanted a woman. He knew better than to let anyone know how he felt, but still he knew it was wrong—and what was he going to do about it. He put her on the bed and was starting to tremble from wanting her so much he needed to get away from her. *What the hell is wrong with me?* he thought, as he put the cover on her and left the room. *I need to get a handle on this, or I'm in big trouble!* Her life would be in danger as well, but he didn't know how to stop wanting her. And want her he did, with everything that was in him; good or bad he needed her.

I had been asleep for days now. I was dreaming of my life in my new home with my dog. I was working in the big yard putting in flowers and starting a new garden in the big field by the barn. It was a hot day, and Tucker was playing by my side as I dug in the dirt to plant the lovely flowers. It wasn't real, but it made me feel good, so I wanted to stay here. I didn't want to deal with the real world. With caves and no way out, I slept instead of waking up to a world I know nothing about. A world I was afraid of—a world where I had no control over my own life.

Orlando told his son, "Kyle you need to rest now. I'll sit with her. You've been up for days now, and you need to eat and get some rest. There's nothing else you can do here right now. It won't do you any good to stay here with her. She might not wake up for a long time, so go get some food and get some sleep. Later I'll have Little One watch over her, and I'll let you know if she wakes up."

Orlando was upset to see his only son starting to have feelings for this upper world woman. He had so many plans for him. But he knew in his heart it was too late; it wouldn't be long, and he would have to let go of him. He would still fight to try and keep him here where he was raised, where he was needed. Even as he thought it, he knew it was already too late. The upper world woman already had his son's heart in her hands without even knowing it.

"Father, I feel so bad she might not wake up again, and it's my fault. I had no idea that I hit her so hard. I guess I don't know my own strength, and now this woman is paying for it." Kyle was tall for an underworld man, but not for someone from the upper world. He was over six feet tall, and no one else here in the underworld was anywhere near that tall. It gave him the feel of a leader, and that was what his father wanted for him someday. He had been shaping him all his life so that Kyle would stand by his father. They could lead the clan until the day his father gave up his rights, and then Kyle would be the new lord of this clan.

The underworld men were dark and all of them had dark eyes—everyone except Kyle, who had dark green eyes; it was like looking at a pond with moss under the water. Kyle had always thought maybe he had eyes like his mother, but his father never talked about her, and as the years went by it didn't seem to matter anymore. Someday he might bring up his mother, but right now wasn't the right time.

Kyle was a good son and would someday be the lord of the underworld. He still hadn't found a mate, but he would in time. It was up to his father to make sure he didn't try to pick the upper world woman. Orlando was the clan lord now, and it was his duty to make sure the bloodlines would stay clean, and that meant he could not mate with an upper world woman.

There was never a time that he could think of that any of the men had ever wanted to mate with an upper world woman. But there was a time when Orlando himself wanted to leave the clan and try to live in the upper world because he could see the women there were beautiful. He would go on the hunt with some of the men to get things that they needed here like some of their tools and sometimes a cow or pig. Once they had brought back some chickens. So now they had eggs that they would not have had if not for carrying a few chickens from the upper world, as well as other things to work with here to make their life a little better. The girls there had beautiful faces and had on pretty things that made them look so different than the girls here. Orlando was young and like any young man wanted to taste the forbidden fruit, so to speak.

But he knew he couldn't have anything to do with any of them or he would be put to death or would have to leave the clan. He could not do that; this was who he was, and he would stay. Now he was a father, and it didn't make it any easier to see his own son want the same things that almost took everything away from him all those years ago. He knew firsthand how hard it was not to take one of the pretty girls to mate with. But if he had done that, he wouldn't have the son he has today.

Orlando had told his son that his mother had died when Kyle was very young; she was a lovely woman and the only underworld girl he had ever seen with those pretty green eyes. Orlando had fallen hard for her and never really got over her; he never took another woman as a mate. There was never anyone who came close to her for him, so he just never tried to mate again. No, he would die with only one love in his life even if she had not been here with him for years now.

And now his son had the same eyes as his mother; sometimes it was like looking at her, and it made it hard on him because he missed her to this day. But it felt good to know he still had a lot of her in his son. Someday he would have to talk to his son about his mother because of the way she had left him. He knew that there were times when Kyle wanted to ask about her, but he had always changed the subject, so he didn't have to go there with him. The truth was that she just left him one day and never came back, and to this day he had no idea where she was, or if she was really dead. Orlando had to be both mom and dad to Kyle, and sometimes it was hard to be both. This way of life was hard for a young man to grow up in, and some of the young boys never made it to adulthood. This world was for the fit only. Mean as that may sound, it was the way of this life; the weak just don't hold up under the hard conditions of life here.

Orlando could see that his son had feelings for this woman; it made him feel sad to see this as it could not work. But how was he going to stop him when he had feelings for her already? Why would he pick this woman when he knew it was forbidden to be with an upper world woman in this clan?

The women of the underworld were not as nice to look at as the upper world woman was, but they were pure blood, and it had to stay that way. In his heart he knew that was not going to happen; he just wished he could somehow keep his son safe from the pain that was coming his way.

Somehow, as the clan lord, he would have to give up the only son he had, and that pain was already cutting deep.

No one knew what would happen if they tried to mix with an unclean. Oh, Orlando knew that a woman was a woman no matter what world she came from, but the rest of the clan didn't feel the same way about it as he did. It was up to the lord of the clan to make sure no one ever took an outsider to mate with. That was a rule that had been here for as long as anyone could remember, and it had to stay that way no matter what.

But as a father it was one of the hardest jobs he would ever have, he could see that his son had deep feelings for this woman. But he could not let him be with her.

It had been a few days now, and the woman was starting to eat and ask where she was. Kyle had been the one to take care of the upper world woman because he felt like he was the one to hurt her, and so he had to be the one to make sure she was all right. But he didn't know how to tell her that she was never going to be able to go back home. She didn't understand why she was brought here in the first place. It was hard trying to get her to understand why they had brought her here from her home, but in time she knew all too well what that meant. Kyle was getting to know the upper world woman as the days went by. He found her to be very smart as well as pretty; he liked talking to her about how this life worked, and she seemed to like talking to him as well. They seemed to hit it off right away, and that was not a good thing for either one of them. He didn't care—he needed to know all there was to know about this woman.

It was time to hold a meeting with the rest of the clan and decide what to do with the woman. If only the men hadn't taken her. After all, he didn't think she knew what she saw anyway, and she had told Kyle that when they talked about why she was brought here. But the clan had the right to keep their world safe if they thought there was someone who could bring harm to their way of life.

It was time to make her one of their clan or she would be put to death.

If they made her one of them, she could never have a man. She would have to be just one of the workers, maybe a caretaker of the old ones or the little ones, when they went out on the food hunts.

Either way, it would not be the life she was used to in the upper world, and it would take a long time to trust her in their world. Kyle had to tell this wonderful woman that she could never have a life here in his world. What could he say to make her want to stay? If only he could tell her how he really felt about her. That he wanted to have a life with her, but he knew that he could never tell her how he felt, and that was killing him, to say the least. She was always on his mind even in his sleep. She already had his heart even if he could never tell her so.

Orlando was the first one to stand and ask the clan what they wanted to do with the woman that they had brought back to the caves.

"I know that some of you are afraid of this woman. But I don't think she is a threat to our way of life. She does not know how she got here and has not tried to harm anyone so far, so I vote that we make her part of the clan." Orlando sat back down to see who else would stand up to have a say in the order; as always it was Cal. He was a mean older man who always tried to make trouble with everything that went on in the clan. When he stood up, Orlando was pretty sure he would say to have the woman put to death.

"I think the woman is a real threat to all of us, and we have to protect our way of life, and if anyone or anything can do harm to our life here, we have to be strong. I say, have the upper world woman put to death as she can and will do harm to all of us if we let her live here in our world. It has always been only underworld people, and it should stay that way if we want to keep our way of life here." With that said, Cal stood there with that evil little smile on his face that Orlando so hated.

Orlando thought he was an old windbag, but he had a point of view, so he would have to let him speak even if he wanted to tell him to shut up and sit back down.

Kyle stood up to speak, and everyone watched as Cal gave him a dirty look. Kyle wasn't going to let Cal have the upper hand in anything if he could help it. He was a snake, and everyone in the clan knew it. But he had the right to speak his mind.

"Well, since when do we just kill without a reason?" Kyle asked. "I've spent time with this upper world woman. I can tell you as I'm sure my father can also tell all of you, this woman is no threat to any one of us and in no way a threat to our way of life here. She didn't ask for this. We put her here, and now we need to give her a chance to live here with us and try to fit into our way of life here. We owe it to her after what we did to her.

"I know that many of you are afraid of her, but I think if you take the time to be around her, you too will see she is not a threat to us. I move that we give her a chance to fit in with our way of life here for a few weeks before we do anything else. Then hold a meeting again to decide what to do. Let me also say that while it's been many years ago since we have had someone from the upper world come here, we did have an upper world man come here. He not only fit into our world, but he also gave us the ability to speak as we do today. He also helped us to live a better life here when he showed us how to do many of the things that we do today. He taught us how to hunt better with some of the tools from his world, as well as many other things, so we could have a better life here. We all know this to be true.

"Until he came to the clan, we had no idea how to make a bow and arrow to hunt with or how to cook our meat underground like we do today. So yes, the upper world can help us, as we know when we go to the upper world to get things like tools to use to make life better for all of us."

The clan was all talking to one another as Kyle sat back down. Kyle had done all that he could to save the woman from being killed; now he had to wait and hope it was enough.

I was not sure what the hell this place was, but I knew that I was underground in some kind of cave. It was so dark, and for light there was just a torch of some kind. It was hard to tell if it was daylight or dark outside because I didn't see any windows anywhere, so I had no way to tell.

And I also had no idea how long I had been here either, and that was not a good feeling. I wanted to yell out to someone to help me wake up because I had to be in a dream and couldn't wake up. This couldn't be real; it was a bad dream—it had to be.

But it wasn't a dream; it was real, and I was living in it. I wished I could do something to feel like I still had a will of my own. What could I do when I was in some kind of a cave, and there were only these strange-looking little people here, and no one to help me get back to my life?

I had never seen anything like it before. The bed that I had been sleeping on looked like a hollowed-out tree; I thought it looked like it came from a caveman movie. I had never seen anything anywhere like this. All the bedding was strange too. Not like the bedding that I was used to in my life because it was all made from animal furs, again not what you buy in stores to use as bedding, or at least not for me.

The man who had been bringing me the food was the one who had put me back into the bed when I had passed out again. Even though I didn't really see him, I knew that it was him.

At least I was pretty sure it was the same man. He was so gentle with me and had been here with me every day so far to try and help me adjust to my new life here with his clan.

He had told me that I could never go back to my own world again because no one could ever know of this place.

If I didn't want to stay, I would be put to death. I had little choice—either live here or die. I was having a hard time understanding why these people wanted to kill me because I wanted to go home. I had no idea what to say to the man who was here most of the time to get him to see that I really needed to go home. I had a life there and a dog to take care of, and anyway, I wouldn't tell anyone about this place, and if I ever did, no one would believe me anyway.

At the meeting, the clan had mixed feelings about what to do with the woman; no one could come to an agreement as to what to do with her at that moment.

So they voted just to watch her for now, to make sure that she didn't try to leave the underworld, and if she did, she was to be put to death.

That did not sit well with Kyle because he wanted to give her some time to get used to living down here in their world. He told them that he was sure that she would fit in after she had some time to get used to their way of life here.

"No, we can't just let her run around here and upset everyone. Almost everyone here is afraid of her. They think that she's a demon and that she will bring bad luck to the clan if we let her stay," Cal said with a hard look on his face.

He was a small, dark, angry man, and Kyle knew very well he was a hard man to get to know.

It was very unlikely he would ever give in to the thought of an upper world woman staying with the clan. You could see the look of hate on his face every time someone said anything about the woman.

But for now, he had to live with what the rest of the clan voted for, and that was for her to be allowed to stay for now.

Chapter 5

It was time for the food run, and all the men were ready to go out for the hunt. Before the clan had brought this woman here, this was a time that had always been fun for Kyle. Not right now—he was worried that someone from the clan might hurt the woman while he was out on the hunt. It was not an easy thing for him to go with the rest of the clan this time. Everyone always looked up to him on these runs, so he had to go.

Kyle had a big knot in his stomach as he tried to get ready to leave this time, but he had to keep up his part of the kill. Or he would never be able to hold the clan together when it was his turn to lead. Kyle was very strong and the best hunter that the clan had; he made most of the kills. He could carry the most game from the kills of all the men in the clan, so everyone wanted him with them when they needed to bring the kills back to the caves. Little One came up to Kyle before he went on the hunt and told him she would stay with the upper world woman until he got back so she would be safe. She could see the relief on his face as he thanked her and left the caves for the hunt.

After the hunt, Kyle went to check in on the woman and found her asleep again, and it was starting to worry him, he wasn't sure what to do to help her. He was pretty sure if she didn't wake up soon, she would die. Kyle said thanks to Little One and told her she could go back to her own work.

"I really don't mind staying with her if you need me to."

"No, you've done enough for me for now, and I don't want Cal telling the rest of the clan that the woman is already upsetting the clan's work."

Kyle knew it was not good for this woman to sleep so much, but he thought maybe it was what she needed to do to deal with this new way of life. Kyle had to do something, but what could he do that the clan wouldn't stop? Every time Cal had a chance to stir the pot, so to speak, he would. That was what he loved to do: start the clan fighting over anything that he could find. The upper world woman was the perfect way to get things going; it made him happy just to think he could stir up another mess within the clan.

If Kyle had his way, he would let her go back home and live her life as before, but the clan thought she would tell everyone about the world that they lived in. And Cal was pushing them to keep thinking like that.

Kyle didn't think she would ever do that, and he wanted so much to help her. As he sat there, she started to wake up; and when she saw that it was Kyle, she smiled at him and asked where he had been.

"I had to go on a food hunt with the other men of the clan," he told her.

"I'm glad you're back, I missed you being here when I wake up. It's nice to see your face when I open my eyes. It feels good knowing that you're with me. I do hope you had good luck with your hunt and that you brought enough food back for the clan."

Kyle had to smile at her because she really did care about his people. He knew she had a good heart.

"Yes, we found food enough for now, so we'll be all right."

"Good, I'm glad," she replied. "Kyle, is there any way that the clan will ever let me go back home? I miss my dog, and I have a life there! Please just let me go home."

He sat there shaking his head, and I knew this was upsetting for him as much as it was for me.

"I hate to keep you here, but the rest of the clan still thinks that you're a threat to our way of life. If we let you go back to the upper world, people would soon come and bring our world to an end."

"But I would never tell anyone that this place is here and even if I did no one would ever believe me. What can I do to make them see that? I would never do anything to harm anyone here. Why would I do that? Please, you have to help me make them see that I'm not a threat to them."

Kyle sat there with his head down and said, "Don't you think I've tried to tell them that you're not a threat to us already? They just won't let you go. I've tried to help you. I know that you're not a threat to us, but I don't' know how to get them to see that. I know that you need to go back home to your own life even though I'd miss you."

"Kyle, I'll come back to see you and help your people any way that I can. I would never hurt any of them. I have no reason to do that, so why would I? . . . I just don't belong here, and I miss my dog and my life."

Kyle told me he would try to talk to the lord of the clan to make a plea to the clan again. But even as he told me that he didn't think it would do any good.

But he was a man of his word, and he found his father and they both went to the clan and set up a meeting for the next day. The meeting went pretty much as Kyle had thought it would with everyone still affirming that the woman had to either stay or be killed. As it was the way of the clan, and that was what had worked for as far back as anyone could remember, so why should they change it now?

Kyle would not let them kill me. Although there was only so much he could do and letting me go was not one of them.

After the meeting, Kyle's father said, "I tried to tell you that the clan would never let her go. That's not our way of doing things here, and you know it."

"Yes, I know it, but I had to try for her. I told her I would do what I could for her."

I was crying when Kyle told me they would not let me go back to my old life.

"Well, can someone at least get my dog for me?"

Kyle thought that was something he could do for me if that was what I wanted, but he had a hard time understanding it because dogs were only food in his world, never pets. But he would give that to me and let everyone in the clan know that the dog was not to be eaten.

Kyle could tell that this was something that I very much wanted. It was late when Kyle got back with the dog. It was not a fun job; the dog had not been willing just to go with him. He had to put the dog in a bag after he knocked it out so it wouldn't bark all the way back to the underworld. It was a nasty biting little dog, and he would have killed it if not for his promise to the upper world woman that he would get the dog for her. The dog had fought him and got in a few good bites before he put the dog into the bag and started home with it in hand.

But it was worth it when he saw the light in my eyes when he gave the dog to me, and the dog seemed to be just as happy to see me.

"Thank you so much for this."

The dog was licking my face, and I was crying and then I pulled Kyle to me and gave him a kiss that said just how much this meant to me. He was caught off guard when I did this and didn't know what to say or do.

He had never felt a kiss like that in his life; it made him want this woman even more.

The dog was a little thing, and it didn't even have a tail as far as he could see, but it sure did make me happy. Kyle had never seen anyone with a dog like this before; he just stood there watching me and the dog for a long time.

All the other dogs that the clan had killed were much bigger than this one, so maybe they wouldn't even want to eat this dog because there wasn't much to eat that he could see. But the woman sure did love that dog. It seemed he loved her just as much; Kyle was pretty much amazed by me and the dog. I called the dog Tucker and said that he was my "Big Boy." There was nothing big about this dog. He was very little. That made him wonder what was so great about this dog that made me act so silly with him. He didn't think he would ever understand me. But he was fascinated by me and the dog.

It was so odd to see the two of them; the dog didn't even seem to dislike Kyle anymore, and he had a hard time with the dog when he found it. All was forgiven as far as the dog was concerned; he was so happy to be with me.

"I thought you might like to see the rest of the living spaces and get to know how things work here because you'll be living here with all of us now." Kyle waited for me to say something, while I was hugging the dog.

He had to ask me again, but this time I glanced up at him and said, "I think I should see the living spaces. When would you want me to come with you? And if it's all right, I'd like to bring my dog."

"Well, let's plan for tomorrow. It's late now and time to eat, and I need to talk to the clan lord about my plan so I'll see you tomorrow." And with that, Kyle left me to hug my dog and get some rest. He had to shake his head as he walked out of my room; it was so strange to watch me with that dog.

The next day was not so easy for the clan. They all kept coming up to me and touching me because they had never seen anyone with such light skin. I had green eyes like Kyle, so that made them all wonder about this upper world woman. Was I more like them than any of them thought?

I was not sure what to expect when I said I would go with Kyle to see the living spaces, but this was not what I thought it would be. The area was so big and the clan was looking at me as if I had two heads or something; it had me on guard for most of the day. But I did love the walk around the caves.

All the living spaces are in one big cave with small rooms for sleeping in and one big room where everyone sat around a big fire pit to talk and eat. In one part of the big room there was a place to fix the food; it had stone slabs to make the food on with stone and wood bowls to put the food into. It was like an old caveman movie of long ago; it was hard to believe that this was real—but it is.

I smiled when I saw how primitive they are. There are a lot of men, but I didn't see very many women and all of them are small. Kyle was much bigger than all the other men. There was one man who was looking at me with such hate on his face that it made me uneasy.

I was right because Cal hated having this upper world woman here in his space, I had no right, and he wanted to kill me himself even though I was the most beautiful woman he had ever laid eyes on in his life. And he was always looking for the prettiest ones.

All the rest of them seemed to be fascinated with me. I was right: Cal was not happy with Kyle bringing this upper world woman into the main cave. It was not right. I was not a pure blood and should not be here. If he had his way, I would be put to death, along with my dog that I was carrying with me. After the clan was done looking at me, they all went about doing what it was they do every day to get by in life here. Some of the women were getting ready to cook for the men. The men were all starting to smoke some kind of pipe. But it wasn't like any pipe I had ever seen. It was long and had a bowl at the end to hold whatever it was that they were smoking in it. They just had one, so they passed it around to all the men around the fire pit in the middle of the room.

What should I do? I thought while they all smoked their pipe. Then Kyle said he would take me back to the room I was sleeping in if I wanted to leave. I wanted to yell "Yes, please get me out of here!" but somehow I needed to fit in, so I would stay.

"No, I'd like to stay and help the women cook if that's all right."

"Wait here," he said as he walked away. He came back in a few minutes and said that one of the women would show me what I could do to help.

The girl who was going to show me how to cook the food was very dark and small; she had big dark eyes and a pretty smile. She said her name was Little One because she was so much smaller than the other women in the clan. That might have been true, but one thing was for sure: she was also the prettiest one of all.

She was happy to show me what needed to be done and to talk to me about life in the underworld. We had a real bond between us from the start. It didn't take long before I was trying to cook on the big fire pit in a back cave that the women had to use to fix the food. This was a hard life; I had sweat running down my face as I helped Little One with the meal.

"How do you stand the heat in here while you're cooking?"

"You get used to it," Little One told me. "Sometimes we don't have to cook inside. We eat the meat that the men have cooked under the ground. It makes it a lot easier to make the meal."

I didn't see how anyone could ever get used to this heat, I thought, but in time I was pretty sure I would find out.

Little One was telling me how it was always fun to cook and make up new meal ideas. But sometimes the men didn't like what she cooked for them, so she only got to cook once a week.

I liked the new friend I had found in this girl called Little One. Little One took me into another cave to get the meat that we would need to make the evening meal. I couldn't believe what I saw here. In this long cave it was a lot cooler than the living part of the cave; they had lines pulled across the cave for hanging some of the meat to dry. And they had furs hanging across the opening to keep out the heat from the rest of the cave.

It had all kinds of meat in it. There was deer, beef, and other types of meat that I was not sure I wanted to know about! But I had to admit it was set up very well, and it seemed to be working for the clan; everyone seemed to be well nourished as far as I could tell anyway.

After we had left the meat part of the caves, we went into another part of the caves that had all kinds of dry food in it. There were all kinds of herbs, some were drying and some were already dry. They had cutouts in the cave wall to hold the herbs and lines to hang the plants from so they could dry. There were long shelves that were just cut out of the cave wall to put the herbs on that were ready to use. We took some of the dry for the meal.

"How do you get all the herbs and other foods that you have here?" I asked with a smile as I was truly amazed to see how well they eat. They had a better pantry than most people I knew.

"We grow most of the things you see here. The rest we find on our hunts. The men take a lot of the meat, and put it into an underground fire pit to cook it."

"How long does that take?" I asked her.

"It stays in the ground usually for a day, sometimes longer," Little One replied. She had a big smile on her pretty face as I talked to her.

"When they bring the meat up, it is so tender that it almost falls off of the bones. We all eat until we can't hold any more. It's one of our favorite foods here."

"Well, I can see why it sounds great!"

The young woman just smiled at me as we went back to work on the dinner. Little One was fast with the food, and she used a long thin knife unlike anything I had seen. It looked like it was handmade because it wasn't smooth like the ones you would buy. Little One said it was made from stone that they worked until it was thin and smooth. But I thought that it was pretty good for a handmade one, and she could cut the meat with ease and very fast. Then she pushed a thin rod through the meat that looked like wood and then put the meat over the fire to cook it. There was also a rock that had been worked into what looked like a large round bowl that went out over the fire, and it was very hot. They cooked meat and other foods in it, and it didn't take very long. I thought it would work well for a big stew and asked Little One if they ever made that.

"I'm not sure what stew is!" she answered.

"It is meat and vegetables in one pot like the one over there," and I pointed to the big bowl-looking thing.

"No, I don't think so," she told me.

I thought if the clan lets me cook I'll fix them a big stew; I'll bet they like it. As we worked, I asked the girl questions about the clan.

"How is it that all of you can speak so well?" Little One thought for a few minutes before she answered.

"We have been here for a very long time, and it is said that many years ago our first clan couldn't speak as we do now and that a man came from the upper world. And that he was the first one to teach us how to speak. It is said that he was a great man; there has never been anyone like him since that has done so much for the people of our clan."

I thought about what the girl had said and wondered why they would not let an outsider be with any of the men here. It didn't make any sense to me. As the days passed I got closer to the young girl, as we traveled to other parts of the caves that were a part of this clan's home.

There were parts of the caves that were so large it was something else to see. Some of the ceilings in the caves were so high it was a true wonder to behold. Other parts of the caves had light from the outside coming through all the way down to the cave floor.

It was in these parts of the caves that they grew some of the food that they ate. It was also one source of their water. It had a waterfall in it with a large pond of water, and there was another part of the caves that had a natural hot springs so the whole clan went there to clean and to just relax. I had never seen any caves in my life like these. They were so enormous and so beautiful that I wished I could paint them. They were so wonderful and so pretty; if only I could put them on canvas. *Maybe someday I'll try to do just that,* I thought to myself.

The hot springs were wonderful. It would become one of my favorite places to go when I was homesick and needed to be alone, and in the days to come I would spend a lot of my time there. It made me feel so good and clean as I lay in the hot water. These days Tucker was with Little One as much as he was with me, and that was all right because the girl loved the dog as much as I did. But when it came to bedtime he was always with me no matter what.

I had no way of knowing, but one day he would become a clan favorite. But for today he was still my big boy and Little One's friend as well.

Chapter 6

The clan had a meeting about me, and it was decided that I would become one of the clan. Even with Cal trying to get them to have me put to death. They didn't think I was a threat to them, so they voted to let me become part of their clan.

But I could never be with any of the men in the clan because it was forbidden in their world. I wanted to say how I felt about not being with any of their men because I only wanted to be with one of them, and that was Kyle.

I had fallen in love with him even though I knew it was forbidden. It was out of my hands, and there was nothing that I could do about it, and I was pretty sure that he had feelings for me as well.

If only they could see how right they were together.

But there was no way to get them to see anything as I was not permitted to say anything at any of the meetings; that right was for the men of the clan only. I was just now let in to be part of the clan, and I knew that there was one in the clan that wanted me to be killed, and that was Cal.

If he had his say, I would already be gone. He hated me with everything in him. It was on one of the men's hunts that I got to ask Little One why Cal hated me so much.

Little One thought for a few minutes before she said, "I think he feels threatened by you because he doesn't understand you."

"Do you think there is any way to get him to see me as a woman instead of a threat?"

"I think it will take time for him to see you as you want him to see you, and I think you have to give it time."

I was happy to call this girl my friend. She always had a way of making one see things in a way that was always in good light. It was nice to have someone like her here when I had no one else other than Tucker, and maybe Kyle. I was really hoping I had Kyle on my side because I wanted that more than anything. I knew that I would hold Kyle in my heart forever even if I could not have him. In my heart, I already had him.

If more people were like Little One, the world would be a better place to live. She just wanted the best for everyone, and we could all use more of that in our lives. I asked Little One why they only had furs to wear, and Little One told me that was all they knew how to make.

"We have always had furs to wear. What else is there?"

"You mean that no one knows how to make clothes?"

"What are clothes?" Little One asked.

I smiled at her and told her that clothes were things that you put on like they put on the furs to cover up their bodies.

"You mean like you have on now?"

"Yes," I told her. "If you want to learn how to make things other than furs to wear, I'd be happy to show you how to make them."

Little One was more than willing to learn anything new and told me that she would love to learn how to sew and asked if some of the other women could learn too.

"Yes, of course, if they want to, but I'll need some stuff from my world to show you how to make them?"

"I don't think the men will let us go to the upper world to get things to make clothes." Little One told me.

"Well, I'll ask Kyle if we can get the things I need then," I replied.

It was after dinner that I went back to the cave that I now called home. As much as I hated to know that my old life was over, I was happy to have this one place in the big caves to call my own. Kyle stopped by to see if I was all right and if I needed anything.

"Well, yes, I do. I was wondering if we could get some things to make clothes with from my world."

Kyle was dumbfounded by what he just heard from me. I could see by the look on his face that Kyle had no idea what I was talking about.

"What are clothes? Why do we have to go to your world to get them?"

"I'm sorry, I keep forgetting that no one knows what I'm talking about. Clothes are what I have on my body."

Kyle looked at me for a minute and then said, "I'll have to talk to the lord of the clan to see if we can get you the things that you need. Then I'll let you know," he told me. "What are the things that you have on?"

"I have on pants, and what is called a blouse and shoes," I replied.

"I like what you have on," he told me as he turned to leave.

But before he left, I said, "Thank you, and if it's all right, can Little One and I go with you so I can show you what I need to get?"

"I don't know if the clan lord will let you do that, but I'll ask." Kyle had to get away from me for now because he had no idea what I was talking about, and he had no idea what to say to his father either. He went to find Little One; maybe she could shed some light on what I was talking about.

Little One helped him to understand what I was talking about and that what I had to have to make these clothes was only in my world right now. So Kyle went to his father and asked if he could take me and Little One to the upper world to get the things that I needed.

"No, are you out of your mind? What would make you think that you could take Little One and the upper world woman to her world? We have told her that if she tries to go to her world we would have her put to death or did you somehow forget that?" Orlando asked him.

Kyle told his father that there was no way the upper world woman would get away from him and the other men whom he would take along. Besides, it would do me good to make some of the things that I needed to feel like I was helping the clan.

"What would make you think that the clan would ever want to make the things that she wears? I mean the clan has always had fur to wear, and it works so why change now?" Orlando just stood there shaking his head wondering what this woman had done to his son. After a few days of thinking, Orlando said that they could go to the upper world and let the upper world woman get the things she needed. Little One could go as well. So Kyle took a few of his men and told me and Little One we would be going in a few days. But Orlando knew that this would be one more thing that Cal could use against the woman to get the clan worked up again.

Tucker was lying on the bed and it looked like he was having a bad dream. His legs were moving back and forth and he was trying to bark at something. I got into the bed beside him and started to pat him; soon he was sleeping soundly and so was I.

Only now I was having a dream, and I was running as fast as I could. Someone was right behind me, and just as someone put their hand on me, I woke up. I was wet with sweat. *What was that about*? I thought as I turned over and went back to sleep. Tucker was sleeping next to me, and it looked like he was still having a bad dream too. He was trying to run away from something. *I guess this was a night for bad dreams for both of us*, I thought to myself. Try to sleep, Tucker, because you're going to have a long walk very soon.

Kyle and a few of the clan men along with myself and Little One made a few day's journey to the big cave that we would be walking through to get to the upper world. I couldn't believe that we had walked so far and still were not anywhere near the upper world yet. How far was this place from my world anyway?

Kyle was followed by the rest of his men, followed by me and Little One.

I asked Little One, "How far away is it to my old home?"

"I wasn't there when they took you, so I don't know," Little One replied.

Great, I thought, *no one seems to know how far this was going to be, and I didn't think I could walk for much longer.* I was not used to this kind of a workout. I asked if Kyle could let me rest for a few minutes and Kyle told the men to stop for a little while.

"Kyle, how far away is my world from where you live?"

"It will take us two more days to get there."

I couldn't believe how far it was. "How did you get my dog back to me so fast then?" I asked him.

"I can run fast, and I'm used to this, but with you and Little One with us it will take a lot longer. That is why we don't take anyone with us to the upper world to get things. Only men go, until now, that is."

"Well, I guess I should feel special then."

"You are lucky and so is Little One to be able to do this. We don't like to take the time to bring women with us because it takes a long time to get there," he told me. After a rest for me and Little One, we started to walk again and now it was through the largest cave I had seen yet. It was much bigger than the one the clan lived in, and the clan had put torches in it for light as they walked through it. I could not believe that no one had ever found any of this. I wanted to ask Kyle how they had managed to keep their way of life from my world. But I was too tired to talk right now. And I was pretty sure that he wouldn't tell me anyway.

I had no idea how much longer we walked before Kyle told the men that we would be spending the night here in this cave. I was so glad to be able to sit for a while; I was pretty sure if he hadn't stopped I would have passed out before much longer. *How do these people do this all the time? Talk about getting in shape,* I thought.

Kyle had a fire going and Little One had food put out for everyone to eat. Then it was time to sleep for the night. I was so tired that I didn't need anything other than to put my head down, and I was out. When I opened up my eyes again, it was the next day. Also, I saw that someone had put a fur over me sometime in the night; I was wondering if it was Kyle or Little One, but I didn't want to ask who had done it. Later Little One asked if the fur Kyle put on me was enough to keep me warm all night.

"Yes, I felt nice and warm all night."

Later I would have to thank him, I thought with a smile on my face.

After we had food, it was time to get back to walking. This time I was enjoying the walk. Little One was walking beside me when we walked around the last turn then up a small grade and out into the sunlight. It was so bright that it hurt my eyes at first and even Little One said it hurt her eyes as well.

We walked for a few more hours and just as I was about to give up and ask for another break, I saw my big red barn and house with the white fence. It was a wonderful sight to see as I ran up the hill to my old home I could see that it was a little run down, but other than that it looked the same. Kyle let me run to the place that was once mine knowing I would have to leave this place and not come back to live in it again.

"What do you need us to get for you?" he asked me.

"I'll show you what I need, and Little One and I will help you carry all of it." It was starting to get dark when we had all the sewing things that I needed. I also had a lot of fabric to carry back, but he had said I could have anything I wanted to bring back with me. The other men were happy to get going back to the underworld. But for me it was hard because this might be the last time I would see my old home. I was all right with that for now because I had Kyle to keep my mind off it. Even if he had no idea that he was on my mind all the time now, I had dreams of him pretty much every night too.

The walk back was not as hard for me maybe because I was not in such a big hurry to get there as I was to get to my world. Now I was going back to his world, and somehow I had to learn to like it there too. Knowing that Kyle would be there made it easier, I thought.

When we got back to the cave and everyone was getting ready for the night, Kyle came into my room to see how I was doing.

"Are you doing all right?" he asked me.

"I'm fine, but thanks for asking. I think I need a few days to rest, but other than that I'm fine. I'm just not used to walking so far. I don't know how you do it," I told him.

"We're all pretty much used to walking and running everywhere and you will be too before you know it and then you won't understand how you ever walked so slowly," he told me with that smile that I had come to love.

"I hope you're right, but I don't see myself doing that anytime soon," I told him.

He gave me a big smile and said, "Trust me, you will."

If only he knew how I really felt about him; I wonder if he would like knowing or would he be upset by it. *I may never know*, I thought to myself. That thought made me want to cry out loud "I love you," but I would keep it to myself for now anyway, and that made me ache for him even more.

I wanted to help in any way that I could to fit into the clan that Kyle called home, so I got up one morning before almost everyone else that day. I wanted to have the meal ready for the clan; I even had the drinks ready as everyone took their places to eat. I knew that I had to prove myself to everyone. I wanted to fit in with the rest of the clan, and right now, that was what I wanted to do, so I was trying to do the best thing that I could to get them to accept me into the clan. I wanted so much to make Kyle proud of me, and I would pretty much do whatever I had to do to make that happen.

"I hope everything is all right," I said as I put the last of the food out. Before anyone could say anything, I left to clean up the mess that I had made before the next meal could be made for the clan. After the cleanup was done, I was about to go back to my own cave when Kyle came up to me and thanked me for the meal.

"It was better than anything we have had before, and some of the other women want you to show them how to cook like that. What is the food that you fixed us called?"

"It is a Stew, and I would be happy to help them with that," I replied.

As he was about to leave I stopped him by putting my hand on his arm. It was all Kyle could do to keep from taking me in his arms and kissing me right there, but he knew better than to do that right then. He could feel my hand shaking as I tried to talk to him.

"I was hoping to be able to go with you on a food run if it would be all right," I asked.

He just looked at me at first as if he didn't understand me. Then he said as nicely as he could, "I'm sorry, but only men are sent out for food. I thought I told you that."

I stood there for a few moments looking confused then said, "Oh, I see, now I feel like a fool."

"No, please don't. It will take time to get used to our ways, but soon you will."

"Will I ever feel like I'm part of the clan?" I had tears in my eyes as I looked at him.

He could not bring himself to tell me that I could never have a family within the clan. "I'm sure with time that you'll feel at home here."

Without another word he was gone again and I was left with a heart that I thought would break if I couldn't hold him close soon.

I wasn't sure if he even had feelings for me. Sometimes I could feel his eyes on me, but when I looked back at him he would always look away. It was so hard to hold my feelings in all the time, and so I tried to keep busy with all the work that had to be done around the cave. Little One was always with me these days, and that made it a little better, but Kyle was on my mind most of the time.

I had to find a way to get him alone somehow and see if there was something there or not, but how? Right now, everything seemed to be so hopeless. I was not one to ever just give up on something if I really wanted it, and right now I wanted Kyle. Yes, I wanted him so badly I couldn't stand it, but I still don't have any idea how he feels about me. *So get it together and find a way to do something about it. Yes*, I thought, *I have to find a way and somehow I will and soon.*

It was the next day as I was going to take a dip in the hot springs that I had the chance I was waiting for.

Kyle was there, and as I got into the hot water I could see that he had his eyes closed so I got in and got as close to him as I could without him opening his eyes.

I just wanted to look at him for a while before he knew I was there. I was wrong. He knew I was there; he could smell me as I got into the water and he wanted to take my scent in. He knew he could never let me know how he felt about me. It was almost too much for him just to keep his eyes closed as I came close to him. Just the smell of me was upsetting for him because I did things to his manhood that no other woman had ever done to him. It was not easy to just stay there with his eyes closed as if he didn't know I was in the water with him.

I was all he had on his mind these days, but he could not let me know; the clan would never let us have a life together. After a few more minutes, he opened his eyes, and I was looking at him with those eyes that he had come to love.

"I'm sorry, I didn't mean to bother you," I said. "I love the water here. It's so nice to relax. It makes me feel so sleepy sometimes."

He could see that I was having a hard time talking to him like this. My hands were shaking and I was talking too fast because I was nervous being close to him. And he was too. There was not anything that we could do about it, and he was all too aware of that.

He didn't say anything; he just started to get out of the water before he lost it and took me right there. He had been trying to keep his distance from me and this was not easy with me so close. How much was he supposed to take; after all, he was just a man, and he wanted to show me that! I was trying not to keep watching him, but he was so handsome with that hard body and those green eyes that made my heart melt every time I looked at them.

"Please don't leave," I said. "I just want to talk to you."

Kyle turned around and sat back down next to me. "What is it that you want to talk to me about?" he asked me.

"I was wondering if I could go out with you to see some of the land and maybe try to find some herbs while we're out."

At first he just sat there looking at me as if he didn't hear me right, and then he said, "I'm going out tomorrow. If you like, you can go with me then."

"That would be great. I'll be waiting for you then." And with that I got out of the water and went back to my cave. He was left with just the scent of me, so he just took it in with a smile on his face. He was going to have his hands full just trying to keep from finding a spot to make love to this beautiful woman. He was so much in love with me that it hurt. Over the last few days, some of the clan women had been giving him the eye. Even though some of them were pretty, and any one of them would be a good clan choice, he just couldn't even give any of them a chance. His heart was already taken even if it were forbidden.

Chapter 7

I had been sewing some things to wear when Little One asked if she could learn how to sew as well. I was happy to show her how to make some things that she would want to wear.

I was happy working with Little One. Even though I wanted to tell Little One that I would be going outside with Kyle, I thought better of it. I didn't know if he would want anyone else to know about it. As hard as it was to not tell Little One about the day trip, I just kept it to myself and just had a good time with my new friend. We made some nice things to wear.

It was not even daylight out yet, but it felt so good to be outside of the cave for the second time since I had been taken. It was cold out, but it felt good on my skin, and the cool air in my lungs was wonderful. I just wanted to stand and take in the sweet scent of the early morning air.

I stood and let it fill my lungs before Kyle told me it was time to move on. It was hard for him to push me; he could see that I was really enjoying the outing. He could see that I had made something new to wear for this outing. It was so pretty on me, it was light blue and yellow, and it didn't cover up my legs as the other things I had been wearing did. It was light and airy and made me look even prettier than before in his eyes. I had long pretty legs and large breasts with a small waist, and all that pretty long dark hair that was flowing gently around my face with the morning breeze. He could stay here just watching me for hours if not for the danger, but he knew better.

It was not safe to stay in sight for too long because there could be other clans walking around. They would see that Kyle was on an outing with the upper world woman. That would be the start of one very big mess, and Kyle wasn't up to that right now, so he had to be very careful not to be seen. We stayed out of the open places for most of the day. As we got deeper into the woods we started going out into the fields more and more, and I found some nice herbs. They would work very well with most of the food that I wanted to show Little One how to make.

As I was gathering the plants, I could feel his eyes on me. I knew that my face was red; it made my face feel hot. I only hoped he couldn't see it. I was trying to think of something to say that wouldn't sound dumb to him. I wanted him, and I had never wanted anyone else like this in my life, but I had no idea what to do to get him.

At about midday, he cleared a spot, and I put out some food that I had made the night before so we could eat before we headed back to the cave. As we sat there eating,

I asked him how he felt about me. When I did, I could see his face get red, and the look in his eyes told me that he had no idea how to answer me. It was hard for me to look at him, but I had to find a way to see where I stood with him now while I had him to myself out here with no one else around.

"I'm sorry, I shouldn't have asked you that. It's just that I have these feelings for you, and I'm not sure what to do about them. I mean I'm not sure if you even have feelings for me or not."

After a few minutes, he got up and came over to me and pulled me up to him and very slowly and gently gave me a kiss that told me how he felt about me. I felt like I would fall if he let me go right now, because the kiss was so long, and it had my heart beating so loud I thought he must hear it.

It was a deep and very needy kiss that took my breath away; it made me want him so much that it hurt. The kiss was taking over as we found ourselves on the ground; he was taking off everything that he had on. I saw how big he was, and how much he wanted to make love to me. He got down on his knees and bent to kiss every inch of my body with a heat that was taking us both to a hot intense desire. He wanted to take his time, but he needed to be in me and feel the sweet release that was long overdue. I was shaking as I heard him moan as he placed hot kisses over me. I could feel just how much we both needed this and that it would be sweet, hot lovemaking.

There was no way we could have stopped even if we had wanted to. His hands were shaking as he took off my top to expose my breasts, and then he took them into his mouth. I let out a low moan that said I was ready for him.

I wanted him more than anyone I had ever known, and I was sure he felt the same way as he slid into me. We both let out a moan. The heat had us both wet with the sweat of passion as he pushed into me slow and held my ass in his big hands to feel as much a part of me as anyone could. It was hot and sweet, and we fit together as if someone had planned for us to be together. We never said anything right then because there were no words, only hot sweet lovemaking.

Afterward, we held on to each other and slept for most of the day before either one said anything. When we did, it was just to say that we needed to be together, and we had known for a long time that we had feelings for each other. It was only a matter of time before this was going to happen between the two of us. I had been in love before, but it was never as intense as this was; these feelings were much stronger with Kyle. I was sure that this kind of love only came along once in a lifetime.

When he got up and pulled me up to my feet, he took me in his arms again. Before we knew it, we were making love again; it was dark before we felt like we had enough of each other to last for a while.

"I want you to know that I love you and have from the first time I saw you," he told me.

I leaned into him with a real need to be as close to him as I could get.

"I feel the same way about you," I told him. "But I wasn't sure if you wanted me or not because you always seem to be so cold to me most of the time."

He held me close and told me that it was so no one else would see how much he really wanted to be with me. He was looking at me now as if he had the weight of the world on his shoulders, then he let out a deep breath and said, "I don't know how to tell you this so you'll understand our ways and know that what I've done has put both of us in danger. I was trying to stay away from you so I could keep you safe. It's too late now, and you need to know that it is forbidden for us to be together like this. I've tried to stop my feelings for you for so long now. I can't anymore. I want you even if it means that we have to leave the clan, and go out on our own and live, and I'll do that before I'll lose you."

"Oh, Kyle, I'm so sorry that I've put you in a bad place with the clan. What can I do to make them see that we should be together? I'll do whatever you think I need to do to make things right with the clan again."

Kyle stood there with his jaw working as he tried to think of something to tell me to make me see things the way they were for both of us now.

Because there was no way out for either one of us now, Kyle shook his head then said, "There is nothing that anyone can do. The clan will never let us be together. It is not allowed. They can have us put to death if they want to for what we've done."

"I'm so sorry. What do we do now? How can I help you make it right with the clan?"

There were tears in my eyes as I said this, and he knew that this came from my heart. He also knew he would never let anyone hurt me no matter what he had to do to keep me safe. He wiped away the tears from my face and held me close until I stopped crying before he told me.

"I'm not sure what we'll do, but we'll be together no matter what else happens, even if it means we leave here."

"I can't make you just leave your clan over me. I'll just stay away from you, and no one will know that we've been together like this. I don't want to do anything to hurt you."

He put his face close to mine and told me that I was his life now, and he wouldn't have a life without me in it.

"I can't and won't ever take this back. I love you and without you I don't want to be here anyway."

It was late when we got back to the caves, and it was so hard just to go back to my room and not stay with him in his cave and make love to him all night long. Why did this happen? I never thought I could feel like this and to know that it is a bad thing to the clan just seemed so stupid. What was wrong with these people anyway?

After everyone was asleep, Kyle took his time trying to get to my room in the cave. Right now, he wished the cave wasn't so damn big. If someone saw him, he would be in more hot water than the hot springs had—and he knew it—but he needed me so much that he would take the chance.

I was in my bed trying to get to sleep, but he was on my mind. I felt hot with a heat that had nothing to do with the room. I could still feel his hands on my breast and the hard fullness of him as he pushed into me over and over again until we both felt the hot flow of his seed flowing into me. And I was sure he had the same thing on his mind too. *At least I hope I'm not the only one who can't sleep tonight*, I thought.

Sometime in the night I woke up to his hand over my mouth. At first I didn't know what was going on. When I knew it was him, I pulled him into me before either one of us could say anything. I wanted him, and he was hot with a need for me as he pushed into me with a desire that said how much he wanted to be with me.

I pulled myself on top of him so that he could take my full breast into his mouth, and hold my ass in both of his hands. He pushed into me with a hot need for as long as he could hold out before he came into me. The night was for us and so as quietly as we could be we had our fill of each other over and over. It was sweet, hot, and we were in love with the feel of each other.

We made love most of the night and sometime very late in the night he got up and left me as I slept. It was one of the hardest things he had done in a long time. He felt me with him most of the time anyway, but now it was so hard to let go of me and go back to his own room.

I had dreams of him most of the night and when I woke up to see I was alone I started to cry. It all seemed to be so hopeless it made me sad to think that I might not get to keep his love all because I was not born into the clan.

The next day I was getting ready to help Little One get the food out for the clan meal. I did my best to not look at him as I put the food out even though it took all I had in me not to. After everyone was in their caves for the night, I got ready for sleep. I was hopeful he would come to me in the night again just the thought of him made me feel warm. It was late when he came into the cave, he found me without anything on in bed waiting for the man I love.

He got in beside me, and I came to him. Slowly he slid his full manhood into me as we came together. I was wet with sweat from the lovemaking as he ran the tip of his tongue around the top of my nipple. Then, slid his tongue up and down between my full breasts as I started to shake, I held onto him as tight as I could. Each time he thrust himself into me I let out a little sigh. It was so good, and each push was better than the last one. I came with a sigh as he fell on me and lay there for a few minutes.

"Please don't leave me right now. I need to feel you in bed with me for a while."

He gave me a kiss that put us back where we started off; I was so easy to take. Most of the other women would not go so many times and could not take all of him in. I was always ready to take him in and with ease. I wanted him as much as he needed me. He was holding me to the wall now with my back to him as he pushed himself into my hot wet spot, and played with my tits with his hands. The nips were hard with desire for more of him as he slid into me harder and faster each time until I was wet all over from the heat we made.

He was a big man with a big and full manhood I took him into my mouth. The delight I felt as I pleased him was a turn-on itself. He went down on me as well; it was as if we couldn't get enough of each other, and it was getting harder to leave each night.

Kyle couldn't wait to push into my womanhood and feel the hot wet spot that was me. He spent most of the day with his manhood hard as a rock; he had to try to keep his mind off me so no one would see how hot he was for me.

As the days went by we spent every night together and made love all night long. It was getting harder to pull away from each other.

One night, as we were making love, and I was on top of him he had his hands on my tight round ass pushing himself into me as hard as he could. I had large full breasts that made him want to suckle me as if he were a baby after milk; with every little bite I let out a moan. He kept pushing harder and faster until I went wild with the need for release. Afterward, we slept and once more he got up and went back to his own cave. But this time he knew he couldn't keep this up. He was putting both of us in danger; he knew what he had to do and now was the time.

Chapter 8

Kyle had to go to his father and tell him about his love for me. It was only a matter of time before someone found out and then it would be a lot worse than it was now. How was he going to talk to someone else about his feelings for me? I was everything to him now, and he couldn't stop being with me now. I was his air to keep him alive now, and no one could understand this. He didn't really understand any of it. He knew he could not and would not live without me in his life, no matter what that meant. Kyle knew exactly what it would mean. It would mean that both of us would have to leave here to have a life together or be put to death if we stay.

As Kyle sat down across from his father, he was having a very hard time saying what he had on his mind. *How do I tell my own father that everything he wanted for me is over? How do I even start talking about any of this?* He thought to himself.

This was his father, and after this nothing would ever be the same for either one of them. But before he could say what was on his mind his father started talking.

"What's on your mind, son? I can see that something is bothering you, and it has been for some time now."

Kyle looked down at the dirt floor for some time as he tried to think of some way to tell his father that everything that he wanted for him was over now. That he would never be the lord of this clan as his father wanted him to be someday. Because he had been with the upper world woman and that he was in love with her and wanted to spend the rest of his life with her no matter what it took. Somehow he had to make his father see that this was what he really wanted, and he would not let me go no matter what the consequences.

"I know what's on your mind, son. I've seen it coming for a long time now. I was hoping that you would find a way to overcome it and go on with your life. I now know I was wrong and that I have lost you to the upper world woman. I've seen the way you both look at each other when you think no one is looking. But I see what is going on with the two of you. You also know that as the lord of this clan, I have to hold both of you accountable for what you have done."

"Father, I have tried for a long time to stay away from her and be what you want me to be. I can't live without her. I'll do whatever I have to do so that Betz and I can be together. I can't help myself. I love her, and I want to have a life with her, and I'll give up everything for her. I know it's wrong, but I can't stop myself and I need to do whatever it takes to keep her safe. Please try to understand how I feel about her and find it in your heart to forgive me for what I have to do now."

Kyle's father got up and turned away from him for a few moments.

He then looked at his son and said, "You have to leave here and never come back, or you and the woman will be killed. I have always wanted the best for you. If you think being with this woman is what you have to do to be happy, then go and have a life that I could never have. But don't forget your father when you hold your first child because I'll be thinking of you and wishing that I could be a part of your life. Understand, I'm the lord of this clan, and I can't stop them from wanting to kill both of you for what you've done. You have broken the one rule they won't forgive. So you can never come back here again. Do you understand?"

"Yes, Father, I do, and I had a feeling that was what you would tell me to do. How do I leave here without anyone knowing it?

"You have to leave right now before anyone is up and looking for you. I'll handle it after you're gone, but son, please understand that if you come back I can't save you or the woman. You will be at the mercy of the clan, and you know what that means."

"I understand, and we will never come back here."

With that, Kyle gave his father a hug and left to get me ready to leave.

Before he got to my room, Little One came out of another room and stopped him.

"Kyle, I know what you're going to do. Please let me go with you. I'll help with anything that you need me to do, but please don't leave me here."

He was in a spot that was not good right now. He really didn't have the time to talk about any of this, so he had to make a decision now and hope he could live with it later.

"You won't ever be able to come back home if you go with us and I can't do that to you. We don't have a choice, but you do and I don't think this is right for you."

"I love Betz, and she'll need my help as I need hers, and I don't ever want to come back here. So please let me come with you. She is the only one who has ever been nice to me. I'll follow you if you don't let me go with you anyway, so I'm begging you, please let me come with you."

He was out of time, so he said, "You have to keep up and do as I tell you. Is that understood?"

She nodded her head yes, and they went to get me.

I was asleep when Kyle bent down and put his hand over my mouth. As I looked at him, I knew something was wrong, so I got up and stood by him and asked him what was wrong.

"We have to leave here right now and you don't have time to take much of anything with you."

"Why do we have to go now? Did something happen?"

"Yes. I went to my father and told him about us and he told me we have to go now, or we will be left to the clan's mercy. That would not go well for either one of us for what we've done."

As he had started to take my hand and pull me to him, Little One came into the cave and told me that she was going with us. I gave her a hug, and as quietly as possible we left the caves that Kyle grew up in for the last time. It felt very strange to me as I left the caves that had been home to me for a long time now; it made me start to cry, but I didn't understand it. When I got there, all I wanted was to go back to my old life, but now as I was leaving I felt very sad to see it for the last time. I thought that it must be killing Kyle inside to know that he would never be coming back to the only home he had ever known. The one thing that made things better for me was that I was with the man I loved and had my best friend by my side. Tucker was safe in my arms as the caves faded into the night.

We had been walking for hours now, and it was getting hot. I needed to stop for a while, but I would not ask for a break. I felt it was my fault that we had to leave in the first place, so I would keep going as long as I could. Poor Tucker had been walking for a while now. I was having a hard enough time holding myself up to walk on my own without trying to carry my dog as well right now.

It was Kyle that called for a break so we could rest, eat, and drink. I was so exhausted that it was all I could do to stay awake. It was hot. Even with food and water I still needed to rest for a while longer before we started walking again. With the day coming to an end, I could see that I was not keeping up with Little One and Kyle. It was not like me to be so tired like this, but I had no way to get any help from a doctor. I had to keep up and hope

I didn't have anything that might make Kyle or Little One sick and have to stay out in the open for too long because of me. *What is going on with me?* I thought as I tried to keep up but just kept falling behind.

Kyle could see that I was not doing very well. He thought I had needed more rest before we went on. So he called it a night. He couldn't push me anymore. I had to rest, so he found some wood and water. And Little One put out some food for us, but I found that I couldn't eat anything. I felt so sick that I was sure I would lose anything that I tried to eat. The only thing that I wanted right now was to sleep for as long as I could. Kyle was worried about me, but he knew that we had to keep moving or the clan might find us, and he couldn't take that chance. Kyle spent most of the night trying to make sure that no one was following us, so he had very little sleep; he was up and ready to get the day started. He was hoping against hope that I would be able to hold up for the next few days because he had to keep us moving to stay safe.

Back at Kyle's father's clan, in the main cave, the whole clan was asking all kinds of questions about Kyle. No one seemed to have any answers. It was not anything that any one of the clan had ever seen before. Kyle was to be the next clan lord when his father stepped down, so where had he gone? Maybe he was just out looking for the next hunting spot.

The clan was trying to understand why Kyle would leave and not say anything to anyone. It was not like

Kyle to act in this way, and everyone was upset, to say the least.

But the leader of the clan was Kyle's father, and he said that it would be to no avail to try and find him as he had left the clan and would not be coming back.

The whole clan was talking about Kyle as if he had lost his mind to up and leave in the middle of the night and not let anyone know. It was not like him, and they could not understand it.

"What should we do?" asked one of the men.

"I mean, shouldn't we go after him, and bring him back?"

Before anyone could answer, Kyle's father spoke up and said, "As the lord of this clan, I say that we let him leave. If he wants to come back, he will have to answer for what he has done. If he comes back, then we can deal with him and the woman as well as Little One, but for now I say we let him find his own way." *I only hope he has gotten as far away from here as he can so the clan won't be able to find him if I can't stop them from looking. Be safe my son,* he thought to himself.

The next day I woke up sick again and before I could eat anything I started to throw up. I felt hot too. What could I have to make me so sick like this? Why was this happening now of all times when we had to keep moving and no way to get any rest. I have got to make myself keep going. *It's because of me that this is happening so I have to keep up, or the clan might find us and that will be because I wasn't able to do my part by keeping up with them,* I thought.

Kyle knew something was wrong with me, but he had no way of knowing that I was carrying his baby. At least not then, but Little One was sure that I was having a baby, and she told me just that.

"It's the baby that's making you feel so sick. Sometimes it's hard on a new mom to carry the baby. It should pass in a few days," Little One told me with a small smile.

"What? I can't be having a baby."

"I'm sorry, I thought you would be happy to know that."

I gave her a hug and told her that I was sorry for yelling at her. "I'm just not myself right now and I'm worried about Kyle, and for the life of me I just can't keep up with you guys on this walk. I feel so sick all the time, and I'm exhausted. I am sorry for taking it out on you. You've never done anything to me other than be the best friend I've ever had, so please forgive me."

"It's all right. The clan men always yell at me for something."

"Well, I'm not the men and I really am sorry for yelling at you like that. You don't deserve that from anyone."

"Well, what can I do for you that will help you feel better?" Little One asked.

"I think I have some stuff in that bag over there, please give it to me, will you?"

Little One gave the bag to me then said, "I have some mint leaves in my bag that might help you stop throwing up. Do you want to try it?"

I didn't have anything else that would work. So I said, "Sure, I'll give it a try. What do I have to lose right now—I can't keep walking if I'm sick so right now I'll try anything."

Little One put the mint in some hot tea for me and gave it to me to try. And it seemed to help me, so we kept some of the tea for later if I needed it. All the time I was walking I kept thinking what if Little One is right and I'm having Kyle's baby? I couldn't help but smile at the thought of a baby Kyle. What a pretty baby it would be if I were pregnant. Just the thought of a baby that looked like Kyle made me smile as I walked.

Kyle knew he had to find a cave for us to stay in at least for the night. I was so sick that it was hard for him to keep pushing me when I kept getting sick. It was getting late anyway, so he found a cave and walked into it to make sure it was clear.

After he got a fire going and Little One put food out for all of us to eat, he sat down by me. He tried to get me to eat something, but I wasn't going to even try. All I wanted was to rest. As soon as my head went down I was asleep. It was a long night for him; all he could think of was this was too much for me, and he didn't know what to do now. I needed someone to help me, but there was no one to find. He kept the fire going and put more furs on me to make sure I wasn't cold. That was all he could do for me right now, and he was hoping that was enough.

The next day I was up and fixing food for everyone. Kyle was so happy to see me feeling better that he took his time getting ready to move, afraid I would get sick again. Kyle hated to keep pushing me to walk, but we had to keep moving. If the clan was out looking for us and they caught up with us, it would go very badly for all three of us. He had to get all of us as far away as he could, hopefully the clan would give up, and we would be safe. That was the only thing on Kyle's mind right now: keeping us safe.

The rest of the day, I was doing fine, so Kyle started thinking of the right place to stay the night as darkness started closing in on us. He found another cave and as the night before he went into it to make sure it was safe. Like the night before I was pretty much out as soon as I put my head down.

It was late the next day when we got started again because Little One was taking her time getting things ready before leaving. Kyle knew that she was worried about me too. He had to smile at her; she was a good friend to me.

Kyle was glad that she was with us. We had walked for days now, and he still had no idea where we were going. Kyle was hoping that somehow the right spot would just show up as we walked, but so far nothing looked like it would work for us to start a new life. We needed to have a place that would make all of us feel safe, and it had to be a big cave to move in to before winter got here.

I wanted to ask Kyle if we could go to my world, but I was afraid of what he would say if I did. So I kept on walking with him and said nothing, but as the days went on I had it on my mind. That night, as we were getting ready to sleep, I got him aside and asked him.

"Kyle, what if we go to my world? I know of a lot of places that we could go and the clan would never come looking for us there."

He had a dark look on his face when he finally said something to me. "Don't you know that is the first place the clan would look for us?"

"No, I'm sorry, I didn't think of that. I was trying to help, but I see that you're right. Still I know that the clan could not find us there. My world has a lot of places to hide if someone doesn't want to be found," I told him, but he didn't want to hear what I was saying right now, so I let it go.

Kyle took me in his arms and held me close for a while before he gave me a kiss. He sat me down and told me that there was no way we could ever go back to my world.

"I would never fit in there, what would I do there? This is where I belong, so you need to make up your mind to stay here with me or go back to your world."

I just stood there with tears in my eyes. "How can you talk to me the way you are right now? I thought you loved me. I was only trying to help us find a place to live, that's all I was trying to do," I said with a huff and sat down in defeat.

Kyle sat down with me and started to tell me that he would find us a place to live, but it had to be in his world. It was the only world he knew how to live in, and then he thought of how I must feel in his world and not my own. He was so damn dumb sometimes it was unbelievable. How could he talk about how he would feel in my world when I had been taken away from my own world and didn't get to have a say in anything.

"Look, I know this has been hard on you, but somehow you seem to have fit into my world or am I wrong about that?" he asked me.

"You're not wrong about that. I love this world, but I want to help you, and I just thought we could try it and see if it would work for us. And sometimes I still miss the world that I grew up in, that's all."

Kyle had to think of what I wanted too; it was not just about him anymore, and he had to think of what was best for me now. He loved me and wanted to make me happy. He didn't think he could ever fit into my world. Even if he could, we could not go back to my place. The clan would go there to look for us first without a doubt.

"Well, it's getting late, so we need to find a place to stay for the night so let's sleep on this. We can talk more about it tomorrow," he told me as he walked into another cave to make sure it was safe for us to stay in for the night.

But as he walked into the cave he didn't really see anything because he had his mind on what I had said to him. He knew he was being selfish about this. He just could not see himself ever living anywhere but right here. That made him feel even worse because he couldn't think of leaving this place, but he wanted me to give up my world. Right now, he felt like a big jackass for doing this to me. What was he thinking? I had the right to live wherever I wanted to just the same as he could. He had to let me go home to my world if I wanted to. Now that we were away from his father's clan, he could let me make up my own mind on what it was that I really wanted to do. That night Kyle asked me what I really wanted to do.

"Betz, if I told you that you could leave right now and go to your world and live the life that you used to have, what would you do?"

At first I just looked at him as if I had never seen him before. Then I said, "Kyle, if you had said that to me not long ago I would have run all the way home. Now I know that I belong here with you, in this world, because I can't imagine my life without you in it anymore. I love you and wherever we are and as long as we're together then that's home to me." I leaned into him and gave him a kiss that let him know I meant what I said.

Kyle had no way of knowing that the clan would not be looking for us. His father had used his role as lord of the clan to keep his son safe. As long as Kyle never came back, he would be left alone, even though one of the clan wanted to go after us and have us put to death. If only he could, he would. Cal had always thought Kyle was too soft when it came to the workings of the clan. It was not up to him so he would go along with what the clan said for now. But there would come a day that he might be able to do something about Kyle if he were the lord of the clan.

And with Kyle out of the picture, that could happen someday. He would wait for that day, he thought with a smile on his evil face.

I was up the next day fixing food with Little One, and we had the help of Tucker too. He was waiting for his part of the food as he sat next to me with his tongue hanging out.

Kyle still could not see what I loved about that dog; he always seemed to be in the way. Kyle didn't want to give up any of what little food we had left right now to a dog; it went against what he had grown up to believe in. Dogs were to eat not to keep as pets. He loved me, and I really did love that damn dog. So he would learn to at least like the dog for me.

Every time he saw the look of love in my eyes he knew he had to learn to live with Tucker. And in time he would, but for now he had to put up with him, at least the dog kept my mind off being sick most of the time and for that he was thankful.

I had been resting under a big tree with Tucker when I saw something shiny a few feet away. I thought it might be something that we could use, but I couldn't really see it well enough. The dog and I walked closer to it and saw what I was pretty sure was an airplane.

"Kyle, come over here, will you?"

"What's wrong?" he asked me.

"I see something over there by that rock." I was pointing at something, but Kyle didn't see what it was until we got closer to it.

"What is that?" he asked.

"Oh my god, it's an airplane," I said.

"What's an airplane? Kyle asked me.

"It's something that my people use to go from one place to another," I told him. "We can fly across the sky in airplanes. There are small ones like this one is that only hold a few people, and then there are bigger ones that hold a lot of people. Anyway, we need to see what's inside of this plane. There might be things we can use."

Kyle looked at me as if he had no idea what I was talking about and I was pretty sure he had never seen a plane before. "How can this plane fly across the sky? Only birds can fly," he said with a confused look on his face.

"That's a very long story, but I promise that I will tell you later, but not right now," I told him with a big smile on my face. "Trust me," I said, "this is a good find for us right now. There might be a lot of good things inside of that plane. Let's go and see if anyone left anything in it that we can use." I pulled him with me to the shiny thing that was waiting for someone to find it. Neither Kyle nor Little One was very happy to be walking into something that they had never seen before. But I was thrilled with this find, and so they went along with me because they trusted me.

As we got closer to it, I could see that it had been there for a long time, and if there was anything in it, I had my doubts that it would still be useful. But there was no way I was going to walk by it without looking to see what there was inside. It was worth looking at. Kyle was not sure if it was safe for us to go inside of the thing.

He could see that I wanted to see inside of it, so he went in first and then I followed him. As he got further inside of the plane, Kyle could see that someone had died here a long time ago. He was still sitting at the far end of the thing that I called a plane, and there wasn't much left of him. There seemed only to be bones and some of the clothes on him. Even that was falling apart.

He had something around his neck. Kyle took it off him and gave it to me to look at. All this was pretty strange to Kyle.

"These are what we call his dog tags," I said.

"What is that?" he asked.

"They are what we call an ID. They tell us who he was when he was alive," I added. "This man's name was Mike Shaw."

I felt sick and needed to sit down for a few minutes. I knew I needed to look around the plane as good as I could; there might be some things in the plane that we could use. As I was about to give up and leave, I saw something in a corner by the back of the plane. It was some kind of trunk.

"Kyle, I need you to help me with this, please." After we had got the trunk out of the plane, I found a rock to hit the lock with and it broke open with just a few hits. I was smiling when I looked inside of it, and I brought out a handful of things that Kyle was not sure he had ever seen before.

"What is that?" he asked.

"Books," I told him. "All these books will help us live a better life, and books to teach with. Someday we might have a family, and I'll need these books to teach our family with."

"This book will help me find out why I'm sick, and it will help me to understand how to make you and Little One feel better when you don't feel good."

"My father has a book like that one over there." Kyle was pointing at a book of names and places of the world.

"So that's how the clan came up with some of the names that I had thought was strange for them to know. Kyle, can your father read the book that he has?" I asked.

"I don't know what 'read' means," he told me. "But he knows what the words mean," he answered.

I smiled back at him and gave him a kiss. "That's the same thing," I told him, "and that is wonderful."

Kyle was still looking inside of the plane when he called me inside of it with him.

"Look at this," he said. He was pointing at another trunk, and there were boxes next to the other trunk. It took all of us most of the day to get the trunks and boxes outside of the plane. I wanted to find some place to look inside of them and all the boxes. I was sure that with some time to study some of the books that our lives would be made a lot better. Kyle found a cave, and we spent a few days there so I could rest and also go through as many of the boxes and the trunks as I could. I knew that I had to keep all the stuff that we had found inside the plane, but I had no idea how I was going to take any of it with us. Maybe we could come back for all the stuff we had found after we found a place to call home.

It had been a hard few days for me as I still felt sick most of the time. Now I was starting to think that Little One might be right about me being pregnant. It was not a good time for me, but I would deal with it as best I could.

I was looking inside one of the trunks when I found what looked like an old letter of some kind. After I got done reading it, I found Kyle and told him that the man in the plane was looking for a lost city out here someplace. I thought he was trying to make a name for himself if he found it. But he had died before he could fulfill his dream of doing that. We took the body and laid it to rest by a nice shade tree, and put up a cross with his name. I had found a lot of things that I was sure we could use like paper, pens, pencils. Under the last trunk, I found some guns and ammunition to go with it.

I knew that this was something that would help Kyle with the food run, but I would have to show him how to use the guns. When I told him about the guns, I thought he would be happy about something new to use in the hunt for food. He just looked at me for a while before he said anything to me.

"We have tried to use guns before and it didn't go so well for the clan."

"What? How did you get guns?" I had a look of disbelief on my face as I asked him.

"The clan found them a long time ago and when we tried to use one of them it went off and one of the clan was killed by it. So we threw the rest of them away so that no one else would be hurt or killed.

I thought about what to say to him to make him see that it was an accident. I was sorry that it happened, but I knew how to use a gun and would show him how to as well.

"Look, Kyle, it's not hard to do, and it's safe if you know how to use a gun."

Kyle thought that I was more than just a woman. I was smart and knew a lot about many things in the world. He would be happy to let me teach him more things of the world. He was still a little worried about the guns. He saw what they could do, and he didn't really want to deal with them, but if it made me feel better to help him than that's what he would do.

We stayed a few more days at the same cave so I could show Kyle how to use the guns. It didn't take him very long, and he was a much better shot than I was. He was handling all the guns and ammunition now as if he had been dealing with them all his life. It was time to move on now and find a place to call home.

I was sitting with my back up against the wall at the back of the cave. It had been a long day, and I was drinking some mint tea and trying not to throw up again. I was pushing up against the wall to get the kinks out of my back when I felt it move a little. At first I wasn't sure if it really did move, so I stayed with my back pressed against it. But when I felt it moved a little more I jumped to my feet and yelled for Kyle to take a closer look at the wall.

"I can't see anything, but I feel air coming through it. I'll give it a push or two and see what happens. I can't move it," Kyle told me. "We need to find something to push the wall with."

"Maybe we can all three try to push it open." With all of us pushing, I could feel more air coming through, so we kept pushing until I could get a rock to hold it open. We all stood there looking at the doorway to some place. None of us wanted to take the first step inside of it.

Chapter 9

Finally, I said, "Oh for crying out loud, I'll go first." I went through the wall into a hallway that had to lead to someplace. It was starting to get dark in the hallway when I saw a torch on one side of the wall and took it. I had found a lighter in one of the trunks, so I lit it and to my surprise it burst into light.

The hallway led up and down and had many turns for what seemed to be a very long time. As we walked, I could see that the path was worn, so I could tell that someone or maybe a lot of feet had made this path smooth as stone. It was done a long time ago because it had weeds and cobwebs hanging everywhere now.

"I wonder if we'll find anyone when we find the end of this," Little One asked.

I thought of that already but didn't want to say anything yet. Why worry everyone before there was a reason to?

"Well, I see light up ahead, so I guess we'll find out, but I doubt that anyone will be here with all the weeds and cobwebs in this place," I stated.

Kyle was not as fast to walk into someplace that he had never been before, but he wouldn't let me go alone. It was a long hallway, and there were steps going down for a long time before we turned back to another hallway. Now it seemed to be going up and turning; Kyle was wondering if it would ever come to an end. He felt like I was right about this place because it had a lot of cobwebs everywhere. He had his doubts that anyone would still live here because if there were still anyone here, he was sure there wouldn't be cobwebs and weeds everywhere. But he would still take his time looking over this place before he would feel it was safe for all of us to start our new life here.

Up a few more steps and then there was bright light as we walked outside in what looked like some kind of courtyard. It was so bright after being in the dark hallway for so long that it hurt our eyes for a few minutes. We all stood there in amazement in what had to be the most beautiful place that any one of us had ever seen, and Kyle knew it was all the more true for him. It was something to see, just stunning to look at like something out of an old movie. All that was missing were people, as far as we could tell. There were no people anywhere, but why? And why would anyone ever leave a beautiful place like this? The courtyard was big with stone caves all around it; everywhere you looked there stood caves looking at you. Some of them were up high, and some were at ground level. It was like a two-story building in size, but so much more beautiful than any buildings that you could imagine; this was great. Somehow these people had built a whole city here from one very large mountain. The front of it was like one big wall of caves with beautiful columns that were standing by each cave opening. It was just stunning to look at.

There was a variety of bushes and trees; they all needed to be taken care of, and weeds needed to be pulled. It was like a dream here; with some hard work we would have something that no one else had here or anywhere else. As we walked around the grounds, it was an unbelievable place to behold. Kyle was trying to get us to calm down until he had a chance to make sure we were alone.

I could hear something that sounded like water falling, and so I went to the sound, and there we stood looking at the most beautiful waterfall I had ever seen. It was tall, and there were flowers and trees as well as all kinds of bushes. If you looked really close, you could see that there was a cave opening behind the waterfall. This was something that you don't see every day. You could easily swim in the big pond or go to the waterfall and stand under it to clean off. I could see myself doing just that if we were lucky enough to live here in this wonderful place. Try to imagine the most beautiful picture of an enormous magical garden that you've ever seen in a magazine or in a movie. Well, this is even bigger and more beautiful than that.

I started to laugh out loud, but Kyle put his hand to my mouth and said, "We need to see if there are others here before we do anything else." He took his hand away and we started looking around the place. It didn't look like anyone lived here and from the looks of the place it had been a long time since anyone had been here. Why would they leave here—it was a wonderful place to live. Kyle could not understand why there was no one to be found anywhere. This was not a place that anyone would want to leave. What could have happened to make everyone leave here?

It was much bigger than the caves that he grew up in, and it had a lot of rooms within the rock walls and it looked like all of them led back to one very big cave. Kyle said that we needed to find one of the caves to stay in for the night and that we could pick up the search of the place the next day.

Kyle took us deep inside one of the caves, so if someone did come, they would never see anything unusual. It had another opening at the back, so we could get out fast if we had to. I was beside myself with the excitement of the place, and no one could blame me. It was the prettiest place that Kyle had ever seen in his life as well. Not even my upper world could out do what this place had to offer us as far as some place that was so peaceful with wonderful views as far as the eye could see.

No one ever came to the cave that night. In the morning light, Kyle took his time going over the whole place to make sure that no one was living here anymore. He knew that this would be a great place to start over with Little One and me; it had more than he had ever thought he would find for us. I wanted to fix everything, but I couldn't do it by myself.

"Kyle, we can have such a great life here and have a family one day. Don't you see that this place is enchanted?

I've seen a lot of pretty places in my world, but I have to tell you that none of them even come close to this magical place. It can be ours to in live in and raise a family, and enlarge the clan. Don't you see we were supposed to find this place? What I'm trying to say is it's meant to be."

"I can see a big garden and pretty flowers all over the courtyard, and we can do so much by the big waterfall. Let's look around in the caves and see what's in all of them. We might find more amazing things in some of the caves so let's go." I had all but forgotten about being sick. I ran around the big courtyard showing them where everything should be planted in a big garden. I was already drawing a line in the dirt so we could see how it should look one day.

Kyle loved the way I always wanted to get everything going. I didn't ever want to wait for anything; I had to get things working now. I have such a zest for life it was hard not to feel the same way when you were around me. As we walked into one cave after another, we soon saw that they all interlocked like one big spider web. We came out into the largest cave with very high ceilings and the walls of that cave had smaller caves within this big room. We thought some of them might make good bedrooms for all of us.

One of the long caves had a lot of rooms to do the cooking in and as we went through more caves we found one that had a natural hot springs in it. I loved that one; it would be a great place for all of us to relax in as well as being good for sore muscles. It was a great find, and it would be used for years to come. I still had very fond memories of being in the hot springs with Kyle even if he didn't know that I had strong feelings for him at that time.

One of the caves was long, wide and would work for the clan to use when we had our meetings and have the meals there as well. Kyle could visualize everything as I talked about what each room would be used for. He had to smile at me; I was so smart and wanted the life we would have here to be the best it could be for all of us as well as the next generation. He was sure that, with me by his side, this lost city we had found would be as wonderful as I thought it could be. We were making a whole new world not only for us but also for the generations that would follow us.

Kyle, Little One, and I spent long hours over the next few weeks getting all the boxes and trunks into the new cave in the city where we would spend the rest of our lives.

I had the biggest cave picked out for us to live in and for all my new books and things that we had found in the airplane. I had a lot of rooms within the cave to pick from so it would work out very well for all of us. It had a large open cave almost like the meeting room in Kyle's home clan's cave. It would work out well for the same kind of meetings for now and for years to come. All of us had been busy working within the big cave with the highest ceilings for the meeting room for the lord of the clan. Now Kyle was clan lord in this new place, and he would hold all the important meetings here. We had built a very large fire pit and placed seating all the way around it where the whole clan could sit and talk and just enjoy.

We had made some of the seating out of stone and some of it was made from logs. At the head of it was the best seat for Kyle which was made of one big stone to sit on and it had another stone behind it as a backrest. None of the other seats had that. This was to signify that he was the lord of the clan. I had taken some of the best furs that we had and used them for Kyle's seat so it would be more comfortable for him to sit on for long periods of time. Unlike Kyle's old meeting cave, this one had a long wide wood table that I had Kyle make out of one of the old trees. We had spent days making it as smooth to the touch as we could and it was very pretty and it would work well for meetings and for dining on. Again with Kyle's seat at the end made of stone with a back rest and more furs for the lord of this clan.

Kyle was proud of me. I had gone from someone who didn't want to live here to someone who was always looking for the next thing that would make our lives better.

He watched as Little One and I put food up in one of the caves. I had found a medical box in the airplane so I had made up one of the caves for that and other things that would help me when anyone got sick.

I was starting to show now, so Kyle now knew that I was having his baby; it made him smile to see me work with Little One. We were laughing as we worked. Little One had been such a big help for Kyle and I that we could not even imagine what our life would be without her here with us to help us shape our new world.

Kyle had also found a cave that would work for the meat from the hunting trips so he would be able to clean and also hang and dry some of the meat in here. He got everything that he had brought with him when he left his old clan and made dugouts in the walls to hold most of his tools. He pulled a rope across the span of the cave walls as tight as he could without any help for now, so he could hang some of his tools. It would work well for hanging up game as well. Kyle was starting to feel at home here; it was a great place to be able to call home for anyone. Right now, Kyle and I as well as Little One were the lucky ones that get to call this wonderful place home.

Even though he wasn't happy about the guns that we had found at first, he was now. He was a pretty good shot now, and it would make it a lot easier for a good kill. But that would take a long time for him because he loved to hunt the way he was brought up with either a bow and arrow or a spear or an axe. He was very good with all of them. He already had game put up, so we had enough meat to get through most of the winter, and he would put up more game as we needed it. Kyle had also been working hard to get an underground pit made for cooking large meat in. It would be something that the whole clan would love using over the years.

Little One and I were out in the courtyard working to make it a nice place to relax and also to grow my garden. I would soon be putting one in because I had found a box full of seeds in one of the boxes from the plane. They would be going into the ground soon so we would have food to put up in one of the caves to help feed us when winter came. Little One and Kyle had been digging most of the ditches for the water to run to the plants. I was getting big with the baby, and he didn't want me over doing it. The baby and I needed to come first, and that meant I had to back off of some of the hardest work for now.

It was all starting to come together and by this time next year the city would be back to what it once was and the baby would be here. Kyle could not believe that soon he would be a father; it was going to be happening soon.

As the days turned into months, all of them stayed busy working within the walls of the city to make it a home for us and the baby. Kyle had put in a large pit in the middle of the main cave to sit and eat, also to talk and plan for whatever was up next. Kyle was the lord of his own clan now; soon there would be one more and in time there would be many more.

As the days went by Kyle had worked through all most all the caves to see if the last clan had left anything to tell who we were and why they had left such a wonderful place. All we ever found was a few graves in the back part of the city, so all we could think of was that they died. One day, while Kyle was working in one of the caves, he found a skeleton. Later he found more of them in another cave, so we now thought they got sick, died, and some of them were buried. The others had no one left to bury them. We laid them to rest under a big tree and placed a stone that said "rest in peace." Kyle thought that was the least we could do for the last of the clan that had made this wonderful place that Kyle, Little One, and I would be calling home from now on.

From what we did find we thought that the people here were just another clan not unlike the one Kyle was born into. Except that these people really knew how to build a beautiful place to live. And for that all of us would be forever grateful. It was a place that anyone would love to call home. The clan that had made this place was very smart and had a vision for this city that no clan that Kyle had ever seen had. They knew how to make a whole city out of a mountain of caves with beautiful columns that had stood for years and would stand for many more years with some work and care.

Winter was long, but Kyle had put up all the meat we would need, and I had the pantry full. We had water within the caves to drink and to take baths and clean with, so we were set up pretty good, Kyle thought. The hot springs was not a good idea for me as far along as I was with the baby, but after the baby came I would meet him there a lot.

I was starting to get big with the baby now, and I seemed to be having a hard time getting around. I still always had a smile on my face. I was happy to be here with him and to be having his baby. As the time for the baby got closer, I kept reading in one of my books to get ready for the birth of the baby.

I was also working with both Kyle and Little One to teach them how to read. I thought it would be good for them to know how and I loved teaching them.

Little One was learning fast, and Kyle was already reading. In one of the trunks, I had found a few blankets, and I had one of them made up for the baby.

At night, I would work on my knitting. I was making something for the baby. Kyle had never seen anyone so happy to be having a baby as I was. It was so nice to see. I had shown Little One how to sew because I wanted them to have things to wear. If we ever did go to the upper world, we would need to have things that looked like what everyone else was wearing. It had taken time, but with hard work we had some things that would work if we had to go to my world someday.

Kyle was still not sure that the clan was not looking for us. He took extra care every time we left the city to try and keep it hidden from anyone who might find the outside cave that led to the courtyard of the city.

He was trying to keep all of us safe for as long as he could. Little One and I had spent many weeks putting together long benches for seating around the courtyard. Kyle had helped with them too; he had made most of them from some tall trees that needed to be cut down. He helped with cutting and making them as smooth as he could so they would be good for seating. Both Little One and I put pretty flowers as well as some of the other plants in and around them so it was as if it was meant to be this way, and maybe it was.

I had spent many months trying to find out who lived here. I had not found anything so far that led to an answer. There were no drawings on any of the cave walls and as far as I could tell whoever they were they most likely were just another clan like Kyle's. Or maybe they just left here. What could have happened to make them leave?

Either way, it was a mystery. I had started making drawings on some of the walls so the next generation would know more than we did right now about who lived here. It was home to us now. I had made up the cave that Kyle and I called our bedroom as nice as I could. I had made drawings on the walls and tried to make as many cutouts as I could to hold some of the baby things. I had put down big animal skins on the floor, so it was warm to walk on, and it would be good for the baby to learn to crawl on.

It was late in the spring when I started to have labor pains, and Little One already knew what to do to help me. Kyle, on the other hand, was having a hard time with it. He had no idea what he should be doing.

I had everything ready for the big day or night, and now it was here. I thought I had a long night coming before the baby would be here. Kyle was uneasy, and he kept walking back and forth outside of the bedroom cave that I was in to have the baby. He had no way of knowing how long this would take, and it was a lot harder knowing that it was his baby coming.

Kyle kept getting hot water for Little One and kept the fire pit burning so it was warm for the new baby. It was just starting to get light outside when Kyle heard the baby cry.

He jumped up and went into the cave to see Little One giving the baby to me, and then she turned to Kyle and said, "You have a son."

He came to me and the baby, bent down and gave me a kiss, then took the baby from me to hold him up to the light so he could see the small body of his first son. He had a head full of hair, and it was dark like both of his parents'. He was a big boy as far as babies go. As Kyle stood there holding his first son, he could see himself going on hunting trips with him and showing him how to do everything that Kyle knew how to do to live this kind of life. He was as happy as he had ever been, and very proud of his new son. The only thing that made Kyle sad was that his father would never get to see or hold his new grandson. That would be a sadness that would stay with Kyle for the rest of his life.

I had tears in my eyes as I watched Kyle with his son. I could see that he would be a good father. He was so gentle with the baby and so proud to be a father.

He put the baby back in my arms and left to let us both get some sleep. Little One was waiting outside of the cave room when Kyle came out.

"Please take care of them for me," he said.

"I will," she replied.

With that, she went back to take care of the reasons that he was still trying to make a life for all of them. He had to make sure that the fire was still going and that everything was ready for them to fix food with the next day.

When Kyle went into the room to sleep, he sat there by me and the baby for a few minutes to just look at his new family. He was a happy man; he had everything that a man could ask for. He knew it as he got into bed next to me and his new baby and fell asleep with a big smile on his face.

The next few days went by fast. I was up most of the nights with the baby and Little One spent her time trying to help in any way that she could. Kyle and I thought for a few days before coming up with a name for the baby and we both liked the name Carson.

It was a strong name that would command respect and someday he would be the lord of this clan, so Kyle wanted a name that sounded like a leader. The baby was happy and getting bigger every day. Life was good for all of us now. Kyle was out on a food hunt one day when he came across something that he hadn't seen for over a year now. It was one of the men in his father's clan. What in the hell was he doing here? Was he here to start a war or was something else going on? Kyle had watched him for over an hour before he let the man know someone was watching him when Kyle came out in the open so the man could see him. He could see that it was Toby, one of Kyle's friends from his father's clan.

Toby came running to Kyle and gave him a hug. "I've been out here for days hoping I would find you alive, but I had no idea if I ever would."

Kyle was happy to see him too, but he had no idea what to do with him because Kyle didn't want to take him to the lost city that we now called home. It was a safe place, and he wouldn't trust anyone who could bring it all to an end. No, he would stay here and find out what this was about before he would let him see his home.

It was late at night when Toby finally fell asleep. Kyle still waited for a while longer before he left to let me know what had happened and see what I thought of it.

I was up with the baby when Kyle got to the cave. "I was wondering where you were," I said as he walked into the room with me and the baby.

"I have something I need to talk to you about," he told me.

"What's up?"

Kyle took the baby and told me to sit down. "I was out on a hunt when I saw something moving and at first I thought it might be a deer. As I watched, it came into sight, and it was Toby."

"What?"

"Toby, you know, from my father's clan."

"Okay, I'm not sure what to say other than why is Toby way out here?"

"Betz, I think I need to take a few days and see what's up, and I want to make sure no one else comes looking around here."

"All right, if that's what you need to do. We'll be fine here so stop worrying about us," I said as I gave him a kiss and pushed him away so I could put the baby back down for a nap.

It was almost day light when Kyle got back to where Toby and he had spent the night. Toby was still asleep, he must have been done in to sleep for that long, Kyle thought as he settled down again he could use a little sleep too.

Later that day as they were eating, Kyle asked Toby why he was here. He could see that it was something he was having a hard time trying to talk about right away, so Kyle let him take his time. When he was ready, he started talking.

"I came looking for you, Kyle. It never set well with me the way you left and besides I don't like the way Cal is talking about you these days. So here I am, but to be honest I wasn't sure I'd find you. It's been a long time since you left."

Kyle wanted to tell him everything, but he still had no idea what was going on with him. "Well, you've found me. What's up?"

Toby had thought for a few minutes before he told Kyle what was really on his mind. He got up and started walking back and forth, and then he stood in front of Kyle and said, "Look, Kyle, I'd like to stay here with you and Betz if it's all right with you. I just can't get along with Cal anymore. He hates you and wants to take over the clan someday. He has made it plain to everyone that when he's lord of the clan, things will be his way. I know it's only a matter of time now that you're not there, and, well, I guess I just don't fit in there anymore."

Kyle was floored; he wasn't expecting this. He had thought that the clan was looking for him, but Toby had said that no one was looking for him. "I'm sure that my father will keep Cal in line. Orlando is a strong leader, so things will be all right there even with Cal still trying to make a mess within the clan."

"Yes, Orlando is a very good leader, but even he can't shut up Cal's big mouth these days." But other than that they had moved on with life within the clan and were not looking for Kyle anymore, and that was a relief to hear.

Kyle got to his feet and took Toby's hand and said, "Well then, welcome to my clan."

Toby gave him a slap on the back and then Kyle started telling Toby that we had been walking for days before we found something that he thought would work for the clan to get its new start. Kyle wasn't going to tell him anything else. No, he wanted Toby to see it for himself.

It took Kyle and Toby most of the day to get back to the city. They brought back meat and some apples that they had found in a field where there were some deer grazing. So it was a good food run for them. After walking for a while, they came to a very large outer cave.

Toby turned to Kyle and said, "So this is the big secret you were telling me about?"

"Not quite," Kyle told him as he went to the back of the cave and pushed open a doorway.

"Wow, what is this?" Toby asked as both of them walked into the long hallway that would lead them to the city.

As they got to the big opening to the city, Kyle said, "This is what I was talking about." As they walked out into the courtyard, Kyle could see the same expression on Toby's face that he had seen on all of ours.

"You have got to be kidding, Kyle." Toby just stood there in amazement like all the rest of us had done. "This is some place you have here all right."

Just then, Little One came out of one of the caves and stopped when she saw Toby standing by Kyle.

"Toby is that really you?" she asked.

Toby had a big smile on his face as he ran to her and gave her a big hug and said, "It's good to see you again."

I came outside with the baby to see what was going on. "Hi, I didn't know we had company. Hi, Toby, it's nice to see you again." He gave me a hug and then asked if he could hold the baby. "Sure," I said as I gave the baby to him.

"What's his name?" Toby asked me.

"Well, that has taken us a little while to decide, but we have now, and it's Carson."

"He's a big boy," he told me as he gave the baby back to me.

Kyle told me that Toby was going to be part of the clan now.

"Well then, welcome home," I said. "I hope you'll be as happy here as we are. I really need to feed this little guy right now, but we'll talk later after you get settled in," I said as I started back to the cave to feed the baby.

Chapter 10

Little One was happy to have Toby here with us; she had always liked him. He always went out of his way to be nice to her when she was in the old clan. The only other people that were nice to her were Kyle and me.

She never had feelings for Kyle like she did for Toby. But she never thought he felt anything for her because she was small and not as pretty as the other women in the clan. Still she could daydream about him. After a few days to get caught up with everything, Toby was fitting in nicely, and Kyle could see that Little One was happy to have him here.

She got red in the face every time he looked at her. Toby was looking at her a lot, maybe there was something there. Time would tell.

As summer came to an end, Kyle and Toby had made sure that everything was ready. They worked well together, and it was nice to have another man around just to talk to. And now he had another man to go on the hunting trips with. It was on a hunting trip that Kyle would find out more about Toby.

Toby asked Kyle if he could talk to him about something when they were out on one of the food runs. Kyle sat by the fire that they had for the night and waited for Toby to talk.

"I'm not sure how to ask you this. It's not something that I thought I would be asking you, but here I am." Kyle sat there waiting for whatever was coming.

Toby got up and stood in front of Kyle and looked him in the eyes and said, "I know you're the clan lord here so here goes. I would like to ask if Little One and I could be mated or married as Betz calls it."

He was out of breath as he sat back down across from Kyle. Kyle started to laugh so hard that he was crying.

"What's so funny?" Toby asked him.

"I thought you were going to tell me that you wanted to leave and go back to my father's clan," Kyle told him. Toby still didn't get how that was funny.

"It's okay; you don't need to get it. How does Little One feel about all this?" Kyle asked.

"I haven't talked to her about it yet. I thought I should ask you first."

"Well, you let me know how it goes and if she wants this then Betz and I will be happy to help you with anything that we can."

With that, Kyle got up and started working with the meat that they had killed. It was going to be a long night for the two of them, but this should be enough to hold them. Little One and I had a great garden and had a lot of fresh and canned vegetables to hold them for a long time.

I had found some jars, and two stock pots for canning in one of the boxes in the plane. I had thought that the man in the plane must have been going to stay for some time. He had a lot of things that he would need to make life easier for his stay here in this wonderful place if he ever found it. I was so glad that Kyle and I, as well as Little One, had been the lucky ones to have done that.

I thought that there was another man in the plane with him, but we hadn't found any more bones, so Kyle was not as sure of it as I was. I couldn't help but wonder if the other man might have been the one who found the clan all those years ago, and helped them to live better lives.

I did have a point because I thought that maybe the other man was the one who came into one of the old clans years ago. And that he was the one who taught them how to speak English that they now know. It was not so farfetched as far as Kyle could see. But all he really knew was that his father had taught the clan and as far back as he could remember his father and mother taught him. So on and so forth down through the years it went, but maybe the man on the plane was the first one to teach the clan how to speak. That was a mystery that would never be solved.

Little One and I were working with the baby when Kyle and Toby got back to the city. He was getting to be a big boy these days and loved to keep his mother and everyone else on our toes. He was so fast now and into everything in sight.

I gave Kyle a kiss that said I missed him a lot. That night he took his time with me as he ran his hands down my white skin and put hot kisses all over my body. He could see the need in my eyes and his need building within him. My dark hair was wet with sweat as he slid into me, and we made love for most of the night.

It had been a while since we had made love, and we both found release at the same time. He lay down next to me, and we slept for most of the night until little Carson let us know that he was hungry.

Kyle started to get up to help with him, but I pushed him back down and said, "No you don't. You need some sleep and I might need more of you later."

I had a smile on my face as I took the baby to a setting area to feed him. Carson was a happy baby and, just like his daddy, always wanting more of everything. He would be a great clan lord one day, I was sure of it.

Kyle was out for most of the night, other than to wake up and take his time making love to me. We always made love like it was the first time. It never got old for us, and there was always a need to get as much of each other as we could almost as if we thought it could be the last time. That made it that much more intense for both of us.

Over the next few months, we worked to get everything ready for Toby and Little One. I was sure that Toby would ask Little One to marry him, and Kyle knew better than to try and stop me from anything when I had my mind made up to do something. It didn't happen that year;

Toby wanted to take his time and make sure it was right for both of them, and he knew when it was right it would happen.

The next year Toby asked Little One to be his mate. She said yes; they seemed to be as happy as Kyle and I were, so it was a good life for all of us so far. Toby sat by himself a lot just thinking of how long he had waited for the right time to ask Little One to be his mate. He had feelings for Little One for years but never said anything because he didn't think she would pick him for a mate. In his eyes, she was the prettiest one of all the clan women. So why would she ever pick him, he thought to himself.

I had told Kyle that I wanted everyone to meet in the big cave for something, but no one seemed to know what that was. As we all sat down to eat, I started off with "There's something that I want to tell you before we go on with the meal. Both Little One and I have talked about this for some time now and from now on she would like to be called 'Lily,' like the flower," I said with a smile. "We both feel that Lily is a better name for her than Little One. That name is more about her size, and she wants people to think of her as person, not just someone who is small."

Toby and Kyle looked at each other and said, "Then so be it."

Toby and Lily made one of the caves on the other side of the big one that Kyle and I lived in theirs. The room was almost as big as the one Kyle and I had, but there was no extra room to sit and just relax or as I did feed the baby. But it was nice, and I was helping her with everything so it would feel like home for them to raise their family in.

I was happy for them. Lily always had a glow about her these days, so I knew that she was happy and so very much in love with Toby. I was sure they would have a little one before very long and that the baby would be as cute as both of them in my eyes. Toby was tall though not as tall as Kyle was, and he was very nice-looking. He had dark eyes and dark hair; he also almost always had a smile on his face. The best part of him was his kindness and, of course, his love for Lily.

No one really wanted to talk about Kyle's old home and clan these days. The life we had here was so good and so easy to live because there was no one trying to start fights all the time like Cal has done in the old clan. All of us wanted to keep the past where we all thought it should be—in the past. Toby had said that things were good with Kyle's father. So Kyle wanted to let them live their lives just as Kyle was living his. Sometimes Kyle had his dad on his mind when no one was around he would sit and think of home and wished that his father could see Kyle's new city and hold his grandchild. He knew in his heart that would never happen, and sometimes it made Kyle sad to know he had everything he could ever want here, but his father would never be a part of any of it.

Carson was walking now and some days everyone was wishing he were still crawling because he was hard to keep up with, and there were so many places to hide from his mom.

Kyle and I thought that all we needed right now was just the two caves that everyone used to sleep in and the big one that everyone used to eat, visit, and talk about what work needed to be done. There were also the water places to get drinking water from and another part to clean ourselves in and also clean everything else that needed to be cleaned. The part that Kyle and I loved the most was the hot springs; we would relax in it often, and would for many more years. When we first found this wonderful city to live in, I had talked to Kyle about where to go to the bathroom. In the old clan, everyone just went down a hill and went and then just put dirt over it. I told Kyle that in the old days in my world people would dig a very big hole. Then we would build walls around it and put a roof on it, and then make a seat for you to sit on over the hole and that's how you would go to the bathroom. We called it an outhouse. Kyle thought that was a lot better than going out in the open, and so we built an outhouse and placed it on a path down away from the main cave.

Kyle and I had been at odds for a few days. I had wanted Kyle to let me go to the upper world so I could get some things that I wanted that I couldn't get here. He was not willing to even talk about it, so things were tense for everyone.

Toby had to ask, "What's so bad about Betz wanting to go to the upper world to get some things that she can't get here?"

Kyle gave him a look that pretty much said to mind his own business. So he was trying to do that, but it was hard when everyone had to work together every day.

Finally, Lily had enough of the tension that was going on, so she stood up at the evening meal. "Look, this is not getting anyone anywhere, so we need to talk about it and move on."

Kyle knew that he needed to talk to us about it, but he sure didn't want to.

"Look," Kyle said, "I know that we go to the upper world sometimes to get things that we can't find here. But without knowing if my father's clan is still out looking for us, I just don't want to take the chance of them finding us. We all know what could happen if they do."

"Yes, but we can't just stop living because we might be seen either," I told him.

It was no use; he would always give in to me when it came to getting things that I needed to make life better, so why should this be any different?

"All right," Kyle said, "but we go when I say we go, and we go together."

"I think it's better to stay together in case something does go wrong," Toby said.

It was set to go to the upper world in a few days, but Kyle was still having a hard time with it. He just never wanted to put me in any danger, but he couldn't stop me from doing whatever I thought was best for the clan. He would go along with this and pray that everything went right.

The baby was walking now but he was just too little to keep up, so it was getting harder to hold him, but we all took turns carrying him on the trip.

The trip took a few days when finally we came to a big cave, and we walked for hours before we came to the back wall where there was an opening in it that led to the outside. Then up a hill and there we were just outside of the home that I had bought years ago, but it didn't upset me to see it now.

It did seem odd that there was no one living here. I still thought it was a very pretty place to live, even though there were tall weeds all over the yard now. The trees needed to be trimmed, and the house was in need of a good paint job. Still, I was glad to see the old place again, even though this wasn't my home anymore. I was happy with my new life now. I had found some money in one of the trunks in the plane, and I still had my old identification with me. I thought it would be easy just to go to a store and get the things I wanted and then meet up with the rest of the clan and go home. I had bought a small easy-to-carry sewing kit and some fabric so I could make things that all of us would need as time went on. With kids coming and the clan growing we would need a lot of things. It would only be the start, but it was a good one for all of us.

It was a good plan, and I was happy to be able to go back into a store again. I only got the things that I needed as I knew that we had to carry it all back. Before I left the store, there was a boy with a box full of puppies, so I took two of them. One was a little black one, and the other was white with back feet. They were both girls; I had to smile as I went back to the woods where the rest of them were waiting for me.

"How cute, Can I hold one of them?" Lily asked.

"Yes, you can. This one is yours," I said as I handed over the black puppy. Lily was laughing as the puppy was licking her face.

"Did you get everything that you needed for now?" Kyle asked me.

"Oh, yes, I got the jars that I told you about and also some yarn to make the baby some things to wear. And I also got things I need for sewing so both Lily and I will be able to make all kinds of things that will help our way of life."

Kyle had to smile as he could see how happy it made me to come back to my own world if only for a little while, and it made him wonder if I thought of staying.

It was as if I read his mind because just as he thought of that I said, "I don't even miss this anymore. I'm ready to go home now," I told all of them, as we started walking back to the underworld.

Toby was as happy about the puppy as Lily was; it made me smile to see them so happy together. Kyle was glad when we got to the spot that would lead them back to the world that he grew up in.

It felt safe to be back in the underworld. He knew he would have to let me go back to see my world sometimes. He was all right with that if that made me happy, although he could not see how anyone could like it. It was so loud, and there were big buildings everywhere and way too many people for him and everywhere you looked there were what I called cars. It was late when we got back. It was time to eat and then get ready for the next day. It still seemed hard for Kyle to understand that he was the lord of this clan and everything that was done made it his job to make sure it was completed. He always liked to watch his father tell the clan what the next day's work would be.

It always seemed to be so easy for him to tell the men what he wanted them to do. But for Kyle it was harder to give the orders. Toby had always liked Kyle and he thought he was a good clan lord.

He was always asking everyone if we had anything that we felt needed to get done. If so, he would put off the day's work that he had going until the next day. Toby was happy to be here and to call Kyle his friend as well as the clan lord. He would do whatever it took to help make this place a safe home for all of them.

The baby was getting into everything these days, and it was getting harder to keep up with him. He wanted to run everywhere and then hide from his mother. At first it was cute, but I didn't find it funny anymore. I spent most of my time trying to find him, and so I was starting to fall behind on a lot of my work to get ready for the next winter. It was time to get the little man under control or I would never get anything done. That would take a lot more hard work to accomplish because he was as stubborn as both of his parents.

Lily came running into the main cave out of breath one day, as I was trying to get Carson to take a much-needed nap, so I could get some work done.

"What's happened to get you so upset?" I asked Lily.

It took a few minutes before she could answer me.

"I think I'm going to have a baby," she said with tears running down her face.

I had a dumbfounded look on my face until I realized what she said.

"Oh, Lily, I'm so happy for both of you."

"Well, I haven't told Toby yet, but I'm going to tonight."

"Well, I'm sure he'll be very happy."

"Betz, I never thought I would ever be a mother like you. I only hope I'll be as good as you are."

I gave her a hug and told her she would be great.

"Now we have to get things ready for the baby. I'll help you with everything," I told her.

Lily was crying again. "No one has ever been as good to me as you have. I'm so lucky to have you as a friend," Lily said through her tears.

"Oh, Lily, you're more than a friend to me. You're my family now."

The summer went by fast and Lily was getting big now with the baby. She had been helping me get the garden cleaned up, and I was showing her how to can some of the food. The pantry was full of food for the winter, and the cold part of the cave had potatoes and other fresh things to cook with. The old clan never had as much fresh food in the winter as Kyle's clan had these days because of Lily and me. We were great when it came to making things grow in the garden, and I made sure that Lily was just as good at it as me. Well, almost as good as me.

I had been busy teaching Lily how to sew and now with the baby so close to being here it was a good time to get things made that the little one would soon need. Lily was going to be a great mother; she had everything ready just as I had done when I was waiting for my baby to get here. It wouldn't be long now and the clan would be blessed with another baby to love.

Carson loved to go to the garden and help himself to carrots and tomatoes. He was getting to be a big boy now, and he was looking more and more like his father these days. He was tall and strong like his dad and always wanted to help with anything that he needed to get done that his father thought Carson was big enough to handle. Carson hated to be treated like a baby even though he was still very young. He would have his time as an adult soon enough, and his mother wasn't in a big hurry to have him grow up just yet. —

Lily had named her puppy "Little One." I couldn't help but to smile every time she called it. The puppy would be fun for the baby when it came. It would have to grow up fast because if the baby were anything like Carson, it would be running a lot just to keep up with the baby.

My own dog Tucker was happy to have two puppies to play with, but not as much as Carson was. He would run until he would just drop and fall asleep wherever he was at that time. Sometimes it was by my garden and sometimes it was by his father where he had been watching him and Toby working on tools or cleaning meat to put up for winter. Either way, he was growing up and was a very happy boy, and he was so loved by everyone in the small clan.

It wouldn't be long and he would be out on the food hunts with his father and Toby, but not today. *No, today he was still my little man, to love and watch over, but one day he would stand on his own,* I thought with a smile. I was wrong about him not staying my little man because he would always come to his mother for help throughout his life. I would be the one who always knew just what to say to make things right again.

Before anyone was ready for it, the big day came, and Lily was getting ready to have the baby. I was still sleeping when Toby came and got me to help with Lily.

"What's wrong?" I asked him.

"I think she's having the baby now," he said with worried eyes. I got up and went with him and tried not to wake up Kyle or Carson.

"Is everything all right?" Kyle asked me.

"Yes. Lily is having the baby, so I need you to take care of our baby if he wakes up."

"All right," he said as he turned over and went back to sleep.

Poor Toby was beside himself with worry, but he did everything that I needed him to do. After about ten hours, he heard the baby's first cry to let everyone know that she was here. She was so pretty, and I wasn't just saying that, the baby had pretty hair, and her skin had a warm glow to it. Not white or an odd color that a lot of babies have to them when they come into the world.

I handed the baby to Toby and said, "You have a very pretty baby girl."

He cradled the baby with tears running down his face. He was a happy father, and then he gave the baby back to Lily.

I started to leave when Lily took my hand and said, "Thank you so much."

"You're so welcome, my dear. Now you both get some sleep with that pretty little girl and I'll see you tomorrow."

It was just getting light out when I got back to my bedroom in the cave. Kyle and the baby were still sleeping so I got in beside Kyle and was asleep before long too. Kyle didn't have the heart to wake me up to tell me that they were going to see the baby. Carson was pulling him away, so he let me sleep; I needed it anyway because I was up all night helping Lily have the baby. He had never heard me snore before, and it was kind of fascinating to him. But Carson won out by pulling him, and if he didn't leave right now they would both wake me, so it was time to go.

The next morning I woke up to the puppy licking my face.

"Well, good morning to you too, fluffy." I picked up the little ball of fur and went to see where everyone was. There was no one to be found in the main cave so I almost went back to bed, but not knowing where everyone was had me wondering if something was going on that I should know about.

Chapter 11

I started for outside to see where everyone was, no one was there either.

"Well, let's try Lily's," I told the puppy. "There they are," I told the dog as we went in to see what was up other than everyone wanting to see the baby. Sure enough, Kyle was holding the baby, and Toby and Carson were playing nearby. Lily was just glowing with pride, and who could blame her; after all, the baby was beautiful.

Lily started to get up when I came in, but before she could I told her, "Stop young lady you stay in bed." Kyle gave the baby back to Lily and told her how pretty the baby was.

"Well, did you think of a name for the baby yet?" I asked.

"Yes, we did. It's Violet. I hope you like it," she said as she held out the baby so I could hold her.

"I love it. She looks like a Violet to me and just as pretty as one too. Well, baby girl, you have lots of people that love you and one little boy that will be happy to have someone to play with other than the puppies and us grown-ups. So you better grow fast, because we all need a helping hand with that little man of mine," I said to the baby as I rocked her in my arms as Lily watched.

The winter was long and hard with a lot of snow, but the dogs and Carson had lots of fun days. Every time Carson would build a big snowman the dogs would run and jump on it until it fell over and Carson would chase after them laughing and rolling around in the cold snow. I loved to sit for hours and watch them as I worked on different things that I needed to get done.

Kyle and Toby both kept busy with stacking up wood and whatever else work that they had to do. Lily was doing the best she could with her part of the work and taking care of her new baby. Life was going good for all of us, but just when you think everything is great it seems that something always happens to throw a wrench into the mix. It was on an early food hunt that Kyle and Toby were on that everything went very wrong.

Kyle came home out of breath and sat me down.

"We have a big problem."

"What is it?" I asked him.

"We found signs that a clan has been near the cave that leads to our city."

I tried to get Kyle to calm down by telling him that I didn't think there was anything to worry about because they didn't find the doorway at the end of the cave or they would have found the city.

"I know that, but they might come back and decide to make that their home cave. If they do that, how would we get back and forth for our hunts? And if they stay in that cave they could find the doorway the same way that you did."

I had to admit he had a real reason to worry. There was nothing that we could do about it right now. We would just have to hope they only wanted a place for the night like Kyle and I had wanted not so long ago.

"Look, I know that you have done the best you can to keep the opening of that cave hidden so stop worrying about it. I really don't think they'll find it." I could see that he wanted to believe that I was right, but even as I said it, I wasn't sure either.

As it worked out, the clan went on their way to wherever they had come from. But Kyle was never at ease after that day; he was always trying to find another way out in case someone did find the doorway to our city.

Toby and Kyle had been looking for some time and it paid off; they found a new way out so even if someone found us at least now we could get out in a hurry if it came to that. Now we needed to watch both openings. Kyle was always uneasy these days, and it put me on edge too, but what could I do to help him? The answer came the next day as I went outside of the city without him knowing about it.

I kept down close to the ground to try to keep out of sight just in case there was anyone around. I was about to give up and go back to the city when I saw someone and then I saw more men. Kyle was right; something was going on, but what?

Why would there be all these men here now what did they want way out here. I wanted to get as close as I could so I could hear what was going on.

It was getting late, but I had to try and find out, so I kept down and got as close as I could. I stayed down and waited for someone to talk, and it didn't take very long before one of the men started talking about how he wanted to just go back. He didn't think they would ever find Kyle anyway.

"I know he's out here somewhere and we can't just go back. He has the right to know about his father, don't you think?"

The rest of the men agreed with him.

"It will be hard for him to know that his father is gone and that Cal has taken over the clan and that no one would stand up to him and put someone else in as the new clan lord."

"I hope he'll want to come back and take his place again," one of the men said.

"Well, we all know that won't happen. He's been gone too long and the way he left has made it impossible for him to come back as the lord of the clan now."

"Still it's his right to know of his father."

I had heard enough to stand up and go to where they were all sitting around a fire.

At first they didn't move, but as I got closer to the fire they all jumped up and started for their weapons. "It's Betz," I said before they could throw me down.

"Betz, we have been looking for Kyle for a few days now," one of the men said.

"I know, I heard most of what you said," I told them.

After talking to them, I told them that I would tell Kyle that they were here to talk to him. I told them that he would come to their fire pit in two days. I took my time getting back just in case they might try to follow me back to the city, but no one did. But it was very late before I got back, and Kyle was waiting and he was not happy.

Kyle was so relieved to see that I was all right, but he was also mad as hell that I would leave like that and not tell anyone. Before he could say anything, I started talking.

"I'm sorry. I know I shouldn't have gone without telling anyone. I thought I should try and see if anyone was still out there around the caves," I told him.

Kyle just looked at me with a hateful look on his face, and then said, "Just what were you going to do if you found someone?" he asked me.

"Kyle, I did find people. Part of your father's clan, and they only want to see you and talk to you about your father. I told them that I'd have you go talk to them at their fire pit two days from now."

"You talked to them? Are you crazy? You could have been killed or taken back and put to death! Why would you do that?" he asked me.

"I was going to just listen to them talking. You know, to see what they were doing here. But then I heard them saying that they had been looking for days trying to find you, and how it was your right to know about your father. I guess I just knew that it was safe to talk to them, so I did."

Kyle had to admit that I had balls and also had more nerve than most men that he knew. But he sure wasn't going to let me off that easy.

Kyle knew that it could have gone very bad, and I could have been hurt or killed. It took the rest of the night before he put it behind him, then he reached for me in bed and he made love to me like it was the last time he would see me.

It was sweet and full of intense passion that left both of us satisfied. It was early when Kyle and Toby left to see the men of his father's clan.

I couldn't bring myself to tell Kyle that his father was gone. I knew how close he was to him and it would be hard for him to deal with it, but he would in time.

After everyone shook hands and told Kyle it was good to see him, Sam got down to why they had come to find him. Sam told Kyle that the clan had been out on a food hunt and somehow Orlando got in the way of a deer, and was kicked in the head as the deer ran past him. They said he was dead before any of them could get to him.

"I'm real sorry for your loss, Kyle, but at least it was fast and he wasn't in a lot of pain."

"Well, somehow it doesn't feel like this is real, Sam, but I know you wouldn't come out here for the fun of it."

"We thought you had the right to know about your father," Sam told him. "It was over before anyone could get to him."

Joe and the other men told Kyle that Cal was taking over now as clan lord and no one was trying to stop him. Kyle had never really liked Cal. He was a bully, and he only saw the worst in everything. It really didn't matter to Kyle one way or another if he was the new lord of that clan now. Kyle had his own clan to watch over now.

"Some of us thought that maybe you would think about coming back and taking your rightful place as our clan lord? If not, well, maybe you'd think about letting some of us come into your clan," Sam asked.

Kyle wasn't expecting this. Kyle looked at them and said, "Look, I don't have a lot to offer any of you right now, but any of you who don't want to go back can stay here with us," he told them. Most of the men went back, but Sam and three others stayed with them.

"Sam, you know that Cal won't like the fact that some of the men wanted to leave his clan to stay here and join my clan. It could cause a war between the two clans over this."

Sam already knew that was coming from Kyle, and he knew that Cal was unstable and that was why he and the others were here in the first place.

"I know. He'll be looking for anything he can to start a war because he hates you for leaving for an upper world woman," Sam told him. "If you want us to leave and go back, I'll understand, but I've known for a long time now that Cal is not of sound mind. That's why we want to leave. He's a time bomb that could go off at any time," Sam stated. Kyle was not one to back down from a fight, so if Cal wanted one, he would get one.

When Kyle got back to the city, all the men stood in the middle of the courtyard and couldn't believe that Kyle had found this place. It wasn't like anything any of them had ever seen. This was a place that any one of them would be happy to be able to call home, and to fight to the death to keep safe for the whole clan if it came to that.

I came out of the caves with Carson and welcomed all the men to the clan. Lily was happy to see some of them but was sad about the death of Kyle's father. Kyle wanted to put up a cross for his father and had everyone in the clan say something about his father. Afterward, Toby and the rest of the men went into the cave and had food as they all sat around the fire pit in the main cave. They talked about all the work and hunts that Kyle had missed in his old clan. It was a long night, and the men would sleep in the main cave for the night and they could figure out everything else over the next few days. Kyle told all the men to get some sleep.

"Tomorrow we'll decide what work needs to be done next to make you feel at home here too." Kyle told them.

I showed the men where they could sleep for the night and they could pick out what cave they each wanted to call their own over the next few days.

In their cave, getting ready for bed, I asked Kyle if he was all right.

"Yes, I'm fine," he said as he started to undress me, taking his sweet time doing it. He put his hands on my breasts and started sucking on each one. Then he ran his hands and tongue up and down my body slowly until I was having a hard time standing up. I leaned back against the wall and let him do whatever he wanted and tonight he wanted to do everything to me. He was hurting and I was what he needed right now to make it all go away for a few hours.

He took me right there and then when I thought he was done he started again before I could get to the bed. Right now he didn't need a bed or anything else other than the two of us and just a wild need that wouldn't stop. Kyle turned me around and pushed me over while he took me as slowly as he could from behind. As he thrust himself into my wet warm place, I came and with harder faster thrusting he came into me as we both slid to the floor and slept there most of the night.

The next few days went by fast and the men all seemed to be enjoying the city. They were all in amazement at how pretty the city was. Everything within the walls of the city seemed to make you feel safe from everything else, even Cal from the old clan.

Kyle knew that it was only a matter of time now, before Cal would be looking for all the men to try and take back what he thought was his. It would be a fight that Kyle wasn't looking forward to. He would not stop fighting for the clan. And he would die before he would let anyone hurt his son or me.

The new men in the clan went to get their women before Cal got wind of what was happening, and so far it was working. The clan was getting bigger all the time now. But it would take time to have enough men to fight and win against Cal's clan.

I knew they would have a hard time trying to find the city and I was sure we could live life without worry for now anyway.

There was always someone working either in the meat cave or with Kyle in his tool cave. Some of the new women were helping clean up in the main cave and also would do whatever I asked them to do. They all seemed to think of me as their new lady of the clan because Kyle was the lord of this clan. It was never as hard as it had been when I was in Kyle's old clan. Now everyone liked me and the women all came to me if they needed anything. They always made time to ask what I wanted them to do. So I had my hands full, but because Lily had lived her whole life in a clan she was a big help for me. She helped me to understand my new role within the clan.

Time had gone by so fast and I was having a baby again and Lily was also pregnant again, but now the clan had other women to help with everything that needed to get done. It wasn't always up to me and Lily to get it all done and that was a good thing. For the first time in a long while I could take my time getting ready in the mornings.

Carson was a lot of help now; he was always trying to help me with anything I might need. He could see that I was having a hard time carrying the baby this time.

"I'm fine," I told Carson, "so you can go and help your father if you want."

"Father told me to make sure and help you all day today," he told me with a small smile on his cute little face. He looked so much like Kyle that sometimes it hurt my heart just to look at him and not grab him and just hug him close to my heart. But I knew he was a lot like his dad, and that would embarrass him, so I never did what

I really wanted to do. No, because he would someday be the clan lord here and Mom's hugs were not for big boys, or at least that is what he kept telling me.

"Well, when you see dad you tell him that I said my work is done and I don't need any more help right now. The next clan lord can go help with what he likes to do the best, running the clan." I could see the pride in his face as I told him he would be the next clan lord. I did the one thing that he could do without, but I did it anyway.

I gave my son a kiss on the cheek that he wiped off as he said, "Thanks, Mom," and ran off to find his father.

Kyle and the rest of the new men in the clan had been working to make the city as good as they could. It was a wonderful place to live now; everything was clean and I as well as all the other women had everything green again. Kyle just stood and took it all in sometimes and thought, *I wonder if it was like this long ago.* It didn't matter because it was now and that was all that mattered.

Soon Kyle would be a father again and so would Toby. Kyle knew that Toby was hoping for a boy this time. Kyle really didn't care as long as the baby and I were healthy he would be happy. He was still standing in the middle of the courtyard when his son found him.

"Father, mother said I could come and help you now, so here I am. What do you want me to do?" he asked his father.

"Well, let's get some more wood in the cave so when the babies come we will have it nice and warm for their birthday. What do you say?"

Carson put out his arms and his father filled them with wood to take in. Kyle was a happy man and if the clan had to go to war with his old clan so be it. This was his life now and he would do what he had to do as a clan lord, husband and father to make sure this life we were living, stayed safe. One day his sons would take over and do the same for the clan.

However back in the other clan these days

Everyone was trying to live under the rule of Cal now and he didn't make it easy to do. He was always looking for someone to do something wrong so he could go into a rant. No one liked him, but what could any of them do? He was the clan lord now and they had to go along with whatever he said if they wanted to live within his caves.

All he ever seemed to do was make every man in the clan go on the food hunts and watch as the rest of the clan did almost the entire cleanup afterward. He never took the time to help with the training of the young either. He only wanted to eat and make love to all the women he could, and all the clan men hated him; he had no respect for anyone other than himself.

Cal had taken the prettiest and youngest women in the clan to mate with and they had all given him children, but he was never a good father to any one of them. He didn't want to be bothered by all the things a real father would do with his kids. He did make sure that the cave had everything it needed to make it safe and warm and there was always food to eat for all of them, even if he was never the one on the hunts to get the food to take care of the whole clan.

So in that way he was doing his part. Cal was as happy as someone like him could be. He was clan lord and had mates to take anytime he felt the need and everyone did as he wished. In the back of his mind everyone was still wishing that Kyle was there and the lord of this clan. Over time it was on his mind all the time and it had put him on the brink of insanity. He would pick fights with some of the men and if he couldn't win the fight he would have the man put to death. But still no one would stand up to him and kick him out of the clan. They just tried to do whatever he wanted in hopes of pleasing him. In the minds of most of the clan, all any of them wanted was to just live a good life within this clan, and let Kyle live his own life like Kyle's father had told the clan to do when he was clan lord. It was just Cal's sick mind that kept them from doing that.

It was on one of the clans hunting runs that one of the men tried to find Kyle's clan and see if he could help them. Cal caught the man and he was put to death for it, and the body was left out hanging on a tree for everyone to see what happens if they tried to undermine him. No one was safe from his wrath. Everyone in the clan had to walk on egg shells if they wanted to stay in the clan, and try not to look at Cal the wrong way or he would have them killed. So their life was not good and it didn't look like it ever would be with him as the clan lord.

Kyle was about to be a father again and he was walking back and forth the same way he did when his son was born. But now he had his boy walking beside him with a big smile on his face.

"I know this is your first time waiting. Not for me," Kyle told his son.

Carson just gave his father a little smile and told him that it was going to be all right. Lily came out and told them that it was a little girl this time and that both of us were doing fine. Kyle went in to see them with Carson by his side.

"Wow, she's so little," Carson told them. "Look, she has dark hair and lots of it."

"Yes, she sure does," I answered.

Kyle held the baby for a few minutes and gave the baby back to me and gave me a kiss then told me that the baby was beautiful.

"Now you need to get some rest and I'll look after Carson," he said as he kissed me.

Lily was tired and Kyle could see it. So he told her to go get some much-needed sleep too.

"Are you sure? I don't need to go if you need me here."

Kyle gave her a big hug and said, "Lily, you're about to have a baby yourself and you're exhausted so go get some sleep."

Toby was glad to see Lily go to bed; Kyle was right—she needed some rest. She loved me so much that she would stay up all night to help if I needed her here and not let anyone know that she was tired herself. Lily was a true friend.

Kyle took his son's hand as they walked into the other part of the caves and said, "Well, let's go get some food to eat, and then we'll make sure your mother and the baby are sleeping."

Carson was always happy to be doing anything with his father.

The next few days were a blur for all of them. Lily had her baby just two months after I had mine. This time she had a baby boy. Toby was beside himself with the joy of being a father again. Because of the other women in the clan now, both Lily and I could take our time getting back on our feet. We both needed to take the time to rest up because with two new babies around it would be a busy place here for a long time. Kyle and I named our baby girl Raven because of all her dark hair. Lily and Toby named their boy Sonny because he made them smile all the time.

Chapter 12

Things had gotten worse in Cal's clan. Everyone was on edge because Cal had killed one of the clan men and hung him on a tree for all to see what would happen if you went up against him. All the clan men were upset over it. The man had not done anything to be put to death over, other than say something about Cal that wasn't in very good light even if it was true. For that, Cal had the man put to death. No one was safe in Cal's clan. If you didn't like something that Cal did, you had better keep it to yourself or take the chance of being put to death if you said what you thought of him out loud.

"We have to do something now, or there might not be any men left in the clan to do anything," Cody said to a few of the men.

Mark stood up and said, "I'll go and see if I can find Kyle maybe he'll help us."

"What makes you think he'll help us when everyone here stood by and let him be kicked out of the clan?"

Cody knew Mark was right, but he didn't see that they had a choice; it was try and get some help or just wait and see who Cal would have killed next. Cody told the rest of the men that he would be the one to go for help if he could get it.

Cal had been with one of the youngest women in the clan for a few days now, so everyone thought she would be expecting a baby soon. That seemed to be what he was doing these days getting one of the women pregnant and then he would find another to be with. It had been going on this way for some time now, and all the men were upset over his lack of respect for the rest of the clan.

That was not the way that they had lived when Orlando was lord of the clan. Orlando was a clan lord whom everyone pretty much respected except for Cal. Then Cal hated everyone other than himself. It took Cody a few days of walking and waiting before one of Kyle's clan found him and then two more days before he got to talk to Kyle himself.

"Kyle, I know that none of us stood up to help you when you needed us and for that all of us are sorry and if we could deal with Cal ourselves we would have. But Cal is one whom you had better have a good plan worked out for, or be ready to die. Because he just doesn't have a heart, and it won't bother him to kill as many men as he can. We only want you to help us come up with some kind of plan to get rid of him. I think we have to kill him because he won't give up being clan lord any other way."

Kyle knew that he was right, for as many years that Kyle had been around Cal he had never seen him in a giving mood. He was always hateful to everyone and always trying to start a fight with someone over nothing.

It took a few days to come up with a good plan that everyone thought would work; everyone knew that the only weakness Cal seemed to have is with the women of the clan. So that was it; they would give him something in one of his drinks when he was with one of the women. That was the only time he ever let down his guard as far as anyone knew.

Everyone agreed he would not think one of his women would try to kill him, so everyone thought that would be the best way to get rid of him once and for all.

One of the women of Kyle's clan gave Cody poison that he could put into one of Cal's drinks; it wouldn't hurt him, he would just go to sleep and never wake up. After all the things that he had done to everyone in the clan, he was getting off easy in their eyes.

The men said their goodbyes and left to go back to their clan. To make it look good, they came back with food so it would look like they had just been on a hunt for the clan. Kyle was hoping that the plan had gone as everyone had been hoping it would for the clans' sake. In Kyle's mind Cal would still be there; he was not dumb, and he always seemed to land on his feet. But he was hoping for his old clan's sake that the plan worked.

There was no way to know right now because Kyle wasn't going to take the chance of anyone finding the city where his clan and family were. No, Kyle knew that he didn't have enough men to fight off Cal's clan right now. It would take more men than he had to win a fight with Cal. But in time he'd be able to hold his own very well and that day would not be far off.

After a few years of working with Kyle's clan, the men could now stand their own in any fight if they had to. Kyle was sure they could fight off his father's old clan if it came to that now. Even his own son had been training with the rest of Kyle's men, and he would be a fighting force that even Kyle himself wouldn't want to go up against in a fight. They were ready.

Meanwhile, back in Kyle's old clan . . .

Cal had a bad feeling about the clan these days. He was always at odds with someone in the clan, and he wasn't sure why, but right now he didn't trust any one of them. He knew that if he didn't watch them closely he might fall prey to any one of them.

Yes, he knew that they didn't want him as the lord of this clan. So he had to watch everything that went on within the clan. The plan that the clan had come up with didn't go as they had wanted it to.

Cal had been having one of the women test everything that he ate or drank to make sure no one had a chance to do him in. No one in the clan had thought that he went to that extreme. So it was a big surprise when they found one of the women dead in Cal's bed. He had thought pretty much of everything so far when it came to the clan. He always seemed to be one step ahead of them.

Of course everyone acted as if they had no idea what could have happened to the woman.

"I know that someone in this clan has been trying to kill me for some time now. I want a name, or I'll make everyone pay for this," Cal said with a sneer on his face.

Before anyone could answer him, one of the older men in the clan jumped up. "It was me, and I'd do it again if I thought it would do any good," Asher said and sat back down. Cal just sat there looking at the rest of the men around the fire pit to see if he could find someone who looked uneasy. To his amazement they all sat there as if they had nothing to do with it.

He knew that was not the case, and he was damn sure it wasn't old Asher, but he had to make a point. So if Asher wanted to make himself a martyr then let him. Cal was true to his word, and the old man was put to death and left hanging so everyone could see how Cal handled traitors.

Word got back to Kyle's clan that the plan went horribly wrong and that Cal had killed another man just to make a point. It was late in the year before anyone heard any more from Cal's clan, but when they did, it was not good. Kyle knew that it wouldn't be long, and he would have to fight or lose his family and clan.

The rest of the clan would stand by whatever Kyle did as the lord of the clan. Carson was a tall young man with his mother's dark hair and both of his parents green eyes, and like his father, he would fight for the clan and his family.

Kyle was proud of his son and knew that someday he would become a good lord of the clan. Kyle had a hard time thinking that his son was almost a man now. Where had the time gone? The boy he had held in his arms and showed how to hunt for food was now a young man.

"I don't want you to go with me this time. But soon you'll be ready for anything that comes your way," Kyle told his son.

"Father, I'm as ready as I'll ever be to fight, and you know it."

Kyle could see the right side of Carson's jaw working as he walked back and forth in front of his father. Kyle knew he couldn't hold his son back with a war on its way even though he wanted to so badly that it hurt.

So he took a deep breath and said, "Okay, but you are to do as I tell you without fighting me every step of the way, do you understand me?"

Carson stood in front of Kyle with his hands behind his back and looked his father in the face and said, "Look, I know you think I'm too young to understand a lot of things. You know I can fight as good as any one of the men here and a lot better than most of them. I wish you would treat me like a man and not like your son when it comes to things like this."

Kyle had a hard time thinking of him as a man even though he knew that he was indeed a young man now.

"Fair enough," Kyle said and shook his son's hand as they walked off together to find me and see what was for dinner.

I was not happy knowing that my son was going to be fighting for the clan already. He was so young, and I was afraid that he would be hurt or worse he could get killed in the fight, and that was more than I could stand.

"Are you out of your mind?" I asked as I stood next to Kyle in the bedroom of our cave.

"I know you still think of him as a boy, but he's not a boy anymore, and he feels like he needs to prove himself to all of us." Kyle could see the hurt in my eyes and put his arms around me and told me that he would die before he would let anything happen to our son.

Kyle thought that all his men were as ready as they could be to go into a war with his father's clan. He was always one to try and get as much out of everyone as he could and wished that they could have more time to get in shape. He had a feeling that time was running out.

Toby was having a hard time getting used to the fact that he was a father of two kids now and the happiest he had ever been in his life. If he died tomorrow, he would die knowing that he had everything he ever wanted. Lily would always love him no matter what he did so he was ready to fight for what he loved, and that was his family, as well as the rest of the clan. He would be proud to die for what he loved.

Kyle had taken his role as lord of his clan to heart. He had spent many hours a day training the men to fight and hunt. He was proud of all of them; they had all worked hard to learn, and now it seemed that they might have to go to war with Kyle's old clan. It was not something any one of them wanted to do, but if it came to that they would. He was still hoping they could avoid a war right now, but in his heart he was pretty sure war was coming sooner than he or anyone else expected.

I found Kyle standing alone by the water. He had his back to me as I came to his side and put my head on his shoulder.

"I know this is a hard time for you right now thinking that you might have to fight your father's clan. But you know that everyone here will back you up with their lives if it comes to that!"

Kyle just stood there for a few more minutes before he said anything. With a sigh, he pulled me close to him and said, "I only hope that we can find a way to end it as soon as possible, without a lot of lives lost."

Carson was watching his father and mother, although he couldn't hear them. He could see that this was hard on both of them; he wished he could stop all of it for everyone. What could he do by himself to help?

Carson was walking back to the family cave when he saw his sister running to him. "Hi, pretty girl," Carson said to Raven as he picked her up and put her on his shoulders for a ride.

Carson loved his little sister and always had time for her; she was such a sweet little girl, and he would always make time for her in his life.

Raven was tall and had the long dark hair like the rest of her family, but she also had the most wonderful smile, and she knew how to use it. She could sometimes be as mean as a snake, but she also had a way of making everyone she knew laugh all the time, she never seemed to have a bad day. If you ever crossed her, that would all change, and believe me when I say you really don't want to see that side of Carson's sister.

The whole clan loved her as if she were their child. She would be a woman soon and someday someone would have a wonderful mate, and she was also a good cook. She was always coming up with something new, and so far everyone ate it without anyone complaining about it. So she had become one of the clan's favorite cooks. But then she had a real good teacher: her mother.

I wanted to go to the upper world for more guns and bullets, but Kyle was not going to have any of that.

"No, we are not going to go top side every time we have something going on here. We will deal with this the same way we have for as many years as I can remember."

I knew there was no use in arguing with him when he was upset, so I let it go for now, but it was still on my mind. I knew with my kind of weapons the fighting would not last long because the other clan didn't have them. So we would have the upper hand in the war.

Kyle didn't want everyone here to have guns because they had lived for many years without them, and they could go on without them.

"Well, I think we should use them to end all this as fast as we can so life can go on without killing each other," I told him.

Kyle knew that I had a point, but it was still hard for him to go with the upper world way of handling things, he could never live like they do up there. But he did want to end this with Cal as soon as he could because he didn't want to see a lot of killing either. He gave it a lot of thought, but in the end he would use what they had always used to fight, and that was with hatchets, bows, and arrows, as well as hand-to-hand. It had been done this way for as long as Kyle could remember, and it would stay that way as long as he was the clan lord.

He was good with a bow and not bad with his hatchet either, and so that would be the way they would fight. I was not happy with Kyle's choice, but I would stand by whatever he wanted to do. It was Kyle's clan, and I would always stand by him. Carson was a lot like his father as far as wanting to keep the fighting the same way it had always been; after all, that's what made them who they are.

"Oh, for crying out loud, what is so wrong with wanting to end this as easy as we can?" I asked them. Both of them just stood there looking at me like I had two heads or something. It was funny to see how much they looked alike.

Kyle turned to Carson and said, "I need to talk to your mother alone so go and find the rest of the men and tell them we will be having a meeting in the main cave tonight." Carson was off before Kyle was done talking. Kyle was having a very hard time staying calm as he stood in front of me. He loved me, but sometimes I could make him so mad that he saw red, and right now was one of those times.

"Please try to understand how things are done here. I know that in your world you go for the easy way out of a fight. But here we have been fighting this way for as long as I can remember. Let me take care of my job and you just do your job and everything will be fine."

"Well, don't ever let me stand in your way. I just wish you could see that this is my world now too, and not just up to you, and if you don't care about what I think then we have a big problem. I have a lot to say about what happens to our children, not just you."

Kyle's jaw was working as he tried to stay calm. "I love the children just as much as any man can, and I would never let them do anything that I thought would hurt them. Our son is not a little boy anymore, and he wants, no, he needs to do his part for him to feel like he is a part of this clan. One day he will be clan lord, and not you, I, or anyone else has the right to try and keep him from growing up."

Kyle stood his ground and tried to make me see that he would let me speak my mind in private, but not in front of the clan and not in front of our children. It was not allowed in his world.

In his father's clan I would be pushed out of the clan if I tried to talk in front of the clan like I was doing to him right now; it was not right to do this.

Kyle was always so good with me, but even he had his limits, and right now I was pushing him to his. I knew that Kyle was very upset with me; for the next few days he was very distant. It was a hard time for the whole clan now as war was right next door to us, and everyone was on edge. It was on a clear day, and everyone was out in the courtyard when someone saw a clan man standing on top of one of the outer caves looking at them.

Kyle told me to take the children into one of the caves for safety, and all the men went after the intruder.

"Where is he?" Kyle asked Toby.

"We've looked everywhere, but he just disappeared."

All the men had to take turns standing guard at all hours over the next few days because Kyle thought the whole clan would be trying to get to them in the middle of the night.

The next few days went by without incident.

"Maybe it was just an outsider who just happened to find our city," Toby said.

"I hope you're right, but I don't think so," Kyle told the men. "Carson, I want you and the rest of the men to keep watch at both of the openings tonight for any sign of movement. If you see anything, I want you to stand down until I have a chance to decide the best way to proceed."

It was a long night for the whole clan, but when it was over Kyle was busy with his best plans to find a place to fight the other clan outside of his city. The last thing Kyle wanted was for Cal's clan to find the city. He had to make sure that never happened; there was no way he would let the fighting start within the city walls.

"I think it's a good strategy," Toby remarked. "If we get them out in the open field by the big rock on the other side of our city, it will be far enough away so that the city will be safe, and hopefully it won't be a long fight because pretty much the whole clan hates Cal anyway. Maybe if they get the chance they'll come over to our side, and we can get rid of him once and for all."

"All right then, we have a plan, so let's get everyone in place right away, and we'll take turns at all the lookouts," Kyle said as he got up and put more wood on the fire pit.

"I'll take the first watch at the main entrance of our city then," Toby said as he got to his feet and started for his post outside of our city.

Chapter 13

L ily and I had put all the books in one of the outside caves to turn into a classroom to teach anyone who wanted to learn how to read and write. Some of the older men had no need of it as far as they could see it made no sense to learn this woman's ways. But a lot of them did want to learn, and all the children knew how to read, write, and also how to do some math.

Lily could see that I was not myself the last few days, and so she asked me, "Okay, what's up with you? It's not like you to work all day and not say anything to me."

I loved Lily as if she was my own sister, so I wasn't afraid to say whatever was on my mind.

"I'm sorry, it's just been a long week with everyone on edge over the upcoming war, and I guess I'm not myself these days," I told her.

"Oh, come on, Betz, I know you better than that. Something is up with you. Are you and Kyle fighting or something?"

"No, not anymore, but yes we did have a fight, and now he acts like I'm not here most of the time," I said with tears in my eyes.

Lily gave me a hug and told me, "You know that he loves you more than anything in this world, but this is a bad time for all of us. Toby is always on edge too. He tries not to let it show, but it does sometimes. You just have to let him work through this, and everything will be as it always has been."

I thought for a few minutes and then I said, "I don't know if we'll ever be the same, after all the things that were said last night."

Lily could see that this was more than just a fight this time. "Is there anything that I can do to help?"

I shook my head. "Not this time I'm afraid, but thanks for caring."

Toby was still gone when Lily got back to their cave and the children were sitting in the part of the cave that was made up for them to sleep in.

Sonny was upset over something, but when Lily asked him what was wrong, he just said, "Nothing, Mom."

"Violet, what's going on with your brother?" Lily could see that she wanted to tell her, but would not go against his wishes, so she just shook her head. "Well, if you two want to talk to me I'll be getting food ready," she said, and left for the big cave.

"Thanks for not telling Mom what I said. It means a lot to me to know that I can trust you when I tell you something," Sonny said as he gave his sister a big hug.

"I'll always be here for you." Violet told him.

Meanwhile back at Kyle's old clan . . .

All the men in Cal's clan were upset over the way Cal was handling the clan. He was the meanest man any one of them had ever seen. He had no feelings for anyone, not even the women whom he had children with. He could just toss them aside like they were nothing to him. He was so full of hate for everyone and everything that all the men wanted to kill him. No one would go that far again because they all knew the last time they had tried, it ended with an innocent man and woman getting killed.

Cal was trying to find a way to fight the other clan without getting himself killed; he knew that everyone in his own clan would kill him if they got the chance to do it. His hate for Kyle was all he could think of. He would take the chance and go to war with the one who had brought that upper world woman into the clan and put her first before his own people.

To Cal, that was unforgivable, and he would do whatever it took to kill Kyle and that upper world woman. He had hated Kyle before, but now it was eating up what was left of his mind. He couldn't see past the hate and that was all that kept him going—well, that and the women whom he made love to.

However in Kyle's clan,

Everyone was always ready to do whatever Kyle thought needed to be done; he was a good clan lord.

"What's up with you, Sonny?" asked Carson. They had been friends their whole lives. Carson had a lot of fun learning to fight when they were boys; even though

Sonny was a better fighter than he was, he had no jealousy toward him.

"Carson, do you think I'm a good fighter?"

"Of course I do. You're even better than I am. Why do you ask?"

"My father doesn't seem to think so. He won't even talk to me about fighting in the war if it comes to that." Carson was not sure how to take what he was saying because he knew how much both of his parents loved him.

"Let me talk to your father for you. Sometimes it's easier to talk to someone else than it is to your child," Carson told him.

Sonny looked anxious when he asked, "Do you think it will do any good?"

"There's only one way to find out. Besides, what do you have to lose by it?"

"Thanks, I really appreciate it, and I'll take any help I can get at this point."

Carson was a man of his word, and later that night, he found Sonny's father and asked if he could talk to him.

"Sure, what's up?" Toby asked as they walked.

"Well, I was talking to Sonny today, and he seemed upset about something. We had a long talk about the war, and he was pretty upset over not being able to do his part."

Toby was not happy about this. "I know I should use him, but I just can't bring myself to put my own son in the middle of all this fighting right now, I guess. Yes, I know he's a good fighter. Your father and I have worked with him for the last few years to make sure both of you can handle any weapon we put in your hands. It's not him, it's me. I just have a hard time thinking of him as a man now, and it's the same with you. I was here when you were a baby, and now to think that you could be killed in some war that doesn't make any sense is just too much for me. But I'll do what I have to when it's time to fight. Thanks for talking to me about this. I know you and my son are good friends, and I also know he's lucky to have you to talk to."

He gave Carson a pat on the back. Toby asked Carson to tell his son that he wanted to talk to him by the waterfall. After Carson had left to go get Sonny, Toby sat by the water to think for a few minutes before his son got there. He never thought he would ever be as happy as he had been since he had become part of Kyle's clan. He would do everything he could to keep everyone safe, even put his own life on the line to make sure life here stayed the way it was right now.

Lily was his whole world—she and, of course, the children. So yes, this was very hard for him to put his son in the line of fire. Sonny sat down by his father and let him take his time.

"Since you were born, I've watched you grow in every way, and I want you to know how proud of you I am." Toby was not one to talk about feelings like this, but this was not just any time. This could be a long war, and no one knew who would be killed in it.

"Father, I'm going to be as careful as I can be. I know you and Mother are worried about me, but I'm a good fighter, and I have a good head on my shoulders. You both made sure of that."

"I have always known that someday I would have to let you grow up, but I just didn't want it to be in a war, but I'm confident that you'll be fine. I'm proud of you, son."

Toby walked back to the main cave with his son to talk to the clan about the next move.

"We have been watching the land around the field that we picked out for the fight, and so far, there has not been any movement," Toby told them. "It's just a matter of time before we see some of Cal's clan making a stand somewhere around the field." Kyle stated.

Kyle knew that Sonny was waiting for someone to give him his orders, and Kyle wanted to be the one to give that right to his father.

"Toby, do you have anything else to say in this meeting?"

Toby stood up and said, "Yes, I do. As everyone knows, I have a son, and now it's his wish, as well as mine, to let him fight in this war. So I move that we let him do his part right now as one of the lookouts."

Everyone said "aye" and it was done. From now on, Sonny would do whatever his clan told him to do in this war, and he was ready to do his part. Lily didn't much like that her son was going to fight the same as the rest of the men in the clan. Although she knew that it was not up to her to say one way or another. So she made peace with it and went on to try and do her part as one of the clan women to make life as easy as she could for everyone when they were in the city, just like all the rest of the women did.

That was the way of the clan, and it would stay that way for a long time if Kyle had anything to say about it. Right now, he was the only one who had anything to say that would make a difference. As the lord of the clan, it was hard sometimes, but he would do whatever had to be done to make everyone's life here safe and happy.

"Betz, I'd like to speak to you for a minute," Toby said.

"Sure, what can I do for you?"

"I know that I've never been the friendliest one here, but I do care for you and the children. I only want the best for the clan, and well, I hope you know that."

"Of course I know that. I've never thought any different."

"Well, I've got a favor to ask of you."

I couldn't think of anything that Toby would want of me, but I was happy to help anyway that I could.

"What do you need me to do?" I asked him.

Toby thought about what he was going to ask me to do for him, for a few days now. "As you know, I'm not the best one to read and write around here, and so I'd like to have you write down some things for me, if you don't mind."

"Sure, but you know Lily can write almost as well as I can now, don't you?"

"Yes, I do, but I don't want her to see this unless I die, so I'd like you to write this for me."

I wrote everything down that Toby had asked me to. Most of it was just telling his wife, son and daughter what he wanted each one of them to have if he didn't make it back from the war.

He wanted his son to have all his working tools and fighting things, and some of the other men to have a few other things. Other than that, he wanted his wife Lily to have the rest of his things to do with as she felt was right.

That night, as I got ready for bed, I wanted so much to fix things between us; I knew that Kyle could be killed as well as any of the other men in the clan. I didn't want things to be bad with us when he went out to fight.

"I know that things have been bad with us lately," I told Kyle as he was getting into bed next to me. "I want to make sure that you know the children and I love you."

Kyle took me in his arms and started kissing me all over and when he was done doing that we made love most of the night like we used to.

"Boy, I should tell you how much I love you more often," I whispered into his ear as he lay beside me afterward.

Chapter 14

It was a good day for the clan at the other side of the world as far as Cal could see. He was a father again, and now he had more children than anyone else in the clan. That made him happy to know that no matter what kind of man the rest of the clan thought he was he would have his bloodline go on for many years. He had made sure of that.

It wasn't as if he wanted to be a good father, more like he needed to know that his bloodline would go on after he was gone. Cal hated most of the clan and only kept them because he needed them to do the work and to keep the rest of them safe in case Kyle wanted to come back into this clan. Although he didn't think that would ever happen now because he had some of the clan watching for any sign of him coming back. So far, he didn't seem to care what went on in this clan.

It was too bad that everyone here hated Cal so much. What could he do about it now? He was not one to say I'm sorry. Even if he did, he really didn't think any one of these men would start liking him all of sudden. Why would they? He knew that he had taken most of the women to give him children, and he saw some of them look at him with hate in their eyes. Over it, some of them wanted a few of the women whom Cal had taken for himself, so that had left a bad taste in the clan's mouth.

Right now, every one of them would like to kill him. But because he was the clan lord here, they would still go with him into battle, and even die to try to keep this clan as safe as their fighting hands could. Cal was having a hard time with the fact that he had to go to war with the other clan. Oh, he wanted to fight. He just didn't want to be one of the men fighting. He would like to send the clan men out to fight, and stay safe here with his women. He had to do this because if he didn't no one would ever follow him, and his rule as clan lord would be over. There was no way that he was going to lose his role as clan lord, at least not if he could help it. Cal was getting older now, and he knew that his time would be up soon, so he wanted to make the most of it. He was making sure he did everything that he wanted now because it could end at any time. No one ever got to stay as clan lord until they were very old. They had tried that years ago, and it was a mess because you have to be in good shape to rule as a clan lord. If not, a younger one can ask to fight for his right to rule. That would just put someone younger in charge. That doesn't mean he should be the one to rule because it takes more than a strong young man. It takes someone who has what it takes to make all kinds of decisions to make this kind of life work for the whole clan, and not everyone can do that.

Back at Kyle's clan

Kyle was thinking that the other clan was getting ready for war. It would be a while before the real fighting would take place, but Kyle had no way of knowing that at this point. He only knew that there was someone watching the clan; Kyle would keep the men watching for as long as it took to keep everyone safe.

Over the years, Kyle and his son and the other young men of the clan had gotten very good at hunting and bringing back some big game meat for the whole clan to enjoy. Of course, that meant a lot of work for everyone, but no one ever tried to get out of their share of the work. No, this was a happy clan. Everyone wanted to do whatever it took to have a good life here, and work was always something that had to be done. So they all did their part to make life here as good as they could.

The hunting always seemed to go well for Kyle, his son, and Toby always had his son with him as well. It seemed like the rest of the clan was trying to get as close to them as they could, and as time went on everyone was pretty close now. The four of them were still very close because it was just them at first. That was a tie that would last for the rest of their lives. The rest of the clan knew that the four of them would stay together for life. Everyone understood it; they knew that it had been just them for a long time so everyone went along with the hunts to help in any way that they could.

I was sick for a whole week. Lily was helping me take care of some of the chores around our cave; most of the time she was there I was in bed. Lily didn't like what she was seeing. She thought I was losing too much weight; she thought that I might be having another baby, but it was kind of late in my life for that.

She was worried about me, so she was there every day to help with everything that needed to be done. Because if I was having another baby I would have my hands full and Lily didn't want me over doing anything with this new baby.

I had been so sick for a while now. The thought of having another baby right now was on my mind a lot because I knew I was getting older, and it would be harder for me this time. I had lost weight, and I was so tired all the time. I wasn't sure if I could do this again.

I had never been this sick with the other children. After a few more days, I started getting up again and doing everything again that I always did in and around the city. Now that my daughter Raven was grown she was a big help with teaching the other children, and she loved to cook, and everyone loved her meals. She was a true blessing these days. It was so nice to know that I had someone who wanted to be a helping hand when I so needed it right now.

"How are you feeling?" Raven asked me as I came into the cave where Raven was teaching the children to read today.

"Oh, I'm all right. Stop worrying about me so much. You have your hands full with all these kids."

"Well, I love teaching them, and I can't help but worry about you when you're sick for such a long time. It's not like you to miss a class with the children."

"I know, but I'm here now. What do you need me to do?" I asked.

"Not a thing. We are done for the day so go get some rest, please. You still don't look like you feel good." Raven knew that I was not back to myself yet.

Raven asked her brother if he had seen me today.

"No, but I was just going to check on her. Why? Is something wrong?"

"I don't know, but it seems to be taking a long time for her to get well this time. It worries me."

Carson put his arm around his sister and told her he would check on me and make sure I was in bed and resting.

"Okay, I'm counting on you to do that," she said with a big smile for her big brother.

Kyle was a happy man to be having another baby, and he didn't care what it was as long as it was healthy, and I was all right. It had been a long time since the clan had a new baby, and everyone was looking forward to the baby. Kyle also pretty much knew that this would be the last baby for the two of us because it was late in life for both of us. Still just the thought of another baby that would look like me made him smile.

"Father, I was looking for you," Raven said as she walked beside him.

"Well, you have found me. What's on your mind?" he asked her.

"I'm still worried about Mother. She still doesn't look very good. She should not be so thin with a baby on the way."

"Your mother will be fine. She is a lot stronger than you think she is, and it won't be long, and she'll be back to normal."

"Do you really think so?"

"Yes, I promise you she will be fine." Kyle could see the relief on his daughter's face, and he gave her a hug and told her not to worry so much.

That night, I was brushing my hair when he got into bed.

"Our daughter is worried about you. She thinks you're too thin for someone having a baby in a few months."

I put down the brush and got into the bed beside Kyle, and put my head on his shoulder.

"I'm fine, it's just that I'm not as young as I was with the other two babies, and it's taking me longer to get on my feet this time. But I'm eating a lot better now, and soon I'll start gaining my weight back, so everyone can stop hovering over me like a mother hen."

I was asleep before Kyle could say anything else to me.

Lily was helping me get everything ready for the new baby.

"What do you think you'll have this time?" she asked.

"I'm not sure, but as long as it's healthy we'll be happy."

Lily had to smile at her friend; she thought I was such a good mother and a good friend to her.

"What are you smiling at? We have a lot of work to do yet, and it will be winter soon."

"Well, we have everything ready for the cold days, so you just take care of yourself, and that baby."

"For the life of me I can't see why everyone thinks I'm so helpless now that I'm having a baby. It's not the first time. Everyone needs to stop fussing over me. I'm not going to fall apart just because I'm having a baby. It's been going on for generations."

"We all know it's not your first baby, but you're not as young as you were with the others either, so you need to let all of us help you this time," Lily told me, and before I could say anything else to her she put up her hand as if to say enough. And for once, I let Lily have the last word.

Chapter 15

"Kyle, I think you need to see this," Toby said as he walked up to him.

"See what?" Kyle asked

Toby waited until they were away from the rest of the men in the clan before he started talking to Kyle.

"Just outside of the city walls is one very large herd of elk."

"Wow, now this is a very good day for some elk meat if you ask me," Kyle said.

"I thought you might like that," Toby said with a smile on his face.

"You go and get the men ready and I'll go and get Carson and Sonny ready for a hunt that they will remember for a long time."

Kyle and Toby were lying on a cliff, overlooking the largest herd of elk that they had seen in a long time. Both of them were like two kids when it came to a hunt like this one. Kyle was lying on the cliff making hand signals to let the men know what he wanted them to do. Carson was happy when he got to go on a hunting run with his father. It was a large herd that would give them a lot of good meat to get through the winter. Kyle had his eye on one of the biggest male elk he had seen in a while. The rack on it was very big and would make a nice wall mount, and there would be a lot of meat from him as well. Kyle took the big male out with his bow and arrow. He hit the big elk, he went down and stayed down, so Kyle moved in and made sure he was dead and not in any pain. It was a good clean kill; the rest of the men took as many as they could as well. All in all, it was a very good meat run for the whole clan, and the fur would be good for many things that the clan used them for.

The hunt was just the thing to take the thought of a war off Carson's mind and maybe even get one very pretty girl off his mind as well. No, he knew that she would stay on his mind, but at least hunting made it easier for a day.

After the hunt, the boys were talking to the rest of the clan about what they had done to help with the kill. *It was nice to see all the men happy and talking about hunting instead of talking about fighting,* thought Carson.

In the next few months, I was back to myself, and everyone was happy to see me laugh again; it had been a while. Kyle was cleaning some of the tools and putting things away until the next hunt when I found him.

"I was wondering if you might be available to go for a dip in the water with me before it gets too cold out," I asked.

"Well, you can talk me into anything right now," he said as he took my hand and walked to the waterfall. "Are you sure you want to do this? It's going to be cold at first."

I was already taking off my things and getting into the water; Kyle thought I was so pretty with a round belly and a smile on my face.

He wanted to make love to me right there, but he would wait until we were alone to do that—or would he? Kyle pulled me under the waterfall so we would be hard to see if someone happened to go by. He took his time with me, and I was ready for him as he pushed into me. I let out a soft moan as he took his time taking me to the top of a river of need that we rode until we couldn't hold out any longer. The release was a long time coming for both of us, but when it did come it was worth the wait.

It had been a while since we had been together like this. We both felt happy and satisfied as we held on to each other for a long time before either one of us moved. Then we went into the water to clean off and play for a while before we got out and went to the cave to get some sleep.

Even though the clans had not gone to war, so far Kyle didn't take anything for granted, it wasn't his way to just sit back and do nothing when one clan was so unpredictable. Kyle's father's clan was not one to ignore. Kyle had been keeping the men on guard for a long time now. He still wasn't sure what would happen with Cal, the lord of the clan that he once thought would be his home for life. He could go off the deep end any time, and they would be in a war that no one other than Cal wanted to be in.

Sure enough, Cal had been stirring up a fight with some of the men in his clan. He was saying that if they didn't start the fight with Kyle's clan first they would be put out of the clan forever.

"Well, I can't say that I'm surprised to see Cal's clan starting to come around again. It has been a long time since we have seen any of them." Kyle knew it was only a matter of time. Toby was not sure what to make of it at that moment, but he was sure of one thing, and that was if it had anything to do with Cal, then it wouldn't be good.

"I think we should keep watching them and see what they're up to before we start a war that we might not need to start yet," Kyle said as he got up to walk around the fire pit.

Toby knew Kyle well and whenever he got up to walk, you knew he was thinking of something that he didn't want to deal with at that moment.

"What do you want us to do if they see any of us?" Toby asked.

"We'll deal with that if it happens. Until then, I think we should be careful and try not to be seen." Kyle asked Toby to stay behind so he could talk to him alone after the meeting.

"I want you to make sure that my son doesn't know what's going on right now. He wants to fight, and he might not hesitate to start a war to do so right now," Kyle said. "I know that doesn't sound good coming from his own father, but I know how much he wants to show me that he can handle whatever comes his way."

Toby just waited until Kyle got this off his mind before he said anything.

"I have been around Carson since he was a baby, and I love him like he was my own son, so I will do whatever it takes to keep him safe. I've got to say that I think you underestimate Carson sometimes when it comes to things like this. He's a good kid and only wants to do his best to please you, but I don't think he would ever go to the extent of starting a war to do that."

"Thanks," Kyle said and he slapped Toby on the back as they left the main cave for the courtyard. Carson wasn't as in a hurry to go to war anymore as everyone thought these days. He had other things on his mind, and he didn't really know exactly what to do about it, but he sure was having a lot of fun trying to figure it out.

He had been watching Violet for months now, and he had fallen in love with her even though she had no idea he was alive right now. Or at least that was what he thought. Carson was watching her swimming without anything on, it was amazing to watch her glide through the water with the grace of a fish, or so he thought. There were no fish as beautiful as this young girl was. He wanted to get into the water with her and have his way with her, but he knew that it was not the right time for that with a war about to start. But he could dream of it, and so he did. She was so beautiful that he couldn't take his eyes off her for long these days. Violet was tall and dark with dark eyes. Her body was stunning to look at: she had long slim legs, large full breasts, and a small waistline, with a beautiful face and full red lips that he could see himself kissing until he couldn't feel his lips anymore. He wanted her with every part of his body telling him so. Carson was trying not to be seen by her as she got out of the water; it was hard for him not to watch her.

She was the most beautiful woman he had ever known, and she was all he could think of these days. As Violet walked by where Carson was sitting behind a tree, she said, "Next time you should come in the water with me. It was wonderful. I'm sure we could have had a lot of fun today. Maybe next time."

He felt like a fool, but he didn't really care because he was in love with her, and so every time he could see her, he would. Someday she would be his, or at least that was what he was hoping for. Carson waited until she went by before he got up from where he was sitting. Carson wasn't sure how he would go about getting her to see him as a man, and not just a kid that she grew up with. Somehow he had to make sure that she did if he was ever going to have her as his mate, and he wanted that more than words could express. He was sure in time she would love him too, just not sure yet how to make that happen. One day he would make it happen, he was sure of it.

Over the next few days, Kyle was on his guard. The other clan was not leaving the area, and he knew that it would not be long now, and the war they had all been hoping would never come would be here. It was Kyle's place to let his clan know what was next, and he would do that, when it was the right time. It would not be easy to go to war with his old clan; he had spent his whole life with them up until he left, and he still felt bad about leaving his father's clan.

"Well, we knew that this day was coming sooner or later, and I guess it's sooner," Kyle said to the men of the clan. Toby was standing next to Kyle, as the rest of the clan all started to talk at once.

"Let's not get ahead of ourselves," Kyle told them, and they all sat back down, and he waited until they stopped talking to get his point across to them.

"Look, we have more going for us than they know. We have a city that to this day none of them even knows exist. As far as they know, we live somewhere out in the open or in a cave somewhere else. So that gives us an advantage over them right now, and that will give us a head start as far as getting to the fighting field, where we want them to go. With any luck, we will get the first blow in before they even know what hit them."

One of the men asked who would be going to get the field ready for the surprise hit to the other clan. Before Kyle could say anything, Toby said he would go and set up a field line, so if any one of the other clan men were to get too close to the outer cave. Then the men who were watching the other clan would let Kyle know, and that would be the start of the war. The rest of the clan would be ready.

"All right then, the meeting is over for now, and Toby, good luck. And the rest of you get the weapons ready in case we need them right away." Kyle had been hoping that this would wait at least until the baby was born, but he had thought the fight was coming soon for a long time now. So it wasn't a big surprise to him when the other clan made their move; Kyle had known for a long time that the war could happen at any time. He had done his best to make sure that all the men were ready, and they were; it was time to fight for their way of life, and they would.

I was getting ready to have the baby, and I had the bedding ready and the sitting area had everything that I could put into it. I could feed the baby without waking up Kyle; it was hard to get everything done when I knew that Kyle was getting ready to go to war with his father's clan. I had been trying to keep busy making clothes for the baby and not thinking of him getting hurt or even killed before the baby even got here. What would I do without him? That was not something that I wanted on my mind. It was time to do some more work before I started crying like a big baby. No, I would not do that. I had to be strong right now for everyone, and I knew that falling apart would not do anyone any good. It seemed like everyone in the clan was on edge over the upcoming war. The women had their hands full, trying to keep everyone from fighting with one another from all the stress. I was always amazed to see how well these women held up when it was needed; they were hard as steel. But they could also be soft when their men needed them to be. This way of life had been hard for me to get used to. Now I couldn't see myself anywhere else other than by Kyle's side and I knew I would fight with everything I had inside of me to help keep my life here safe as well.

Violet was happy that she saw Carson watching her swimming today, and she had also seen him watching her at other times too. She wanted to be with him too but had no idea how to go about it right now, and it seemed that he wasn't going to say anything to her about his feelings. So what could she do to make it happen? It was not a hard thing to do. The next day, as they were out in the courtyard, she went to him and asked him if he would follow her, and he did. When they were out of sight from the rest of the clan, she went to him and gave him a kiss that let him know what kind of feelings she had for him.

That was all it took for him. He pulled her behind a rock and started by kissing her until she couldn't breathe. He was shaking as he pulled her down on the ground with him and started taking off everything that they both had on. As he stood there with nothing on, she was watching him.

He was beautiful. He had a hard body, and his manhood was full and hard with the need to have her. He took his time with her even though he had a hard time slowing down. As he went into her, he could feel her let go and go with him as he rode her. She had never been with a man before, but it only hurt for a little while. Then the feelings took over, and she felt the hot lust that carried both of them away, until nothing else mattered but the feelings they had for each other.

He pulled her up on top of him and held her ass as he pushed into her. She let out a small cry, as they kept pushing in and out, up and down, harder and faster until they had their fill of each other. Then they just held on each other and fell asleep, wrapped around each other. Before they fell asleep, Carson told her that he loved her.

"I love you too," she said as she fell asleep next to the man who would be her mate one day. It was dark before they got back to the city, and the clan was looking for them.

"Where have you been? We've been looking for you for hours now?" Kyle said as Carson walked back to the cave where his family stayed.

"I'm sorry I didn't know that you were looking for me. What's so important that you had everyone looking for me anyway?" Carson asked. Kyle was trying not to show how upset he was right now, but it wasn't working very well.

"There has been movement by the field, and I think it's time to get ready to fight."

Carson wasn't expecting this now, but he was as ready as he would ever be, he thought.

"I'm ready for whatever you need me to do," he told his father.

"Well, it would be nice to know where the hell you are at when there is a war about to take place. No one can even find you. How was I to know that the other clan hadn't killed you or had you to torture, to get us out in the open so they could start the war?"

"I'm sorry I guess I didn't think of that. It won't happen again, I give you my word." Kyle was still upset with Carson, but he could see that Carson still had some growing up to do. But as his father, Kyle was proud of the way Carson stood up and was ready to take his place by his father's side in a war that might take both of their lives.

In the meantime, back in Cal's clan, Cal was putting more and more of his men out in the open by the field.

Kyle had said that would be the place where they would stand their ground to fight if it came to that.

"Well, I don't see any way out of it now because Cal is doing this to get the word to you that he is taking the land that you want for your own. This is only the beginning of it, if we don't let him know that he can't just come here, and take whatever he wants," Toby said as Kyle put more wood on the fire.

"Well, this is it, I guess. It's time to take our stand now and let him know that this is our land. Get the men in place, and the next time I see you, we will be fighting to keep our place here," Kyle told Toby.

He gave Kyle a nod and went to get everybody ready for the fight.

I was waiting not far by with Lily. I knew this was the time that I had been hoping wouldn't come, but now I knew it was going to happen right now. I rubbed my belly as if to try and let the baby know that it was all right even as I thought that I knew my whole world could be changed by a war that none of my clan really wanted. I also knew that every one of the clan would fight to the death if that was what it took, to keep this beautiful place safe for my whole clan to live out our lives here.

As I rubbed my belly and tried to calm myself, I told my baby, "Kyle and all the rest of your clan will keep you safe no matter what we have to do to make that happen."

I could feel the baby kicking inside of me as if to answer me, *I know, Mommy, I know.*

Chapter 16

Cal didn't take any time putting his men in place to force Kyle to take a stand, and if he didn't he could lose his clan to Kyle. All the men in Cal's clan were ready even though they really didn't want this war. They had no choice; it was either fight or you would be killed for not fighting. It was early the next day when Kyle's men were in place to start the fight if Cal's men came any closer to the line that Kyle had drawn. The men were lying on the ground overlooking the place where Cal's men were hold up.

Kyle whispered to Toby, "Take the guard out first, and then the ones close to him as fast as you can and stay down."

With that Toby was gone, and soon the rest of the men were in place to do whatever Kyle needed them to do. Carson was next to his father and ready to do his part in this.

"What do you want me to do next?" he asked. Kyle pointed to one of the men setting back from the rest of the clan. Kyle told Carson to make the kill as clean and fast as he could without being seen if he could. Carson nodded to his father and was gone without another word. It was starting to get light out now, and Kyle could see that the other clan hadn't seen anything wrong yet, and that was what Kyle had wanted—to make this as fast, and clean as he could without being seen for as long as he could. Kyle's men had already taken out a few of the men around the other clan. Now it was time to let them know that Kyle's clan was ready to keep their land. Kyle took out another man, but this time he made sure that the other clan saw the man drop. As soon as they saw the man drop, the rest of the clan started running for cover.

Kyle's clan was already out in front of them, so they had no place to go. The fighting had been long, and a lot of Cal's clan was gone in a few hours' time. Pretty much the rest of Cal's men were hurt, but so far Kyle hadn't seen any of his men go down. Cal's men had fallen back behind the line that Kyle had drawn so with that Kyle's men moved back behind the line, and it was a standoff for now. Cal's men were hurt and a lot of them dead. He was not going to stop this fight over it. He hated Kyle and would keep on fighting until all the men were dead if that was what it took to get rid of Kyle's clan.

Cal had more men than Kyle had, so he could lose a lot more of his men than Kyle could. It was not a big deal to him. Kyle put some of the men in place to get ready for the next hit if Cal was going to keep up the fight. Kyle was a better leader of his clan. His father had taught him to see that his men were his best weapon, so take care of them, and they'll take care of the rest of the clan. Kyle had done his best to make his whole clan as happy as he could, and it was paying off now. Every one of them would fight to their death if that's what it took, and there was nothing more anyone could ask of them. On the other hand Cal's clan all hated him, and only wanted this to end, and were hoping that it would with Cal's death. There was no one who would stand by him to fight to save his life. That was not a good thing when you were in a battle like this one; he could be killed at any time. No one would even care, and he had only himself to blame for that. Everywhere he looked he saw his men either dead or dying. He really didn't care about any of them; all he wanted was for them to fight long enough to kill Kyle and as many of his men as they could. Then what was left could all go home and Cal would not have to worry about Kyle again. He was so full of hate that was all he had on his mind instead of worrying about his own men and trying to help the dying he was yelling at them to keep fighting.

Meanwhile, back at the lost city . . .

I was trying to deal with what I had seen Carson do when the men got ready to leave to fight. Carson gave Violet a hug that said much more than a hug you would give a friend; this was a lover's hug. I was sure of one thing, and that was that my son and Lily's daughter had feelings for each other, and not just as friends who grew up together either. I was sure of that. I had no idea how long they had been close to each other, and that was what was upsetting to me. Oh, I thought the world of Violet and thought that someday it would be nice to be one big family, but I really never thought that it would be so soon. I was pretty sure that no one else knew about it either. I needed to get to the bottom of this as soon as I could without telling anyone what I saw or what I thought. Right now with the war going on I didn't want to get anyone upset over something that I myself wasn't really sure of.

Lily was working with me today, so it was a good time to find out if she knew anything or not, and if she did how she felt about it.

"Well, the day will be a long one with almost all our men fighting," I said as Lily was putting some more food on a shelf.

"Well, let's hope the fighting will not last long, and that we don't lose many of our men," Lily replied.

"How are Sonny and Violet doing?" I asked.

"Just fine," she said. "You know how they both like to help with everything. But with the war going on, Sonny was so happy to be going into the fighting that it makes me afraid for him."

"Well, don't be. He'll be fine. You know how good he is when it comes to fighting, and Kyle will take care of him."

Lily was starting to cry when I put my arm around her and said, "Look at me. It will be all right."

"How do you know?" Lily asked.

"I just do. So let's get this done, and go find the girls, and help them with the teaching." Lily was hoping that I was right but not as sure of it as I was. The girls were in the middle of reading when Lily and I got to the cave.

"Well, this should make you feel better," I said as we stood and watched the two women with the children. They were so good with them, and so grown up now that it brought tears to my eyes.

"Don't you start now," Lily said as she gave me a hug.

"I know, I'm just a big baby right now, aren't I?"

"Yes, you are, but I love you anyway," she said with a laugh. Soon we were both laughing so loud that the class was all looking at us.

"Oh, sorry," I said. "We didn't mean to disturb the class."

Violet and Raven both just looked at us, and went on with the day's lessons. The children all loved to have us watch the classroom; as the day went on, all the children kept waving at Lily and me until Raven told them that class was over for the day.

"Well, I guess you can both see that all the children still love to have both of you around. But next time please let us know when you're going to come to class so we can have you be a part of it instead of just watching."

"Thank you and we will let you know ahead of time and we're sorry to have upset the class today," I told my daughter and left. On my way back to my own cave I thought that Lily didn't know anything about the love birds so I would keep it to myself for now or at least until the war was over with. I was pretty sure that was the best thing to do right now for everyone.

Back at the fighting field

The fighting had come pretty much to a halt as night fell on the men. Kyle was trying to let as many men rest as he could without putting the whole clan at risk. Some of them needed to have their wounds cleaned, bandaged, and some of them just needed to rest, and drink water for a few minutes. Kyle was happy with the way the clan was holding up to the fighting so far, and he let them know it.

"With the first light we'll take out as many of the men as we can before we're seen," he said.

Toby gave all the men a little pep talk, and then he let them rest for the rest of the night.

Back in the lost city

I thought it was up to me to keep a record of the war for the next generation if for nothing more than to learn from it. So I had been keeping as much of it as I could on paper.

"I'll help you with the writing if you would like it," Raven told me, "so will Lily and Violet."

"That would be nice because there is a lot to put to pen and paper." I was so proud of the girls; they had grown to be wonderful people. It was still hard to look at Violet the same way that I did before I saw her and Carson hugging. Now she was not just Lily's little girl; she was now my son's girlfriend. It sounded so unreal to say it or to even think of it right now. Maybe in a few months I could deal with it, but not with the fighting going on; no, now was not the time to dwell on it.

At the fighting field

Kyle was ready to finish this war one way or another if that's what it took, but it was Cal that had put a stop to it for now. Kyle had thought that it was because his clan was so poorly trained to fight. He was right; as the men of Cal's clan started for home he could see that he should have put more time into the training of the men than making more babies. Without men to fight he could lose his reign as lord of the clan. *I've underestimated you, Kyle, but I'll learn from this and next time it won't go so well for you,* Cal thought to himself. As the men left to get some much-needed rest from a war that if Cal had anything to say about it wouldn't end with Kyle as the conqueror.

It had been a long time since Kyle had seen me and the rest of the clan. He wouldn't leave even for supplies as he thought he should be there on the field with his men as long as the fighting was going on. It had been a week now, and no one had come back to fight, so he gave the order to head home. Everyone was happy to hear that it was over for now at least. Carson had only one thing on his mind, and that was one very pretty girl named Violet; he felt his stomach roll as he thought of seeing her again. With the war going on he had to keep his mind on fighting, but now that they were on their way home again she was all he could think of.

"Violet, I'd like to see you for a few minutes if you have the time," I asked.

"Of course," she said. "Just let me put some of the books away, and I'll be right with you."

As soon as they had sat down I asked, "I was wondering how long you have been seeing my son?"

Violet's face got red before she could say anything to me.

"Well, I guess I have my answer, don't I?" I said to her as Violet put her head down to hide her red face.

"Oh, for crying out loud, Violet, it's all right. I've had a feeling for some time now. I'm not mad about it. In fact, I'm pretty happy about it. I wasn't expecting it right now when there's a war going on, and all the men are out fighting, I mean it worries me because they need to keep their minds on the fighting. But these things sometimes happen. It's not like anyone wanted this to happen when there's a war going on. Carson is strong. He'll be fine."

"Look, I wanted to tell you as well as my mother and father, but Carson asked me not to right now, when we had the war at hand. He didn't think it was very good timing right now," she told me.

"It's all right, Violet. I'm not going to say anything to your parents or Carson's father. I wanted to give you something."

"What?" Violet asked.

I couldn't help but to put my arms around the girl. She was so cute and so afraid of me right now it tugged at my heart.

It reminded me of when I fell in love with Kyle; no one would let us be together, but we had found a way to be together. So would Carson and Violet, only they would not have to leave their home to do it like we had to.

I gave her a dress that I had made for her to wear if they got married. It was all lace and hand-sewn. It was beautiful, and it made Violet cry when she saw it.

"I love it! Thank you so much."

I gave her a hug and said, "You're so welcome. You don't have to wear it if you do get married to my son, but if you like it you can. You know, if you two want to get married someday."

"Shouldn't you save this for your daughter?"

"No, I have something else for that day, if she wants it."

"I love it, thank you so much, and I'm sure when the day comes Mom will love seeing me in this."

Just then, Kyle walked into the cave. I was so surprised to see him that I just stood there for a few minutes before I ran to him and started kissing him in front of Violet.

"I can't believe that you're really here. I thought the fighting would still be going on," I said as I put my head on his shoulder and started crying again.

"It's okay. I'm here now so we can sit down and talk." We were so into each other that we didn't even see Violet sitting there watching us kiss.

"Well, I'm happy to see that you're home safe, Kyle," Violet said as she started to go.

But I stopped her before she could go and said, "Will you please have my son come to the main cave for me if you see him?"

"Of course, if I see him," she answered and left the cave as fast as she could go. Glad to be away from the two of us, she wasn't ready to talk to anyone about her and Carson yet.

Not until she had a chance to tell her own mother and father. Carson found Violet by the water crying when he went looking for her.

"Hi," he said as he got close to her, then he saw that she was crying.

"What's wrong?" He asked her.

"First of all, I'm so happy to see you home, and it looks like you're unharmed." She gave him a big hug then they sat down by the water to get caught up on everything.

"I don't know how to tell you, but your mother knows about us, and now I feel the need to tell my parents before anyone else does."

Carson wasn't expecting this when he got back at least not right now, but here it was. He had to do the right thing for both of them. He knew that he was in love with her, and wanted to have a life with her, so he felt the need to tell her mother, and father.

"I'll go with you, and I'll tell them about us right now if that's what you want me to do. Or we can wait until everyone has a chance to get settled in again before we talk to them. It's up to you," he told her.

Violet thought about it for a few minutes then said, "You're right, we should wait until things are back to normal around here first."

"I'm glad you see it that way because some of the men are hurt pretty badly. I don't think they need to know this right now, do you?"

"I'm not sure I mean; maybe it would be good to hear that we want to be together. It's not a bad thing. I think it's a good thing, don't you?"

"Of course I do, but not right now with everything a mess with the war and some of the men hurt," Carson told her.

Lily knew that something was wrong with Violet, but she had no idea what it was; only that she was upset over something. She could see her and my son Carson talking about something, and it seemed to upset her more, whatever it was.

After dinner, that night the whole clan was glad to be back with their families. Kyle was telling the clan that they would be back on watch in a few more days as soon as everyone was back on their feet. He knew that some of the men would be laid up for a few weeks, but the rest of them would be all right in a few days. Kyle had put two men on watch, at the fighting field, and he would have them change out every other day until the rest of the men were back on their feet.

Back in Cal's clan, most of the men were upset with Cal because he didn't want to take the time to bury the men who had died in the field fighting. He didn't care; he thought it was a waste of time as they needed to get back to take care of the ones that did make it out of the fight, but were hurt.

"I'm telling you that he has to go one way or another. He didn't want to take care of our dead," Tory said. "And all of you know he won't give up the fight with Kyle until all of us are gone."

Some of the men agreed, but none of them had any ideas as to what to do about it.

The winter was long, but as with all things it finally came to an end. Cal had been pushing pretty hard on the men to get them ready for the next fight because there *would* be another fight, and it would be soon. Cal's children were getting big now; some of them were almost young men, and he would put them in the fighting field too. He didn't care how many of them would be killed. Not even his sons if that's what it took.

One of the women in Cal's clan ran away to try to find Kyle and ask him to please help her and the rest of his old clan get rid of the monster that was running the clan now. Kay knew Kyle when they were kids, and she thought of him as a friend, so she thought if she could get to him he would help her if she asked him to. Kay had been walking for a few days now and was looking for some water when she came across one of Kyle's men.

"Please help," she said. "I only want to talk to Kyle. I'm alone, and no one knows that I'm here."

Toby knew Kay and told her he would see to it that Kyle got the message that she needed to talk to him right away. He told her to stay in the same place so Kyle could find her. Before he left her, he made sure she had enough food and water to last.

Toby got Kyle by himself, and told him about Kay, and asked what he wanted to do. Kyle knew Kay wouldn't be out here if it wasn't very important so he said to tell her he would come to the big rock on the other side of the field tomorrow.

Kay was happy just to be away from Cal even if it was just for a few days. Kyle waited for a few minutes just watching to see if this was some kind of a setup. After a few minutes, he got up and walked into the camp where Kay was sitting, waiting for Kyle to come.

When Kay saw him, she got up, ran to him, and gave him a hug. Kyle was happy to see her and to see that she was all right.

"So what's up? Why did you need to see me?" He could see that whatever it was, she was pretty upset about it; so he needed to take it easy on her for right now, he thought. It took Kay a few minutes to settle down enough to talk, but when she did, Kyle could see that this was nothing new. It had not been that long ago when some of the other clan men had found him and asked for help with Cal.

"I'm sorry for all that you and the rest of the clan are going through, but what do you think I can do to help?" Kyle asked. "I left my father's clan a long time ago, and now Cal is the lord of that clan. I can't get involved with your fight. I'm sorry, but there is nothing that I can do other than invite any of you who want to leave there, to join my clan. That is all I can do to help you. I wish I could do more, but you know that my hands are tied."

Kay was not happy with what Kyle had to say, but she did understand it, and she would go back and see if any of them wanted to leave Cal's clan. Kyle had to wait until Kay had been gone for about an hour or so before he left to go back to his city.

Back at Cal's clan

Cal was so busy trying to get the men ready that he didn't even notice that Kay was gone. That was a good thing because if he had, he might have had her put to death like everyone else that tried to cross him.

Cal's clan was starting to look like they could stand on their own this time in a fight with the other clan. That was what Cal had been after with all the training over the last few months. Now all he had to do was pick a time to go back to war with Kyle's clan. This time, he was hoping to make him pay for the lives of his men with some of Kyle's. It made him smile to think of Kyle being hurt or maybe killed—that would be even better. Cal hated Kyle, and nothing would be better than to see him die.

Back in Kyle's clan, I was getting big with the baby now, and this time, I was working harder than I had the last time; Kyle couldn't understand why. I had a lot of people to help me with anything that I needed to have done, but I seemed to want to do most of it by myself.

"Why are you trying to do everything by yourself?" Kyle asked while I was making up a place for the baby to sleep by our bed, where I could get to the baby fast if I needed to.

"I'm only doing what I want by myself, not everything!" I told him as I pushed past him to get more things for the baby.

"Well, I think you're doing too much!" he said. Kyle knew me so well, and when I was in a mood like I was right now, he knew that he wouldn't get anywhere with me. So he threw up his hands and went to find something that he could control. Right now, that sure wasn't his wife. After he left, I sat down and tried to rest for a few minutes before I started working again. *What was wrong with me?* I wondered as I put the last of the baby things in the room next to our bed. It had been a long winter, and now it was almost time to have the baby, and still I felt on edge all the time. I wasn't even sure why myself. But I knew that something was wrong. What could that be?

Lily and the other women had been busy making me some blankets for the baby; even Violet was helping with it, and that was not something that she would usually do. Lily was always happy to have her daughter with her no matter what the reason was. All the women in the clan wanted to help with whatever Lily needed them to do to help me so I would have everything that I needed for the baby. Before the baby came, that was what a clan did: they would work as one when someone in the clan needed something.

Violet was taking a dip in the water to clean and relax for a few minutes alone when she saw Carson get into the water and swim to her and pull her under the water to take her mouth, then pull her top off and play with her breasts before he pushed himself into her as they tried to stay afloat. It was not easy for them to hide how they felt from everyone. So it was good when they could just be together and satisfy the need that they had been putting on hold for a while now.

They got out of the water and found a place to lie down and take full advantage of the heat that was between the two of them. It was like a wave that you couldn't stop until it came to its full power. Violet knew that they would have to stop doing some of this while the clan was watching them all the time, but when they could get a chance to be like this, they couldn't help themselves.

They took their time riding the wave as long as the two of them could. It was always as hot as fire, and it felt like it would melt them with a need that was not going away anytime soon.

"Carson, we need to take this to a better place because the clan could find us here if they happen to be passing by to get clean."

Carson didn't care if they did; he wanted this more and more all the time. He wasn't going to stop this kind of lovemaking for anyone.

"We'll go to our families in the next few days, so we can be together without hiding from all of them," he said as he pulled her to him again. He started to kiss her breast and down to her soft spot and found it wet and ready for him to take her again. They spent the rest of the day getting enough of each other so they could go through what was left of the day without feeling such a strong need to be together again.

All the children were playing out in the courtyard with the older dogs and puppies. Tucker had been pretty busy before he died, and now there seemed to be puppies everywhere, but no one seemed to mind it. The whole clan had come to love the dogs now as much as I did. It gave the children more to play with. It was a good place to live; everyone was always trying to make it a better place. Some of them liked to garden; some took the time to keep all the weeds under control. But no matter what it was, everyone took part in the work that it took to keep this wonderful place looking as good as it did. Carson gave me most of the credit for their way of life; I had done most of the planning to make the city what it was today. As Carson got closer to my cave, he was wondering how to go about telling me about his love for Violet, and if I would be upset over it and want him to stop seeing her. He knew he had to talk to me first because he knew I would understand him better than anyone else could. I knew what it felt like to love someone as much as he loved Violet. And he was pretty sure I would tell him to do what he thought was right.

I was getting ready to take a nap when Carson found me.

"I was wondering if I could talk to you for a few minutes," he said.

"Sure, come and sit down here by me and tell me what's on your mind," I told him.

Carson was having a hard time saying what he needed to say. As always, as his mother, I was one step ahead of him.

"Well, let's make this as easy as we can. I'll start off by saying that I know about you and Violet. I think it's great. She's a wonderful girl, and she will make a very good mate for you. If you need me to, I'll talk to her parents for you. Will that help?" I asked him.

He had to smile at me; I was always on his side, no matter what.

"Thank you, but I think I have to do this myself, but I'd like you to be there with us if you don't mind."

"I'd be happy to be there with the two of you when you're ready," I replied.

"All right then, we'll let you know when," he said. With that behind him, he left me to get some much-needed rest.

After he had left, I had to smile to myself. I was so proud of my son; I should be—he was a good man. He would be a good clan lord one day. I had no doubt that when it was his turn, he would do his best to keep the clan as it is today, with everyone safe and happy with the life that they have right now, in the city that no one even knows about. All the other clan had was a mean clan lord that didn't care about anyone in his clan; other than maybe his women because he couldn't stand the thought of being alone. He would make as many babies as he could to make sure he would live on in them.

Kyle was worried about me; I could have the baby any time. It was hard on him because he was worried about me, and with the other clan so unstable, he knew they could be back at war with Cal at any time now. Kyle didn't want me to be trying to take care of a baby and worrying about him, as well as the rest of the clan. I would try to do everything when he was not here to stop me. He had Lily, and she would do her best to take care of me and the baby until he could get back. He had to leave it in her hands and hope that I would let someone else help for once. I was a strong woman and would take care of things that had to be done here until Kyle was back. It was up to me as his mate in this clan; I would always be more than happy to do more than was expected of me. He had said that was one of the things that made me special in his eyes.

With another war at the door, so to speak, Kyle was always on edge these days, and even though he tried not to show it, he was sure that there was one who knew exactly how he was feeling. That was his mate and only love, Betz; there was no way to hide anything from me. But right now he was wishing that he could hide this war from me so I could have the baby without thinking of Kyle being killed. If only he could keep me away from the pain that only comes with a war and not knowing if he was all right, as well as the hours of waiting, but I was his mate, and I would stay strong. That was one of my best qualities, and yes, I would hold up just fine until he could come back home to me and the baby, as well as the rest of his clan.

Chapter 17

Lily could see that both Carson and Violet were in some kind of deep conversion when she walked into her cave.

"Okay, what are you two up to?" Lily asked. She could see that they didn't want to look at her, and that was not like her daughter to look away from her when she was talking to her. Carson, on the other hand, never did like to look Lily in the face for some reason; she didn't understand that. Over the years, she had gotten used to it, and it didn't bother her. Right now, she had a feeling that she needed to know what was going on.

"Mother, we need to talk to you and Father. I'm not sure how to start. So I have to just get this over with. We have been seeing each other for a while now, and we want to be together so we were hoping that you and Carson's mother would help us. We want to be together. I love him, and I want to be Carson's mate, and he loves me too. Can you help us with everything and help us find our own living space in the caves? Please give us your blessings."

"Oh, Violet, I'm so happy for both of you. But I just don't think this is a very good time for it. I'll be glad to help with everything after the war is over with, but right now is not the time to be doing this. Kyle has told all of us that we could go back to war with the other clan any time, and Carson will have to go with the rest of the men to fight. It would be much better if you could wait until the war is over with. Then we can have a wonderful wedding for you, and we can take the time to fix up a cave for both of you, as well."

"Mother, we know the war can start up again at any time. We want to be together. No matter what happens we will stay together for life. So please will you be a part of this with us?"

"Well, it looks like you're going to do this no matter what." Lily gave her daughter a hug and a kiss and said that she would do everything that she could to help them.

"I'll go now, and tell Betz, and see what we need to do to make everything work, so you can have a wonderful day, so don't worry about anything."

Lily was out of breath as she tried to get everything out about Violet, and Carson wanting to be mated or married as I put it. That was all new for Lily because before she came into this clan it was always taking a mate. I had told her that in my world it was called getting married. Either way, it was still the same thing to Lily.

"Well, this sounds like a good time to tell the men, and get things ready for the big day," I said as I got up to go find Kyle. Then he could set up a meeting to let the whole clan know about the wedding. But when I got up my water broke, and Lily saw it.

"I don't think you're going anywhere right now, so let me help you back to your room. I'll find Kyle, and let him know that he's about to be a father again."

"I feel so bad about having the baby right now when the kids want to get married. There are things that I need to do for them."

"Now you stop that. The wedding will wait for now, but this baby won't, and it's not anyone's fault that the baby wants to come into this world now. Everyone understands that. Now I need to go and tell your mate that it's time to have a baby."

"Oh, Kyle, I'm glad I found you. Your lady is having the baby right now, and she's asking for you." It took the whole night to get through the pain before the baby came. When he did, everyone was so happy to see him and to know that I was doing better and that the pain was over with. We had a healthy baby boy.

"I don't think we'll be able to have any more children after this one. It was so hard on me this time. I guess I'm getting too old to go through this anymore," I told Kyle after everyone left them for the night to go to their own caves.

"I know that and it's all right with me. We have wonderful children. It's time for some of them to have children of their own now, don't you think?" Kyle asked me as he brushed my hair out of my eyes. It was still wet with sweat from the work of labor.

I was still so beautiful to him, and I had a glow to my face as the baby suckled at my breast. Over the next few weeks, the baby and I were getting to know each other. Kyle could see that I needed to rest a lot more than I needed to with the other children and thought it was because I was older this time. It was harder for me to keep up with the baby at all hours of the night. I would figure it out and be back to myself in no time, he was sure of that.

At the next meeting, Kyle told everyone about Carson and Violet wanting to be mated, and everyone was happy for them and gave them their blessings. Kyle also told the men to keep watching for any sign of Cal's clan.

It had taken a few weeks before I was ready to help with the preparations for Violet and Carson's wedding day. But when the day came it was wonderful; Lily and I had flowers made into an archway by the waterfall out in the courtyard. It was lovely, they both looked so happy to be able to be together. Kyle and I were both happy to have Violet in the family.

"Well, I guess we are family now," Lily said to me one day when we were getting things ready for the baby's bed.

"Yes, we are, and I'm happy for it. I couldn't ask for a better daughter if I tried."

Lily started crying. I was surprised to see her crying.

"Are you all right?" I asked her.

"It's just that I never thought I'd even have a daughter, and now she's with your son. I'm so lucky."

I gave her a big hug and said, "Well, we feel very lucky too. I have always thought of you as my sister anyway, and now I guess you are. So please stop crying before I start, and then we'll never get anything done."

They both started laughing as they got back to work.

It had been a few weeks since I had given birth to my last child. We couldn't be happier with him. He looked like both of his parents, and he was a good baby, we decided to name him Slade. It was a strong name, and he would need that to sit beside his brother in the clan as well as his father. He would be like his father and big brother, he would love his life here and take pride in this way of life, and he would work hard and fight hard to keep it safe for the clan.

"Well, I think he's the most beautiful baby I've seen in a long time," Raven said when she picked up her new baby brother.

"I think you might really like being a big sister," I told her. Raven was very happy to see the baby and someday wanted one of her own.

"How are you doing?" Raven asked her.

"I'm fine, just a little tired. It's been a long few weeks for me since I had the baby."

Raven knew that I was strong, but she also knew that it was a lot harder for me to give birth this time.

"I know that I've come to the place in life where I have to stop having children. The time has come to watch my children make me a grandmother now. And yes, I'm fine with that. Right now, this little guy wants to have something to eat so go and let me feed him," I said as I pushed my daughter out of the room.

Raven was looking for her father when she found Sonny instead.

"Well, what do we have here?" she said as she watched Sonny trying to hit the mark with his hatchet. It was too much for her just to walk away without showing him that she was just a little bit better than he was when it came to hitting the mark. Her hatchet hit and knocked his out of the way of hers.

"Well, I guess we know who can throw a hatchet better than I can, don't we?" Sonny stated. "It's too bad that women aren't allowed to go on the hunts."

"Yes, it is, because if they were I'd put you to shame when it comes to hitting the mark." Raven had always liked Sonny, but she had also always had the need to prove herself to him, and that was something that she couldn't understand. "Well, now that I've done that, what else can we do that I'm better at than you are?"

Sonny had run after her his whole life. Now he wanted to catch her by the side of the caves and kiss her if she would let him without hitting him in the face.

"What is wrong with you that you have to win in everything that we do around here?" he asked her.

"I just don't like to lose. Is there something wrong with that?" she asked him, even though with him so close to her right now it was hard for her to breathe.

"I love it when you have a hard time talking when I'm this close to you. It makes me want to kiss that pretty face of yours."

Sure enough, she hit him in the face again like she always did when she didn't know how to handle things like this.

"Well, that's what you get when you try to have your way with me," she said with a nervous laugh. He wasn't laughing this time, and even though he had blood on his face he still pulled her to him, and very slowly, gently kissed her. For the first time in her life, she wasn't in control.

But it was all right because she wanted this as much as he seemed to need it. The kiss seemed to last forever. When they came apart, she was shaking all over, her skin felt so hot that she thought he could see what he had done to her. When she opened her eyes, he was gone, and she was alone, so she fell down on the ground and had a good cry.

What was wrong with her? She had never felt like that in her life before, and she had no idea what to do about it either. The next few days went by very slowly for her; she couldn't seem to do anything right now. That was not like her. Raven was in love with him; she was smart enough to know that, but for the life of her she had no idea how to handle it. The only one she wanted to talk to right now was me because I always knew just what to say to make her feel better.

I was feeding the baby when Raven got to the room where the baby and I were laying down.

"Mother, I need to talk to you when you have some time," she said.

"Sure. Can it wait until I get done with him?" I asked.

Raven waited for a few minutes until the baby was asleep before she took a deep breath and said, "I think I'm in love," ending in a whisper.

I smiled, "I'm not surprised because I've been waiting for this day for a long time now and had thought it would be sooner than this." I was happy to see that it was here. "Well, do I have to guess who the lucky guy is?" I asked her.

"No, but I'm not so sure you're going to like it," she said.

"Oh, for crying out loud, I'm sure I'll be happy if he makes you happy," I said. "Well?"

"Well, what?"

I had started to laugh at my daughter. "Who is it?"

"Oh, well, it's Sonny," she said.

I had a big smile on my face and put my arms around Raven then said, "You are such a silly girl sometimes. I've known that he loves you for most of your life. I just didn't think you cared about him the same way."

Raven stood and looked at me like she had never seen me before in her life. "Really?" she said.

I made her sit down and had a long talk with her. "Over the years I've seen Sonny run after you and it was pretty easy to see that he was smitten with you. But you never seemed to feel the same way for him, as far as I could see anyway. It was not a big surprise for me to know that he's still in love with you."

When Raven left my cave, she felt like she had been on another planet. How she could be so smart and so dumb at the same time, she wondered. Sonny was still feeling the pain of the hit that she had given him but not as much as he felt that kiss. The look on her face was all he needed to know that she wanted him too. He would take his time with her. But he also knew it wouldn't be easy to keep his cool with her because he had wanted her pretty much his whole life. To be this close and not really be with her would take everything he had within him to put his feelings on hold for now.

He knew that this was new to her, and she would need to find her own way with these kinds of feelings. He was sure she would be his mate when she was ready. And that was enough for him for now. The hardest part would be for him to stop thinking of that kiss when he had other things that he should be thinking of. Somehow he knew that kiss would be on his mind pretty much all the time no matter what else he had to deal with.

Kyle knew that I was still feeding the baby when he got up and left the bed. I needed the rest of the women to help me out with the food for a few more days. Lily was more than happy to get all the other women together to help with the cooking and cleaning around the main cave until I could get used to taking care of a new baby. What good was being the clan lord if he couldn't get the clan women to help his wife with the little things that had to be done around the cave? That was the least he could do to help me. He had a big smile on his handsome face as he went to find Lily to get things worked out for the next few days for me.

Everyone was happy to help, and so everything was going well. Lily saw how hard it had been on me to have another baby, so she took care to not get pregnant again herself. She knew that I was about the same age as her, and so she wouldn't have any more babies now either. She wasn't upset over it. She was happy with the children she already had, and so was Toby. All the children were running after the puppies when Lily saw something by one of the cave walls and went to see what it was.

Oh no, it was one of Tuckers puppies. He was just lying there, and when she went over to him she tried to pick him up, but he didn't want her to do that. He would start whining. She could see that he was hurt.

"Okay, little guy, I'll go and get some help." She ran to find Kyle because she didn't want to upset me right now with a new baby to take care of; this wouldn't be good for me. Kyle was working on tools when she found him, and she told him he had to come with her right away.

"What's wrong? Is Betz and the baby all right?"

"It's not them," she told him. By that time, they were where she had found the dog laying. He was still there. It didn't look like he had tried to move. Kyle bent down to take a look at the dog and could see that he was bleeding from his side. He picked up the dog and took him to one of the caves where he could take a better look at him.

"Is he going to be all right?" Lily asked him.

"I really don't know right now. It looks like he's been cut by something. It looks like a clean wound."

Kyle cleaned and dressed the wound, and then put him down on a made-up bed he fixed for him. He told Lily not to tell me right now because he thought it would be too much for me to deal with.

The puppy was up and running around in no time, and I was none the wiser. That was good because Kyle had his hands full with the training of the men right now. He didn't need me upset over anything. Because he needed to keep his head clear, he had a feeling that Cal would start a fight again, and he wanted all the men to be ready if it happened. No one wanted to go back to a war that was so unnecessary in the first place. But if that was coming he had to make sure the men in his clan were ready. The training was going good, and he was sure that the men would be ready to fight if it came to that again.

Back in Cal's clan

Cal was sure that this time he could take out some of Kyle's men, and hopefully Kyle would be one of them. He had made sure that all the men had a lot of hard training this time. He was pretty sure they would give Kyle's clan a good run for their money, and just maybe Kyle's clan would not be as ready as his clan was. Kay had been trying to get as many of the women to talk to their men to try and get some of them to make a break with their clan and side with Kyle's clan. So far, it wasn't working as well as she was hoping for. It wasn't that any of them liked Cal. More like they pretty much hated him, but they didn't want to leave their home. They had been born here, and most of them would die here. It was home, and you just don't leave your home. That was how most of his men felt.

Kay understood that. She loved her home too, but what else could they do to live without fear of Cal going off the deep end and killing someone for no reason other than because he felt like it. She was so sick of seeing the cruel way that this man ran the clan. It would be a long fight this time because Cal had all the men ready. So he had planned on starting the fight as soon as he felt winter was over with. He was busy with the women again, and no one could get in the way of him building his bloodline.

Back at the lost city

Kyle was doing everything that he could to make things easy for me; he knew I had my hands full with the new baby boy. It made him smile to think of another son, and he was a big one too. Slade will be a big help to his big brother when the time came to hunt and to fight. Kyle would make sure that he could do both of those things very well. That was his job as lord of the clan and as his father. He loved to help his sons. Slade was starting to crawl now. Soon he would be running around everywhere and into everything that he could get his hands on, which was the fun of being a baby. In addition to living here in this city they called home, it was full of fun things to explore. There were caves, water, hot springs, and lots of other things to find and play with. Slade would be like his brother; he would love all of it as much as he had.

I was having fun with the baby these days as he wanted to crawl everywhere now, so I had to watch him all the time or he would be getting into everything he could. Lily was always trying to do more than she needed to because she loved me and wanted me to have as much help as I needed to raise the baby. Over the years, I had done everything that I could do to make life good for all of them and to help the next generation have a better life here.

There were books to help teach with. You could always find me reading as many books as I could get my hands on so I could teach the women how to cook better and how to can food and to show them how to grow things that they would have never been able to do if not for me. Most of them could even sew now, and a lot of them could make blankets now as well.

There were only a few that could help with the sick. That fell to me, Raven, and Lily. Violet was pretty good with that part too, but I also knew that I needed to teach more of the women how to help with the sick. It was on my to-do list, right at the top. Raven had already started teaching them about which medicines to give and how to make some of the medicine. One of the most common to be given was mint for an upset stomach. It worked the best most of the time. Just put some of it into tea, and it worked for most of them. Also, they could cut a piece of willow and chew on the inner bark for pain; this was a natural aspirin. We used all kinds of herbs and roots for healing, and the hot springs did wonders for a lot of other discomforts. One of the best things about being able to go to the upper world was to get some medicines that we could not make here. So now and then, they would go and get a lot of things that would help all of them live a better life here, like penicillin to stop infection.

Kyle was about to give the men a workout when he ran into Sonny and Raven in the courtyard kissing, and he didn't want to make a mess of things. So he went around them as if he didn't see them then got on with the training that he had in mind to make sure that the men were ready for a fight if it came to that. Kyle would always take the time to enjoy his new son Slade. He was always happy to be able to ride on his father's shoulders when he had the chance to do that. Kyle would keep him on his shoulders for most of the day as he walked all over the city to make sure that everything was working as it should. It was a great place to live; everyone here was lucky.

I was also happy to have some time to get some of the work done that I had been putting off since I had the baby. Whenever I got the chance, I was helping the women put up food or helping teach the children or reading a book that I thought would benefit the clan's overall life here. Today I was taking a dip in one of the hot springs. I was still having a hard time getting back to myself. I thought it was my age, but I wasn't sure. Lily was in the springs with me; both of us were lying back in the water with our eyes closed almost asleep when Kyle found us.

"Well, if that's not a pretty picture, I don't know what is," he said as he put down the baby and gave me a kiss before he put the baby back on his shoulders and left us alone again.

"Betz, I was wondering if you might let Raven take a look at you, just to make sure everything is all right."

I knew that everyone was worried about me, so I just nodded my head and said, "If you'll set it up for me."

Before I could say anything else, Lily was out of the water and off to find Raven to get this done before I changed my mind. The next day, I went to the cave that was set up for looking after the sick; Raven was there with everything ready for me.

"I don't think there's anything wrong with me other than my age and taking longer to get back to myself because of it." Raven was almost as good as I was. She took her time; when she was done, she had a smile on her face and told me, "You're right." It was just taking a little longer to get back to myself. After I had gone back to take care of the baby, Raven sat down and started to cry. She really did not think that I was all right, but she was not qualified to care for everything, and she didn't know what was really going on with me. It made her feel helpless. She had to get me to the upper world so I could get the right help, and that meant that she had to go to her father. Kyle had told Raven that I would be fine; it was just taking a little longer for me to get back on my feet, but I would.

"So please don't worry about her. You'll see she'll be all right in no time." He gave his little girl a hug as they walked together. Raven felt better after talking to her father; she felt he knew me better than anyone else ever could, so she knew that if he wasn't worried, then she shouldn't be either.

Meanwhile, back at the other clan . . .

Cal was waiting for all the men to sit around the fire pit for the meeting, and he was not happy about waiting for them.

"Well, now that we're all here we can get started. As all of you know, it's almost time to go back to war with the other clan. I need all of you to be at your best," he told them.

One of the men wanted to know why they were going to war with Kyle again. "I just don't see what we have to gain by doing this again," he said.

Everyone else could see that Cal was not happy about asking him this. "As long as I'm the lord of this clan, I'll tell you when we need to go to war and you only need to know when and where that is, not why. Do I make myself clear?"

The man only shook his head. After the clan meeting, the men all thought the same thing. *What the hell are we doing going back to* war *with Kyle again when they had lost a lot of their men last time? We just don't understand why he hates him so much, and if we do this again, there might not be any of us left when it's over with this time.*

Over the next few months, Kyle's clan had set up the field line again and kept some of the men watching for the other clan to make a move. When they did, everyone was ready and waiting for Kyle to give the word. It came on a clear, hot day, and the fighting would go on for what would seem like forever this time.

Carson was in front of the men when the fighting started up again, and Sonny was next to him. It was a long hard fight this time as the other men were better at fighting than the last time, so Kyle was losing some of his men, and some were hurt. It would be a long time before the war would be over. That was the way of war for as long as he could remember. His men were strong, so they would fight as long as it took to keep what they had safe. And they had a lot to fight for—their families and the city that all of them had come to love; yes, they had a lot to keep fighting for. The rest of the women and I were busy taking care of the hurt men; this time around, some of them we just couldn't save. But at least Kyle had kept the other clan out of our city, so the women and children were safe from it, for now. Only time would tell if what we had would stay safe.

Kyle was telling Carson to move back when he got hit with a hatchet in the leg and had to have Carson take over with the orders for the men. Sonny was now under Carson's orders.

"I need Toby to take my father back to the city for medical treatment." Before he could get all of it out, Toby was helping Kyle get to his feet and was leaving. When Raven and the other children saw that it was Kyle that was hurt this time, they all came running to help Toby with him.

"Daddy, are you all right?" Raven asked him with tears in her eyes as she helped him into the cave.

"I'll be all right, little girl, don't you worry about your old dad," he told her.

I was caring for one of the other men when I saw Kyle being helped into the cave. I got up and ran over to help put him on one of the beds. My hands were shaking as I cleaned away the blood and dirt from his leg so I could get a better look at it.

"It's not as bad as it looks, so everyone can go back to whatever you were doing before. You will sit here and let me take care of you for a change," I told him with a frown on my face that let him know I meant every word.

"Well, I wouldn't have it any other way," Kyle said as I cut off what was left of his pants to get to the wound. I was good at whatever I did, and this was no different; it didn't take very long, and he was sleeping like a baby.

"I gave him something for the pain. So he'll sleep for a while now, and from what I see, he needs the rest. Toby, I think it's about time that you both let the younger men do the fighting. The two of you need to just teach from now on."

Toby knew better than to get me going when I was upset, so he just nodded to me as if he agreed with me. He knew that it wasn't in Kyle to give up just yet, but he also knew that when it was the right time, he would step down without a fight. But that was not now. Toby had to admit that I was a hard worker, and I was not young anymore either. I still held my own when it came to taking care of the hurt men and also the sick. He had to admire me for what I was capable of. He thought I was a lot more than just another woman. I had strength in me that he had never seen in any of the other women in either of the clans. He could see why Kyle had fallen in love with me. He felt sorry for his old clan because they never really gave this wonderful woman a chance, and it was too bad because Betz would have given so much to their way of life. It made him feel sad to think that they never really got to know me.

Cal was not a good clan leader,
When it came to fighting, he spent most of his time yelling at the men to get back out there and fight even if they were hurt.

He just didn't care about anyone other than himself. One of his men was telling the rest of the men that they had to take a stand with Cal, or they would be killed in the fighting, and for what—to make Cal happy. As it happened, they didn't have to wait very long because Cal thought he would take a stand with his men, and fight, the other side made a run. One of Kyle's men had hit Cal with a hatchet, and it was a good hit. Cal had taken a hit to his head, and within the hour he was dead. And no one was unhappy about it.

"Well, let's tell the other clan that it's over as far as we're concerned," Cody said to what was left of the clan men.

Carson saw the white flag and sent one of the men to the line to see what was up. When Sonny got back to the men, he told Carson that the clan wanted to end the fighting because Cal was dead. They didn't want to continue the fight any longer. Carson wasn't sure of the men on the other side, so he said to wait until the next day and see what his father had to say about all this. It was going to be a very long night for both clans.

Kyle was upset with me for letting him sleep when his men were still out there fighting for all of them while he was asleep.

"I really don't care if you're mad at me or not. I did what I thought was right for you at that time," I said, my arms crossed in front of me. "I'd do it again if that's what it took to get you to rest."

Toby was back in the city to see what was up with Kyle and to let him know what had happened overnight. Kyle and I were in the middle of an argument as Toby walked up to us. "Sorry, but I need to talk to Kyle," he said.

After Toby told Kyle what had happened, Kyle got up and said, "I need to talk to the men, then talk to the other side and see if what they say is what's really going on."

I was not happy when Kyle got up to leave the city again. He was not in good shape.

"I'll be all right. Don't worry about me."

"Well, I'd love to not worry about you. And if you'd do the right thing I wouldn't have to worry. Sometimes you are too damn pig-headed for your own good, but go because I know damn well I can't stop you," I told him as I stomped off to help with the other men who needed help.

Kyle was starting to get mad so he just got out of there before he said something that would only make things worse. The men were all sitting around the fire pit waiting for someone to either start fighting or for Toby to get back.

"Well, I'm glad to see that you're all right," Carson said to his father as he sat down by his son.

"Well, I would have been here before now if your mother hadn't given me something that put me out like a light," he said.

Carson had to smile, because he knew how his mother was about things like that. If she gave him something, it would be because she thought he needed it or else she would never have done it.

"Well, I'm not about to get into that one with you two. Look, you guys will get over this in time like all the other times."

Kyle gave his son a pat on the back and told him he was right; now was not the time to talk about that anyway.

"Well, let's see what's up with the other side," Kyle said as he got up and sent one of the men to get Cody over here to talk to him. It was late when Cody and Kyle got up and shook hands, both men went their own way. It was over for now as long as both clans could talk, work things out; there would be peace for both sides now.

Now that Cal was gone none of the other clan wanted to fight with Kyle; they all pretty much told Kyle that as far as they were concerned this war was over. They all felt relieved that it was.

"I'm proud of you for taking over in the middle of the fighting," Kyle told his son.

"Well, I'm happy that it's over, and we can go on now, and maybe someday soon we can be friends with the other clan."

"That will take some time, but someday that will happen." Kyle said. Over the next few days, the clans spent their time burying the dead and taking care of the men who were hurt. It had been a bloody war this time, and there were a lot of dead to take care of as well as a lot of wounded.

On one of the last days of fighting, Sonny had been injured; he was hurt pretty bad, but not bad enough that he needed to be sent back to the city. The clan had everything that they needed to clean the wounds and even put stitches in if they had to. If it was real bad, they would take them back to the city for me and the others to treat.

Sonny had a bad cut on one of his legs, but it was healing, and it was being kept clean so it would take a while before he would be back to normal. It was another week before Kyle, and the rest of the men left to go home; it took two more days to get there with so many of the men hurt. When they walked out of the long dark hallway of the cave that led to their city, every one of them let out a sigh of relief to be home. With the war over this time hopefully for the last time now that Cal was gone.

The children were the first ones to see the men coming, and then Raven saw that Sonny was hurt as she came running to help him.

"I'm all right so please no waterworks, okay?" he said as he put his arms around her and held her while she cried.

"I'm just so happy that you're all right. I was afraid I'd never see you again to tell you that I love you too," she said as he gave her a kiss in front of everyone.

Chapter 18

"Well, it looks like we have another wedding to plan," I said as I helped Kyle get to the cave that we called home.

All the children ran up to Kyle and asked him if he would tell them the story of his old clan, and how he lived, and what it was like as he grew up. He had told them all kinds of stories about when he was a young boy growing up. Soon he would tell them about the hunting trips that he had with his father, and how those times were the best memories of his young life. Kyle was not one who liked to dwell on the past, but as he got older he found that he had so many fond memories of his life with his father. All the young children loved to hear the stories of who he was and how he grew up.

"You can count on it," he told the children as they ran off to play. It would be good to take a trip down memory lane again, but not today. No, not today, because everyone needed to rest, and there was plenty of time for stories. They had a lifetime to tell the children stories, and he would.

I was happy to have him back in bed to rest for a few days. I knew him so well, and I knew it wouldn't be for long; he was not one to rest for long. I had my hands full trying to get this stubborn man to rest so he could heal. Sometimes he could be so hard-headed that it was infuriating for me. But I was just as stubborn as he could be. I was not going to let him win this one because if he didn't take it easy, I would tie him down for however long it took to get him back on his feet, without making the healing take twice as long as it should.

Sonny found Raven by the hot springs getting ready to go into the water without anything on. He couldn't help himself, so he got into the water with her; at first he just let the healing waters run over his sore body for a few minutes before he got a hold of her. He took her lips to his then ran kisses over her body, and then he held her to one side of the wall by the water so he could take his time with her. At first he just kept kissing her breasts, and then he suckled them. Then he ran his hand down to her womanhood, and found her ready for him, but he still didn't take her.

He wanted to make it last as long as he could. He just let her moan with a red hot need for him until he couldn't wait any longer; then he pushed into her. He pushed into her over and over until they both felt the release, and then they lay back in the water to let it relax both of them.

"It was the hardest thing that I've ever done in my life when I saw you today not to start hitting you with everything I have in me," she said as he kept his eyes closed.

After a while, he said, "I know that, and I'm so glad because I don't think I could have taken it today."

Pretty soon they were both laughing so hard that they were crying.

"Well, I'm so hungry right now that I could eat anything, even Carson's food."

With another laugh, they went to eat. At the fire pit that night it was so quiet that Raven was having a hard time trying to sit there.

Raven was pretty sure that she was going to have a baby, and she needed to tell everyone about it, but there never seemed to be the right time. She kept it to herself for most of the winter, but as she started to show, she knew that the time was going to be up soon. It wouldn't be long until everyone would see that she had a big belly.

Over the next few days, the men started getting back to the way they had been before the fighting had taken them away. All the women and I had to put up with all the sore men and let them take their time getting back to normal before they could start the wedding plans for Raven and Sonny.

By the time winter was getting cold they were together in their own cave and planning on having a family soon. I couldn't believe that Kyle and I would have Sonny as a new part of our family. It was nice to really love the people that our children were with; it would be a happy time when the grandchildren came. Both Kyle and I were looking forward to that day.

All winter long Sonny and Raven had been making love so much that it felt like having a honeymoon that never came to an end. Not that either one of them had a hard time with that. It seemed like that was all they had on their minds. Sonny had never thought this could be as good as it was and last for as long as it had. That was all about to change now.

Sonny had Raven against one of the bedroom walls and was having his way with her from behind; she was wet with sweat from the lovemaking. But it was the best way to sweat. It was after the lovemaking that Raven told Sonny that they were having a baby. They really did need to have the wedding soon, or she would be too big to wear the dress that I had given her. She really wanted to look pretty on that day.

At one of the clan meetings, Kyle was asked to let Sonny stand up and tell everyone something, but at that time Kyle had no idea what it was Sonny was going to say. From the look on his face, he wasn't sure he wanted to know. He had sweat running off his face as he got up to speak.

Kyle could see that Sonny was upset about something, but he didn't know what that was. As the meeting was coming to an end, Kyle said, "At this time Sonny would like to make an announcement to the clan."

Sonny stood up, and cleared his throat, then looked at everyone who was sitting around the fire pit, and said "I'm not sure how to start, so I'll just get to it. Raven and I are going to have a baby, and so we really need to have your blessings, to get married right away. Before the little one comes, we want to be mated before that day."

Everyone stood and shook the boy's hand then when Kyle took his hand he was having a very hard time looking him in the face. After all, this was his little girl that he was making love to, and now she was having his baby. He really didn't know what Kyle would do to him.

He could very easily kick his ass for doing this to his little girl, but Kyle had a big smile on his face as he gave Sonny a hug and a slap on the back.

Then he said, "Well, Betz will be happy to get the big day ready for the two of you, and just plain thrilled to becoming a grandmother at last."

Sonny went back to the cave to tell Raven that he had told everyone at the meeting that they would be having a baby soon. So they really needed to get married before the baby came.

"Oh, thank you, I was so afraid my father would be really upset with us, and not let us get married. Daddy can sometimes be a little dramatic about things so I wasn't sure how he would take the news. You did fine, so I guess he was happy to hear that we're going to have a baby. Now all we need to do is tell my mother."

"Are you kidding me? You thought that your father was going to have a fit in the middle of the meeting? Why would you tell me to talk to everyone then?" He was yelling at her as he stood in front of her.

"Please don't yell. I was hoping that with everyone there he would have to behave so that he couldn't hurt you. You know how my father can be if he doesn't like something. He makes a bigger deal out of things than he should," she said with a small little sigh.

He just looked at her for a minute before he responded to that.

"I can't understand you sometimes. I mean you don't even hesitate to hit me in the face if you get upset over anything, but when it comes to your dad, all of a sudden you don't have a backbone. Do I have that right?" he asked her.

"Well, you don't have to be so damn mean about it, do you?"

"This is too much." And he started laughing until he was crying.

"Just what is so funny?" she asked.

"I just didn't think you were afraid of anything. And all this time, all I ever needed to do is tell your daddy on you." He was still laughing and crying at the same time. "I'm sorry, but it's just too funny to me. I still love you though."

She had to smile at him, and he gave her a kiss that said everything that she needed to know.

The big day came with me telling everyone what to do, but then that was pretty much what happened on every other day, as far as Kyle could see. I was so happy to do this for our little girl. Raven looked so tired that Kyle felt for her, but she wanted this. What could he do other than try to get me to mellow out just a little bit before someone else tried to kill me for being such an ass, with telling everyone to do this and do that.

If I didn't let up a little bit, there wouldn't be anyone to help with any of this stuff that I had everywhere. I had flowers all over the place, pretty much like the last wedding, other than this time it was indoors in the main cave, with all the low light it was something to look at. Kyle knew how I could be when I wanted everything to be the best it could be for them, and this was my little girl.

Finally, it was Raven who said, "Mom, we need to go a bit easier on everyone before we have to do everything on our own."

"Oh, for crying out loud, I'm sorry if I'm being a big bitch, but the day is here, and this has to be done. Oh, all right. Everyone take a ten-minute break."

The rest of the day went by fast, and everything was just the way both of the girls in Kyle's life wanted it, so pretty. Raven looked so lovely in the dress that I had made for this day. The dress was all white lace. It was long, and the front of the dress was low cut, but the sleeves were long and had a loop that went over her middle finger, so the lace went right down to her fingers. It was all white with small rose buttons running down the back of the dress; it was beautiful and fit Raven just right to show off her body. She was just stunning in it. It was hard to believe that I had made such a beautiful dress like this by hand. But Kyle had seen me working on this dress for months so I would have it whenever Raven decided to get married. Kyle was sure that there wasn't another dress as beautiful as this one even in my own world with all the stores. That could hold a candle to what I had made by hand for my little girl to get married in. He was always so proud of me.

Both Sonny and Raven were so happy, and that was the best part of all this. Well, that and the fact that they would have a baby for everyone to love. Kyle and I were both happy to know that we had a grandbaby on the way and that our baby girl was now married and happy. Life was good right now.

Carson was having his own fun with Violet. And she was already starting to show, but it seemed to be making her want him even more than before she got pregnant. When winter was over, there was a new baby boy, and Carson and Violet named him Sam, but his mother liked to call him Sammy. Raven was starting to show that she was very much having a little one of her own. It was good to be having babies and not making war with Kyle's old clan. He was still unhappy knowing that his father was gone, and would never see any of his grandchildren. But who knew, maybe somewhere he was watching right now; he liked to think that anyway.

He would have loved them and would have told them stories that Kyle couldn't about his childhood. He was worried about his father's clan because the fighting had been over for a while now, and he wished he knew who they had voted in as the new lord of the clan. He was hoping that it was someone who would be a good leader like his father was.

In Kyle's time within his father's clan, the clan had done well with everything and everyone pretty much got along other than Cal. He had always been a cold-hearted man, so no one really liked him because of that. Cody was voted in as the new lord of the clan, and the men were happy to be done with Cal. Everyone was other than one of his children, that is.

Chapter 19

There was one of Cal's children who happened to love his father, and that was Lewis. He was not happy about Cody being the new clan lord. He still thought that the clan should have stayed to make sure that Kyle was killed. He wanted to make more of Kyle's clan pay for killing his father.

No one wanted to listen to him; he was just too young to understand what was best for the whole clan. They had told him when he said to stay and fight. He thought they were all a bunch of cowards if he had his way the clan would have stayed and killed Kyle for what he had done to his father.

Well, it had been almost a year now; he was as big and as strong as any of the men now. He wanted to get even with Kyle and he would no matter what the rest of the clan had to say about it. He felt the need to get revenge because no one else seemed to care that his father was gone. Everyone he talked to said the same thing: the war was over, and the clan wanted to live in peace now.

Well, if they wouldn't help he would go on his own and kill the man who killed his father. Lewis was not sure why he felt the need to defend his father because he was never there for him when he was growing up, and everyone else pretty much despised him. There was something inside of him that made him want to defend him. He was going to do that, no matter what anyone said: Kyle would die. He knew that Cal was not a kind man. But he was still his father, and so he thought it was up to him to hurt someone for killing him and for leaving him without a father as well as taking away their clan lord.

Lewis had no one to turn to other than his mother, and she felt like the rest of the clan, that it was time to get on with their lives. He made up his own mind about what was right or wrong; right now he was wrong to go after the other clan, but no one was going to change his mind. So it just kept eating away at him until he had to leave and make someone pay, and that was Kyle. He really never had a good relationship with his father, but he always wanted to have one, and now he would show them all that someone did care that he was killed.

Back in the lost city

Kyle was older now and not as fast as he used to be. When the men wanted to train, he was finding himself asking his son Carson to do more and more of the training these days. It was not something that any man wanted to admit, but he was not as fast anymore. He just couldn't do the same things as easily as he could a few years ago, and that was what the next generation was for. Kyle just happened to hate the fact that his time was coming to an end as clan lord, but he didn't feel like giving up his control just yet.

Carson and Sonny were pretty much the ones that did most of the hard training stuff these days. Kyle could see his time was coming to an end, and soon he would be naming Carson as the new lord of the clan. He was okay with someone else taking over the clan now. He knew that it wouldn't be long anyway, and someone would have to take over.

He could feel the pain every time he tried to do any really hard work these days. He just couldn't keep up with the younger men now. So it was time to step down and let the young run the clan. He would talk to me about naming someone else to take over, but not today. *Not today*, he thought as he walked to the cave where his wife would be waiting for him and where he could still put a smile on her pretty face. That was something that he was looking forward to doing more than anything else, other than hold his children and tells them he loved them.

It took Lewis a few days to find the field that they had fought in, and he had gone by himself to find the man whom he had come to kill. When he was dead, he would be on his way back to his own clan. Some of the men had been standing guard like Kyle always had them do no matter if they were getting ready for a war or not. Kyle would never take anything for granted again. You never know when it could all come to an end. So he felt the need to stay on guard for now. It was just to make sure that their city would stay safe. So far, it had worked for years now, but that was all about to change.

Sonny was watching the field on the other side of the big rock to see if anyone had been looking for the clan when he saw Lewis sitting by a fire eating. He couldn't really see if there was anyone else sitting by the fire. He had no way of knowing that he would be followed by someone who wanted to change everything that Kyle had worked so hard to protect all his life. Sonny started back to the clan without being seen, or so he thought. He was wrong. This time Lewis was waiting for someone to lead him to the man whom he was going to kill. Lewis was good at watching for signs when out in the open; this time was no different, even though Sonny was always so careful not to be seen.

This time he was, and he had no idea he was being watched and followed back to the city. Lewis watched as Sonny walked to the back wall of the cave and then he pushed the wall, and it moved. Sonny pushed the wall again and this time the wall opened up and Sonny walked into the mountain. Lewis had never seen anything like that before, but if he was going to find Kyle he had to try and go through the wall after Sonny had a chance to get a little ways ahead of him. So he wouldn't be seen.

So he sat down for about an hour before he went to the back wall and tried to push the wall like Sonny had done before him. It took him a while to find the right spot, but when he did the wall started to give way just like it had done for Sonny. He pushed again, and then he went into a long dark hallway. He found a torch on the side wall that was still lit, so he took it so he could see to walk down this hallway. It had a lot of turns and went up a few times, then down and then another long hallway. After about an hour or so, the hallway started to open up to a bigger hallway. A little while longer and he could see it was getting lighter and lighter as he walked, he could see that there was a big opening up ahead.

Lewis didn't want to be seen so he would wait until it was really dark then he would go out and see where he was, and if he could find Kyle.

"Wow," he thought as he walked out into the open. It was like nothing he had ever seen, and he would love just to walk around this place, to take it all in if he were here for a visit to see an old friend. But that was not why he was here. No, this was going to be payback for his father's life, and he knew who had to pay the price, and that was Kyle. That made him smile and when he did he looked just as evil as his father before him.

Lewis had waited until dark before he started into the city, but it wasn't as easy as he had thought it would be because they had dogs everywhere. So he had to be very careful not to be seen by them; he knew that they would bark and give him away before he was ready to be seen. So for the next few days he kept out of sight and just watched the clan in their nice city with everything all clean and bright. It was like nothing he had ever seen in his life, but it didn't matter how nice the city was; he was there to kill one man, and go back home. Kyle was walking with some of the children when he saw someone in one of the caves. He didn't see him for very long, so he wasn't sure if it was one of his own men or not.

He would tell the men to keep on the lookout for anything unusual over the next few days anyway. It was putting everyone on edge not knowing if there was someone here, and if there was, who was it and what did he want.

I was sure that I had seen someone in one of the caves too, and I was pretty sure that it wasn't one of the clan. It had put me on edge for the last few days also. Enough so that I had started carrying one of the guns that I had saved from one of the trunks that we had found in the plane all those years ago. *Whoever it was would be in for a big surprise, because I will not hesitate to shoot you, and believe me, I know how to use this gun.* I thought.

I didn't tell Kyle about what I saw because he would get upset with me, and that wasn't something that I wanted to deal with right now. Besides, I was sure that what I saw was a man in one of the caves that did not belong here. But I couldn't bring myself to say anything right now because if I were wrong no one would ever let me live this one down. No, I would wait until I was sure of what I saw then I would deal with it.

The days were starting to get longer now, and that meant that summer was on its way. I was happy to see that because I loved to get the garden ready to plant every year.

What would we put in it this year that would help make the meals better, and that the children would love to eat? Sometimes that was a big deal because if it wasn't sweet or sour it could be hard to get them to eat. I had put in some fruit trees a few years ago and was babying them until they could take hold in the hard ground here, and it was starting to pay off now. Each year the trees were getting bigger, so it wouldn't be long, and we would have fresh fruit. The children would love that; I was sure of it.

Raven was about to give birth to their first child, and she was antsy most of the time now, and I didn't want to do anything to upset her right now either. So I didn't tell her that I had seen a man who was not of our clan either. Not even Lily. No, it was best not to say anything for now in case I was seeing things. Kyle was out watching the men train with his two sons. It was a good feeling to know that what he knew would be living on in them, long after he was gone.

Slade was as fast as anyone whom Carson had ever seen, and he didn't have any fear either, so he would be one to look out for in a fight. Slade was a good-looking kid too, with the same eyes as Kyle's. He was always training for a war that was not coming for a long time now, or at least that was what everyone was hoping for. As the lord of a clan, it was up to Kyle to make sure everyone was ready at a moment's notice. That was how Kyle had been for a very long time now. You stay on top of everything because you never know when things will change so be ready if you want to keep the upper hand, and he did.

Sonny would be happy to see the baby come because it was taking its toll on Raven, and most of the time she was either crying over something or mad as hell about something. He was hoping that the baby would come soon so he could have the life that he wanted to have with his mate. And have a baby to raise, and teach everything that he knew to his child. If it were a boy, they would go on hunting trips, and he would know how to kill as well as clean the meat. He would also teach him how to fight. He would know how to do many things; he's going to be good at all of them. If it were a little girl, he would be as gentle as a man of his size could be he'd be there to help her with whatever she needed through the years. And someday he would give her away to some lucky man to have as a lovely mate; she would be as beautiful as her mother. Sonny would love the child and do his very best to be a good father.

The first Tucker dog had gotten sick and died years ago. It was very hard for me to put my friend to rest, but he had a good life with many puppies to take after him, so I took one of his puppies, and he became the new Tucker. In no time he started to act and look just his dad, so he fit right in; soon he was going everywhere I went just like my old friend had done. I loved the dog as much as I did old Tucker dog.

I was one of those lucky women who keep their looks through life. Even though my hair had more gray in it now than the dark that used to be there, I was still nice-looking, and most of the men still watched as I walked by. To Kyle I was still the most beautiful woman he had ever seen; it made him smile to see that I was not even aware of it now, any more than I was when I was young. All the children were grown now and having children or getting ready to have them.

All of them except Slade; he only had his mind on hunting and training to fight right now. Or so I thought. Slade did have his eye on one of the women, but he had never told anyone about it. He didn't want to be teased about it right now, and anyway he wasn't sure if she even knew that he was alive yet.

Willow had a mind of her own, and she didn't want to be with someone who would try to make her into one of those women who only lived to take care of her man.

No, not this girl, she thought to herself. It was a hot day, and Willow was about to take a dip in the cool water to clean her hair under the waterfall. Before she got into the water, she took a quick look around to see if there was anyone around before she took off everything that she had on before she went into the water. She didn't see anyone, so she took off her things and jumped in.

It was so cold, but after a few minutes she was swimming to the waterfall to clean her hair before she got out. It was then that she saw him watching her, but it was too late to get away. He was too fast for her while she was in the water. He grabbed her as soon as she saw him behind the waterfall.

He pulled her through the waterfall with him. She was told to keep her mouth shut or he would shut it for her; either way was fine by him. He had no feelings for this young girl so either way would not upset him at all, he said as he let her go so she could pull some rags on that were lying nearby to cover up with as he watched her. Willow's face got red as she knew he was watching her put on her things.

Then he told her, "You don't have to worry about that. I'm not here for that," he told her. "Besides, you're not my type anyway."

Willow hung her head down as she tried not to let him see how his tone made her feel.

"Well, I wasn't ready for this, but we'll handle it now, won't we?" he asked her as she shook her head back at him.

"Who are you?" she asked him.

Lewis was tall and dark with the same hard dark eyes that his father had, and he had the same kind of hate on his face that was always on Cal's. Again she asked him who he was. He just looked at her as if he was looking right through her, and it was unsettling to say the least.

Before she could get an answer he hit her on the head, and the lights went out. She hit the ground harder than he had wanted her to; he wasn't here to hurt anyone other than the man who had killed his father, and now he had this young girl to deal with. *Well, this is a mess, but I'll deal with it, just like I deal with everything else that comes my way,* he thought to himself.

It was not in his plans, but he found some rope and tied her up and put a gag into her mouth so he wouldn't have to answer her if she wanted to talk. Things weren't going the way he had thought it would go, but he was so full of hate that going back without doing what he had come for was not an option either. Lewis was trying to fix something for him and the girl to eat and he was having a hard time trying to think of what his next move would be. This young girl was not in any of his plans, but she was here, so he had to get past it and do what he came to do. He had only been eating dry food these days because he didn't want to start any fires that the clan might see. The food wasn't very good, but it would keep him strong, and that would have to do for now.

At the evening meal, everyone was eating when Willow's mother asked if anyone had seen her daughter. No one had. Kyle and I didn't like the idea that one of the clan was missing for a meal. It didn't mean anything right now to anyone other than another young one doing whatever they wanted instead of eating with the rest of the clan.

Slade was worried about Willow because he had never seen her miss the evening meal; as far back as he could remember she was always there to eat with her mother and the rest of the clan.

"What do you think of Willow not being here with the rest of the clan to eat?" Slade asked his brother.

Carson wasn't sure what to make of it as he had never really paid much attention to her, so he didn't know if this was something unusual for her or not.

"I'm not sure what to make of it. Do you think something is wrong?" Carson asked him.

"I don't know, but it's sure not like her to miss an evening meal with her mother. I've never seen her miss a meal before, so I think something is wrong."

Kyle was more worried than he let on. Because he was sure that he did see someone now, and he was pretty sure that the man had Willow. He would be on the lookout for sure now.

After the meal was done, and everything was cleaned up, I went outside. I walked around to see if I could see anything out of place or maybe see the man again that I now knew I had seen. Everything seemed as it should. But somehow I knew something was wrong. I was worried too. This outsider might have his hands on Willow.

Betty was crying by the outside of the main cave. "I'm sorry," she said to me as she wiped her eyes and started to leave.

"No, you don't have to leave. It's all right to be upset. I would be too. Willow is probably off somewhere by herself and just forgot the time, that's all."

Betty shook her head and said, "No, she wouldn't do that to me. She knows how much I worry about her, and especially not after losing her father. No, I know something is wrong."

"Well, the men will find her, and she'll be all right."

"Do you really think so, Betz?" she asked.

I gave her a hug and said, "I know so, now you need to get some rest. You don't want your daughter to see you crying, do you?"

"You're right, she hates to see me cry." She thanked me and walked off to go to her cave to wait for her daughter to come home.

Kyle was busy walking around the courtyard to see if there was anything out of place. It was as it should be, and he didn't know what else to do. I found Kyle walking in the courtyard when I walked out in the open to look for Willow.

"I was hoping I would find something out here," he told her. "But as you can see, everything is the way it should be."

I put my arms around him and gave him a kiss that told him I still wanted him.

"What was that for?" he asked me.

"Oh, just to let you know that I'll always love you as much as I did when I first met you. That's all."

He picked me up and held me as close as he could before he let me down.

"I'm glad, because I feel the same way."

"Even after all these years?"

Carson and Sonny, as well as Slade, were all watching the two of them carrying on as if they just fell in love with each other.

"Now that is more than I really wanted to see," Slade said to his brothers.

"I have to agree with you this time. It just doesn't feel right to see that kind of thing when it comes to your parents," Carson answered.

The boys had all walked away before either Kyle or I saw that our sons were there watching the two of us.

The next day I was going to the cave to help Raven with the children. She was getting so big with the baby that I knew it would only be a few more days and the baby would be here. I didn't want her to overdo it being so close to having the baby.

"Well, children, we have some help today, and so we will start the day off with reading, and then go on to math."

The children all loved Raven and me. They had heard their parents say that I was the one who started the school for whoever wanted to learn, and now after all these years all the clan wanted the children to be taught. So no one even thought of not coming to the classroom. It was nice to know that after I was gone they would still come here to learn how to read, write and be able to do some math. It would help them have a better life.

That night the men had a meeting to talk about Willow and what to do to find her.

"I think we should all take turns looking around the city, and then meet back here to check in to see if anyone found anything," Slade said to all the men.

Kyle was still lord of the clan, but he didn't mind someone having his say when it came to things like this. As Kyle watched his son, it occurred to him that he had feelings for this girl. He was sure that he was in love with her, and so he wanted to talk to him about what the next move was.

After the meeting, Kyle asked Slade to stay behind so he could talk to him.

"What's on your mind?" Slade asked his father. "I just think that was a good call on your part to have everyone look then check in. I'm proud of you."

Kyle knew that he had to be very careful with what he said right now, because he didn't want to push his son to find out if he had been seeing this girl. He had better take this one slowly.

"It's a good plan, so let's get going on it right now before something happens to that girl," Kyle said as he gave his son a push out of the meeting cave.

All the men in the clan were looking for Willow. It was making Lewis very uneasy, but there wasn't anything he could do about it, except keep a watchful eye out as he could not get caught. Willow was going to try and get her hands free then she would make a run for it when he was sleeping. She was thinking of her mother because by now she must be so worried about her, and that hurt her to think of worrying her mother. She had already been through enough with the loss of her husband, Willow's father. Willow was all that she had now. To think about her crying thinking the worst had happened to Willow was too much for her to deal with. She had to get out of here and go home and tell her mom that she was all right.

It was late when Lewis closed his eyes. She was hoping he was really sleeping, not just resting his eyes, or whatever men said when they wanted it to look like they hadn't nodded off. She was working hard to try and get herself free and do it as quietly as she could. It was not easy because he had tied some really hard knots. She had to work them loose a little at a time and only hoped he wouldn't wake up before she could work them all free. It took a lot longer than she had thought it would, but she had her hands free now, so the rest would be a little easier, and she would be out of here. She could feel bleeding from the ropes, but she couldn't think about that right now; she had to get out of here.

It was almost daylight when the men gave up and called it a night. Everyone except for Kyle that is who was still looking for Willow. Just when he was going to give up, he saw Willow running out of one of the caves that they had already looked in but didn't find anything. But there she was running as if her life depended on it.

"Stop, and don't scream," he told her before he took his hand off her mouth. "Where is he?"

She was trying to calm down before she told him what he wanted to know.

"He's in the cave that I just left. He was asleep, but I don't know if he still is," she told him.

"You go, get help, and I'll try to get him before he wakes up if I can."

With that, she was off running to find help for him as fast as her legs would go. She couldn't think of who to get, so she went to find Betz, and maybe some of the men would be there too.

"I can't understand you right now. You need to take your time and tell me what's going on," I told her.

After she had finished telling me about the man in the cave, she took a deep breath before saying, "Now we need to get some of the men to go help Kyle with this man."

I told her to get my sons and any of the men whom she could find to help.

"What are you going to do while I'm doing that?"

"We don't have time to talk right now so please go, and do what I told you to do, and don't stop until you find the men."

Willow was running as fast as she could to try and get help before that man woke up and tried to kill Kyle and Betz.

I was out of the cave going as fast as I could as quietly as I could. When I got to the cave, it was still pretty dark, and I couldn't see much, but I went into it anyway. I could feel the hair on the back of my neck start to stand up because I was anticipating a fight with this man. I wasn't sure how I would handle facing this guy, but if he was going to hurt Kyle, I would fight to the death to save him if that was what it took. I was walking as fast as I could without running, and at this time not knowing what I was going to find. I did not want to live without Kyle in my life, and so I would die to save him without even thinking about it. He was my whole life. Right now, I couldn't think of things like that; I had to be clearheaded if I wanted to help Kyle stay alive. It seemed to take forever to get to the end of this damn cave; it was as if time had slowed down. I could hardly breathe for fear of being heard.

I could hear my own heartbeat, and now I thought I heard someone talking, as I got closer to them. I could hear the man talking to Kyle about how long he had waited for this day, now that it was here he was going to enjoy it as much as Kyle had enjoyed killing his father.

Who was his father? I was wondering when the man said, "Oh, don't tell me you don't know who my father was."

"Look, son, whoever he was, I don't think he would have wanted you to do this."

"Oh, yes, he would. He hated you and wanted to kill you himself, but he never got the chance to do it. Now he's dead, so I'm going to do it for him. My father was Cal," Lewis yelled.

"I never like killing anyone, not even someone as hateful as your father was. He only had feelings for himself, but still I was not the one who killed him. I'm not really sure who the man was that made the blow that killed Cal, other than that it was over fast, so he didn't suffer. It was fast, no time to feel any pain. So be glad for that," Kyle told him.

"Don't try to make me think that you had nothing to do with his dying in that field. I know better than that. I was there that day. You may not have been the one who actually killed him, but it was because of you that he was there in the first place."

"You're wrong about that part. It was because of his hate that all of us were there that day. Your father was so full of hate that he couldn't think right anymore, but that doesn't mean you have to make the same mistakes as he did. You can do the right thing and put down that hatchet and leave here and go on with your life, son. Or you can die like he did for nothing. It's up to you," Kyle told him.

"Don't call me son. I'm not your son and now I'm going to kill you," he replied. I watched in horror as Lewis.

Ran toward Kyle with an ax in his hand, Kyle was ready for him and hit him in the face. He fell back a few steps but got up too fast for Kyle to react, and he hit Kyle with the ax in the right arm.

Kyle let out a cry as the man came at him again. Kyle lost his footing and fell backward, but he rolled to the side to avoid being hit with the hatchet, but Lewis was fast, and Kyle wasn't that fast anymore. I could see that Kyle wasn't going to win this. Before the man could hit Kyle again, there was a shot, and the man fell on top of Kyle and stopped moving. Kyle looked up to see my face standing over him with a smoking gun in my hands.

Kyle got up and tried to take the gun out of my hands, but I was in shock; he couldn't get me to let go of it.

"Betz, it will be okay. Let me have the gun." He was sure that I didn't even know where I was right now.

He was trying to get me out of the cave where the dead man was lying on the ground when the rest of the men got to the cave.

"She'll be all right. She's in shock," Raven said as she helped me to the bedroom of my cave. When Raven and Lily came out of the room where I was sleeping, all the men were there to find out if I was all right.

"I told you that she was in shock, didn't I? So why are all of you still here? Go back to your own caves for the rest of the night, and she'll be back to herself by tomorrow," Raven told all of them. But when she saw the look of hurt on her father's and brothers' faces she melted a little and said, "You can go in to see her. She's sleeping now. I gave her something so she would rest, so don't any one of you even think about waking her up. She needs to rest so her body can deal with this."

"Daddy, you need to let me deal with your arm. It looks bad. I might need to put in some stitches, and it has to be cleaned as well."

Lily had to smile at Raven; she was most definitely her mother's daughter.

"Okay, what is up with you, and that damn smile on your face?" Raven asked Lily.

"Not a thing," she said as she got ready to go back to her own family for the rest of the night. Before she got to the opening of the cave, Raven ran up to her, gave her a hug, and said, "Thank you for everything."

Lily gave her a big hug then said, "You're so welcome. Now stop crying, and go take care of your mom and dad for all of us," she told her.

Lily knew how Raven always tried to come off like she was as mean as a snake, and it worked with almost everyone, but she knew her a lot better than that.

She had been the one to help with that girl when she was little; she had spent almost as much time with her as her own mother. So no, she was not mean; it was just her way of dealing with whatever she was having a hard time with, and right now with her mom like this, as well her dad being hurt, it was very hard on her. She really only wanted someone to tell her that they would be fine.

"Your mom and dad will be just fine, so stop worrying and go back and take care of them."

"Thank you for being here for us," Raven told her as Lily wiped away a tear from her pretty young face.

Raven went back to my bedroom to look in on her one more time before she got to work on her father's arm, and then it would be time to go home to Sonny. He was waiting up for her to come home.

"How are your parents doing?" he asked.

"I'm not sure yet! But I think they'll be fine, Mom just needs to rest as much as she can so her body can deal with all this, and Dad needs to rest so he can heal." Raven was so exhausted right now from the whole ordeal, as well as just knowing that her father could have been killed if her mom hadn't been there. Who knows what would have happened?

She fell asleep with her head on Sonny's shoulder. Sometime in the night he carried her to bed; the sun was up, and it was hot out when she woke up. It was time to check on her mom and dad. As Raven went into the bedroom of our cave, she saw that we were both sleeping soundly, so she backed out as quietly as she could, so she wouldn't wake us up.

She felt a lot better knowing that both of us were sleeping like babies; we both needed as much of that as we could get right now. Raven only wished that she could get some more sleep herself.

She ran into Lily on her way back to the main cave and told her to tell everyone not to bother either one of her parents the whole day. If someone did, they would have to answer to her. Lily had to smile at her as she knew very well that would do the trick because no one wanted to get Raven upset right now. Raven went back to her cave and was only going to rest for a few minutes but fell asleep and didn't wake up for two hours. When she woke up, she felt so much better. She was sure she could deal with whatever else came up now. It was funny what a little rest could do for one's body, she thought with a smile as she went to see about some food.

The next week or so was hard for me; I was having a hard time knowing that I had killed someone, even though I had no choice. Because if I hadn't he would have killed Kyle, and I wasn't going to let that happen. Kyle was trying to let me come to terms with what had occurred on my own. He knew that it would take some time to do that. I was a good person and hurting someone was something I would have never thought I would have to do. Word got back to the other clan that Lewis had been killed trying to kill Kyle.

Chapter 20

It took Kay a few days to get back to the field where the fighting took place, and this time she didn't come alone; she was with some of the men in the clan.

They thought they should be there to let Kyle know that Lewis had acted on his own. The last thing they wanted was to go back to war with Kyle's clan.

Kyle, as always, had some of the men on lookout just in case someone else wanted to get into the city. Toby told Sonny to go back and get Kyle to tell him that Kay and some of the men from the other clan are here to see him. Kay and the men made up the campsite for the night. They had no idea how long it would take for Kyle to see that they were there, so they had brought enough food for a few days as well as gifts to show Kyle that they wanted peace. Kyle's clan was happy to have the other clan willing to trade with them; it would be good for both clans, and Kyle was happy to see that Kay was mated with Cody. He was a good man and would make a very good clan lord of his father's clan.

He liked both of them a lot so the clans could come together sometimes now to share stories, and trade.

"Kyle, what's wrong with Raven?" Sonny asked.

"She's getting ready to have the baby, but other than that, not a thing that I know of. Why do you ask?"

"I'm worried about her. She hasn't been the same since the night that Betz killed Lewis. I just can't seem to help her deal with this. I thought she was just worried about her mother, but now I think that this was just as hard on her as it was on Betz. I was hoping that you could talk to her, to see if you can find out what's up with her, and what I need to do to help her."

"I'll see what I can do. She is a lot like her mother, and both of them like to work things out by themselves, so don't hold your breath," Kyle said as he walked away.

Over the next few days, Raven and I were both pretty much back to normal, other than the fact that the baby was due, and everyone was starting to get worried about Raven. Kyle knew his girls and knew that both of us would be just fine in time, and time was all that we really needed. We just needed to heal from everything that had gone on over the last few months. Kyle knew that Raven was a lot like me; she was strong, so they would be back yelling at everyone soon.

I was having a hard time trying to get Raven ready to give birth to the baby.

"She'll be all right," Kyle told Sonny. "Betz will take good care of her, you just have to be patient, and soon you'll be a father."

"I'm so worried about her. She seems to be in a lot of pain and has been all night long," he told Kyle.

"Well, that's the way it goes sometimes," Kyle said with a pat on Sonny's back. "Believe me when I say this, I've been through this more than once and sometimes it takes a while to have the baby. Raven is strong like her mother is, and she'll do fine. So stop worrying and try to relax. After the baby is here, neither one of you will be getting a lot of sleep for a while," Kyle told him as he slapped Sonny on the back again as he walked away.

Raven was trying to get through the labor without yelling at everyone who got near her, but as the contractions got worse it was getting harder and harder to do.

I felt sorry for my daughter, but there wasn't much I could do other than what I was already doing to reduce the pain. As the labor went on, I thought that I needed to try and find out if the baby was breech or not.

But to do that, I needed to have some help. Lily was in her cave when Sonny came and got her. It only took a few minutes to see that the baby was indeed coming out feet first. With both of us women working on her, the baby was born, and both the baby and Raven were doing just fine.

Sonny was so happy that he was giving everyone a hug and telling them that he was a father.

"Can you believe it?" he said to everyone around him. "I'm a father."

Kyle had to smile at him; it didn't seem so long ago when he was a father for the first time, and he knew how happy he was, so he could understand how he felt.

It was something that you had to live through to understand it. I was wet with sweat when I came out of the cave and told everyone that it was a little boy and that both of them were doing fine. Even as I said it, I was not sure if that was the whole truth. *I only hope she'll be all right,* I thought.

"Well, I have to say you're the best-looking grandmother I've seen in a long time." Kyle gave me a light kiss on the lips as I went to get something to drink.

"Kyle, I didn't want to say anything in front of the rest of them, but she lost a lot of blood. I'm not sure if she'll be able to have more children or not. It will take some time for her to get back on her feet, and then we should know more."

Kyle was not sure what to say other than "I believe in you, and I know that if anyone can fix her it's you. So stop beating yourself up over this. I know you, and I know that you have done the best that you can."

"I wish it were that simple," I said as I sat down to rest. "I'll keep a close eye on her and make sure that she doesn't overdo it if I have to tie her down."

"Now that's the woman I know and love," Kyle told me as he bent to kiss my mouth.

Over the next few days, Raven was starting to get up to walk around and soon she was back to herself. And that was as mean as a snake to most everyone other than the baby; her mother, father, and of course Sonny was always on the receiving end of her yelling.

Kyle watched as his daughter got stronger and stronger with each day, so he thought she would be all right now. Lily and I weren't as sure. Raven was doing a lot better now, so I was starting to relax. "I think she'll be all right," I said to Lily.

"I think so too," she answered.

"I hope they wait a while before they try to have more children," I said, more to myself than to Lily.

I hate to feel this way, but I feel that she still has a long way to go before she'll be back to herself.

Chapter 21

Kyle was taking all the children to watch the men train; it was good for them to see it and also good for the men to have a fan club watching them. All the children were cheering them on as they worked. Sometimes this still made him want to get in there and show them how it was done, but he knew that was just his male ego talking. He had learned to curb his attitude a long time ago. He knew that it was time to watch and let someone else do the fighting these days, and he was all right with it just as long as he could still demonstrate to the clan sometimes.

Raven was giving the baby a bath when I got to my daughter's cave.

"Can I help you with him?" I asked.

Raven looked like she was happy to have some help.

"Yes, you can," she told me.

"I was hoping that you would come today. I'm so exhausted, if I could just get a little nap in. I'm sure I'll be fine."

I felt her head and said," I think you have a fever, so go lie down for a while. I'll take care of the baby."

"Mother, please do not treat me like a child. I'm not a baby anymore." But as she said it she started to fall. I had to catch her before she hit the ground.

"I'm your mother, and I'm not babying you. I am telling you to rest, as your *doctor*."

"Well, that's different," she said and went to lie down.

After Raven was asleep, I went to get Kyle so I could talk to him about our daughter.

"I don't care what you think about this. I know that she isn't getting better after having the baby. I want to take her to a real doctor in the upper world."

Kyle knew that if I felt that determined to go there I was really worried about her. So he said that he would talk to Sonny, and they would make the preparations to go as soon as possible. Kyle was pretty upset over what I had just told him. He knew me, and if I was this upset there was something going on with Raven, but he would keep the worry to himself because what good would it do to upset everyone else right now? No, he would just do as I said and get her to an upper world doctor.

With the fever and Raven being so tired, it was a long trip for all of them. Finally, Kyle made up a pull for her. They put together two long poles, and tied them together with rope, then put some furs on it so it would be more comfortable for her to lay on as they pulled her on it.

The rest of the walk went a lot faster. It was a very long way to go, and they only hoped she would be all right until they got her to an upper world doctor. Raven was out of it for most of the trip. Lily, the others, and I had our hands full trying to take care of the baby and trying to walk to the upper world at the same time.

But after a few days we were there, and now I had to find someone who could help us. I found a phonebook and called a doctor. When we got to the office, the doctor took one look at Raven and told me she needed to go to the hospital right away. She was very sick and would need the staff of the hospital to take care of her and run some tests; they would put her on an IV right away. He said she was dehydrated.

Raven was in the hospital for a little over two weeks, but she was strong. She made a full recovery, in no time they were going back home, and now Raven was taking care of the baby while she walked.

"This has made me think that your world has its good points after all," Kyle told me when we were alone in our cave.

"I know that, and I'm glad we have both worlds when we need them. I'm glad I saved that money from the plane so we could pay the doctor as well as the hospital in full before we left."

Raven was happy to be back at home as well, and so was everyone else. It did make all of us think how lucky we were to have my world to go to and get help if we couldn't fix something here.

Even though it turned out to only be a very bad infection, it still could have killed her if we hadn't taken her there. That was something that the clan had to think about. Life was starting to get back to normal now, with

Raven back to herself; everyone else was starting to feel like their world would be good again. I had taken the time to get some intravenous fluid just in case this ever happened again. At least I could give the much-needed fluids, and also the good doctor let me have some penicillin after telling him we lived a very long way outside of town, and that could make all the difference in someone getting better or having to go to the upper world doctors.

Kyle was getting ready to leave for trading with the other clan when Sonny came and asked if he as well as some of the other men of the clan could go with him.

"Well, I don't see why not if you want to. Sure, we'll leave early in the morning, so tell the men to be ready."

I had sent some of my canned goods to trade for some of their blankets. I also sent some of my clan's blankets to let the other clan see how our women made ours with a lot of color in them.

"Well, we can only hope they'll get along now that Cal's not the clan lord."

"Oh, I'm sure that they'll all get along with each other."

"I guess," replied Lily.

"What's up with you? You don't sound like you think they'll get along."

"I'm sorry, but I still don't trust the other clan yet," Lily told me.

"Well, Kyle thinks this is good for both clans, and I trust my husband." Lily had to agree with that.

It was a long walk to the clan that Kyle had once called his. When the men did get there, everyone was happy to see them. They took a few days to catch up on everything that was going now that Cody was clan lord; when Kay put out food for the men Kyle could see that she was expecting.

"When is the baby due?" he asked Cody after she left the room.

"In early spring, I think."

"Well, I'm happy for you both. It's a wonderful thing to become a parent."

Kyle could see that Cody was happy and that the clan was doing a lot better now that Cal was out of the picture.

"How are Cal's children doing?" Kyle asked.

"For the most part he was never a father to any one of them, that's why it was such a shock to see what Lewis did. He never had anything to do with him either, so why he thought he had to try to get even for his death is something of a mystery to all of us," Cody said.

"Well, I just hope the other children can live a good life now, and grow up without the hate that was a big part of their father," Kyle said as he got up to put another log on the fire. It was nice to be here in his old clan again, even though it was just as a visitor now.

Kyle was glad that they came, and it was nice to know that both of the clans could get along and also trade with each other. Over time, that would prove to be a great gift, for all of them. Kyle was sure that I would be happy with everything that they were bringing back home, and to know that all the women loved my canned goods and the blankets that I had sent. Kyle was sure that over the years both clans would have good trades and it would be nice to have the other clan see their city now. Kyle would put a whole pig in the ground; it would be a good time for everyone. Kyle was looking forward to telling me about everything he had in mind for both clans as far as getting along and having fun each time the clans got together.

While the men were gone, I took the time to help Raven get used to being a new mother to her son Roy. He was a big boy with a full head of dark hair already, and a set of lungs to let you know when he wanted something. That was what he was doing right now as his mother was getting ready to feed him. I was happy to be a grandmother again, and Kyle was having so much fun being a grandfather. He always had his grandson on his shoulders walking around the city with the boy waving to everyone they saw; it was the cutest thing to see.

Time had gone by so fast, I thought as I watched my daughter feed the baby that she held in her arms.

"I think it's time that your father and I give up as lord and lady of this clan," I said to Raven.

"Oh, I don't think it's time for that right now," Raven responded. "I know that you feel like you don't want to do this anymore, but I know that no one is ready to let you and father go just yet."

"How do you know that?" I asked my daughter.

"Hey, I have my ways of finding out these things," she said. They both had a good laugh at that, and it was time to go get the evening meal ready.

"Have l told you that I am so proud of my little girl?"

"Thank you, Mom. I'm proud of you too."

I had taken the time over the last few years to put some of the clan's history down. The next generations would have something to go by as far as where they came from, and how this clan had made its own rules to live by.

I was proud of the things that we had done to become who we were today. Almost all of them could read, write, and do some math. All my children could do both very well and had gone on to teach the rest of the children as well as anyone else that wanted to learn. The city that we had found and made our home was like nothing else that I had ever seen. It was more like something out of one of my favorite books or movies, so beautiful. With a lot of work over the years, the whole clan had helped to make it even more wonderful than it already was. From the tall stone columns on the face of it to the pretty waterfall, and even the inside of the caves were very pretty too. We had done a lot in there as well. The caves had more lighting, and all the walls had cutouts. They had images carved everywhere so whoever walked into them would know about the clan that had lived here, and how much this world meant to us. We had a wonderful life with our families and clan, and our youngest son was all grown up now.

Slade was a strong young man with a lot of heart when it came to his family; he was always ready to fight for them. Now that he was with Willow he had learned to take a lot more than he ever would have in the past; she was hot-tempered, so was he. So sometimes it was hard to get anywhere with the hot-headed two of them; they would fight at the drop of a hat, and most of the time it was over something dumb. It would be a lot easier just to let Willow have her way sometimes, but it was not in his nature to do that when he was right.

Willow thought that she might be going to have a baby, but she wasn't about to tell anyone right now because she was so damn mad at Slade that she wanted to hate him. If only she could, she thought.

"Well, I see that we're still mad as hell," Slade said to her as he walked up on her in the cave that they shared.

She was doing her best to act like she didn't hear him.

"Okay, I give up. What is it that you want me to do to make this go away?"

"Well, isn't that just like you to make me out to be the bad guy when you're the one who started the whole thing?"

"I don't want to fight with you right now, so please tell me what it is that you want from me, and I'll do it," he told her.

Willow was never one to cry, but she was crying like a baby, and that had him on his knees trying to get her to stop.

"I'm so sorry. What did I do?"

Now she was laughing so hard that he just looked at her like she was crazy. "I just do this sometimes now, that's all" she told him. But she was sure it was the baby making her do this.

After a while, she stopped laughing, got up, and told him "I love you" and gave him a kiss. "Now I'm going to the hot springs. If you want to come, I'll be there waiting for you," she said as she took off everything she had on and left the room.

He was not sure what had just happened, but he wasn't going to give up good lovemaking if he could help it. As she got into the hot water, he could see the steam coming off her full breasts as she went under and then came up out of the hot water. He got into the water with her, and she straddled him so she could ride him and he could suck her breast while she was going up and down on him as hard as she could. Then she would slow down, and let him push into her as he kept sucking on her breast. It was so hot, so fulfilling for both of them, it took them a while to get to the top of the wave that they had been riding, but it came, and with it the release came as well.

They both just drifted on their backs through the hot water and just held on to each other for a while before either one of them said anything.

"Boy, I don't understand you sometimes, but I sure as hell do love you." Slade said.

With that, they both laughed then he took her to new heights. It was late when he let her go back to their cave so they could get some rest for the night.

"How is it that we can be so good and so bad at the same time?" she asked him before they fell asleep.

"I don't know, but we'll work it out. We have our whole lives," he told her as they both fell asleep.

It had been a very long week for me without Kyle here, but he was home now, and I was happy to see that everything went well with the other clan.

"How did they like our things?" I asked him.

"Well, I have a lot to tell you, but I really could use some sleep, so if it's all right, can we do this later?" he asked her as he fell into the bed.

Before I could answer him, he was asleep. Over the next few days, Kyle told me everything that had gone on with the other clan.

"I really think we are in a good place with them as far as trading with them, and, well, just getting along for a while."

"I hope you're right about that. I really hate to think that we could be going back to war anytime soon."

Kyle had been watching me and saw that I was starting to get some gray hair at the temples of my face. It made him smile to think that we had been together for that long already.

"By the way, have I told you that I love you lately?" he asked me.

"Oh, you are such a big flirt these days," I said with a laugh. "But I will always want to hear that you still love me because you're stuck with me forever, big guy."

Chapter 22

The other clan was happy to have Kyle to trade with and also as an ally. For the next few years, both clans would work well with each other, but that would change, and like it has been since the beginning of time there would be another war between the clans. That was a long way off and for now life was good for everyone.

I was happy to have little Roy with me today. Because Raven was getting some work done with Violet, and the children they were both so good at teaching that it made a big difference in the way all the children did outside of the classroom these days. Today some of the children wanted to take the two young women on a small picnic to thank them for everything that they had done for them over the years. Both of the girls were so happy knowing that all the work that they had done for years was appreciated by the children. There was no greater gift for a teacher then to have the children say thank you for what you have done for us. So they all had a wonderful day with all the kids playing in the big courtyard and the teachers standing by talking about the year ahead and what they had planned for the next school year.

Kyle was taking his time getting all his tools cleaned and ready for the next hunt when he felt some kind of a pain in his chest. It was so bad that he went down on one knee before he passed out from the pain.

"Has anyone seen Kyle today? I need to get him to eat lunch," I told Toby as I walked by him in the courtyard.

"I think he's working on some of his tools," he told me as I walked by him.

"Okay, thanks, Toby," I responded.

I found Kyle lying on the ground, in his shop where he had been working on some of his tools; he had passed out, and no one could wake him up.

After almost an hour, we had made up our minds to take him to the upper world to get him some help. We were hoping that it wasn't too late. I was so upset the whole trip to the upper world that I had not taken the time to eat anything, for days now. It wasn't that I didn't want to eat, more like I just didn't think of it. All I had on my mind was Kyle, he had to be all right; he was my whole world. The trip to the upper world was long, but I never said anything. All I could think about was *This man is my whole world; please don't let him die.* After the clan had reached the upper world, I found the hospital and the doctor said I got him there in time to save his life. That was the best news I could have gotten; I started to cry with relief. The hospital was a nice one, and everyone was so good with me and the family. In a time like this I was glad we had this world to come to.

"Can you hear me? Kyle, can you hear me?"

"Yes, I can hear you. Why are you yelling at me?" He tried to get up but found that he was in a bed with all kinds of things hanging out of him. "Where am I?" he asked.

"Please don't try to get up. You're in the hospital." It took him a few seconds to understand what was going on.

"I'm in the upper world?" he asked me.

"Yes, I thought it was too late, but you're very strong, and you made it here. The doctor said that he couldn't believe that you were still alive when we got here."

"How long have I been here?" he asked.

"For almost a week and the doctor said that you should be back to normal in a few more weeks."

"What do you mean? I can't stay here for a few more weeks!" As he said it, he was starting to drift off to sleep again.

"Kyle, you've had a heart attack. But the doctor said because you're in such good shape it helped save your life."

I started to cry; it seemed like that was all I had been doing for the last few days now. I was so worried about him that I wasn't sure if I could stand it if anything happened to him. He wasn't sure what was going on right now because he kept drifting in and out of a deep sleep, and that was almost too much for me to see. Every time he came to, I would try to tell him what was going on, but he would be out again before I could explain what had happened. It was a few more days before I got to really talk to him, and even then I wasn't sure if he really understood me.

"Kyle, I want you to listen to me, I want to take you to my old home. It's still there, and while I was waiting for you to wake up I bought it again. I did some checking with my old bank and found out that we have a lot of money. All my old bank accounts are still there. All the money that I had put into them all those years ago, well, let's just say we don't have to ever worry about money. The interest has grown a lot. I've taken care of everything, and even the children are all for it for now. You will need a lot more medical help over the next few months."

Kyle was having a hard time understanding what I was saying as he drifted off to sleep again. Raven and the other children were there to help me with anything that I might need. They were also very concerned about me because I wasn't taking care of myself, and so far I had lost weight over all this. It was hard to get me to leave their father's side long enough to eat something.

And it was hard for them to stay in my world. It was so loud, and there were so many people that it wasn't something any one of them wanted any part of. They knew I needed them, and they were happy to know that there was this place to go to.

"I know that all of you want to help me and be here for your father. We both love you for it, but you need to let me take care of things here right now. I want all of you to go back to our home world for now, and take care of things. When you have, then you can take turns coming back to see us. You know where we'll be over the next few months, at the old house and it's an easy way to get to the underworld."

The children didn't want to leave me here by myself, but they all knew that I could handle this because this used to be my world. It was not their world, and so they did as their mother told them to do. They knew I would be all right, and would take care of their father better than anyone else could.

As I took care of the house so it would be ready for Kyle when he came home, I was amazed to see how little it had changed over the years. Oh, it was dirty and needed a lot of yard work. But it was still in good shape. So it didn't take me very long to get everything ready for the day that Kyle got to come home.

It seemed somehow funny to think that Kyle would be coming home to the place where years ago he had taken me away from. It was happening, and I was hoping he wouldn't fight me every step of the way. I was doing what I had to do to make sure I still had him around for as long as God would allow. I knew he would be as stubborn as a mule, but I would not give up. I had to win this fight; it meant both of our lives, not just his, and that was what I had to get across to him if I was going to get anywhere with him. I was shaking just thinking about having to talk to him about why he needed to stay here for a while.

"Wow, this place is something to look at," Raven said as she helped me put clean sheets on the bed that was going to be our bed while we were here. "You know that he'll have a fit about staying here in this world, don't you?" Raven asked me.

"Yes, I know that he won't like it at first. In time I think he'll see that this is where we need to be right now. Besides, Carson and the rest of you can take care of things back home. He'll feel a lot better knowing that all of you are there to keep everything going smoothly until he's back on his feet, and we can go back home."

Raven just shook her head, "I still don't think he'll go for it, but I'll do whatever you think is right." Raven knew that she couldn't upset me right now when all I was trying to do was take the best care of her father as I could so he would be able to go back home. She had so much respect for everything that I always seemed to be able to handle; I was a very strong woman, and always her hero. Raven and some of the other kids had been helping with all the cleaning that the place needed so it would be ready for us to stay here.

Every time I went to the hospital to see Kyle, he was more and more ready to fight with everything that I had to say about staying here; he hated it all. There were too many people, and way too much noise; how anyone could even think around here was beyond him. Kyle thought he would go nuts if he didn't get out of this place. Where was his wife anyway?

"Well, it's about time you got back here. I'm going crazy here I can't stand all the noise, and everyone making a big fuss over me like I was a child," he told me.

"Well, the doctor has told me that you can go home in a few more days, but you have to do what they tell you to do if you want to get out of here."

"I'll do whatever it takes to be able to go back to my home," he told me. I let that go for now because I didn't think it would do any good to get him upset right now when he was just starting to get his strength back.

I would have my hands full when the time came, but I was up to the challenge. After all, I had gotten him here in time; I would show him that this is the place for him right now. Even as I thought it, I wasn't sure I could win this myself.

"Doctor, I can't keep him in here much longer, he's going crazy in this place."

"Well, if he continues to improve over the next day or so, I'll let him go. If he has any pain at all, you need to bring him back in."

"I promise to do that."

Doctor Owen had never seen a man as strong as this man was. Anyone else would have been down and out for months over a heart attack like he had, if not dead from it. Not this guy. He was something else, and it made him wonder how someone could be as strong as this guy was. *Well, I can only hope I'm as lucky as this guy is when it's my turn,* he thought to himself as he made the rest of his hospital rounds.

I was at home when Raven and Carson brought Tucker to me with one of his puppies so he would have someone to play with.

"How are things going at home?" I asked Carson while Raven put food on the dining room table for them.

"Everything is fine, Mother, so don't worry about things there," he told her. "You have enough to deal with here with father. Mom, I'll do whatever I can, but I'm with

Raven on this. I just don't think he'll ever stay here even if it kills him to go home."

I was so tired of fighting with everyone over this. I got up and put my hands on my hips and said, "Look, I know your father better than you think I do, and I'm telling you that he will be all right. Yes, it will take me some time, but he will listen to me when he sees that this is the only way right now to keep him alive. He has to be near medical help."

"Okay, I stand corrected as usual when it comes to my mother," he said in defeat. "Besides, if anyone can get him to do anything, I believe you're the one to get him to do it." He gave me a kiss on the cheek then sat back down to eat.

It was good to have the kids here right now with everything that was going on. All the kids were so good with me when they knew that I needed help they were always right there to help in any way that was needed. I was so thankful to have children like the ones we have. The next day, after the children left to go back home, I walked around the house for a while before I got ready to go to the hospital to see my husband. Just to clear my mind and make sure that we had everything ready for Kyle's homecoming day.

It was starting to rain as I got into the new car. I had bought it to drive back and forth to the hospital to see Kyle as well as to get things that we would need to live here. The car was small, so it would be good on gas, and it had four doors, so it would be easy to get in and out of. I had paid cash for it, so there were no payments, and

I also paid cash for the house. I had gotten a really good deal on both because of paying cash for them. We had all the money that we would ever need. Having left money in different accounts while I was gone had been a good investment even though it was never meant to be left in the bank back then. It was and now when we really needed money, it was paying off big time. With that and the money that I had found in the plane, we had all that was needed to live very well.

I had the children bring some of Kyle's tools and other things that would keep him busy and was hoping he would be all right for a few months until he was back on his feet.

Then I would let him decide if we should go back or live out our lives here. There was only so much that I could do to help him and to try to save his life. If he wanted to go back to the underworld, he might die, but I had no way to keep him here other than everything that I had already done. It was up to him now. I was hoping with all my heart he would believe me when I told him we needed to stay for a while.

Back in the underworld

Carson had his hands full with everyone in the clan right now because they wanted to see Kyle and see for themselves that he was all right. Carson was a good leader so far, and he wasn't going to let any one of the clan tell him what to do. But he also knew that the longer the clan lord was away it would be harder to handle some of them.

"I'll talk to my father and see if he's up to seeing anyone yet," he told them. He knew that wasn't what he had in mind to do. No, first he would talk to his mother and see what I thought he should do.

"Well, your father will be out of the hospital soon, and then you can talk to him about the clan," I told Carson.

It was strange to the children to ride inside of a loud car to the hospital to see their father.

"I don't think I'll ever get used to sitting in something to get somewhere," Slade said to his family.

I had to laugh at them as this was the only way that I had been able to get around for years. It was kind of funny even to me these days.

"Well, we needed to get this car so I could get around and to get your father home when the doctor says it's all right."

"We know that, mother. But for us, it is pretty hard to get into this thing. On the other hand, it does get us to where we need to go a lot faster. If only it wasn't so loud here. There are so many of these things that you call cars."

I had to laugh at Slade, but I also knew that he was right. After being in the underworld myself for so long, it was hard for me too.

"I love your father so much, and I want him to be all right, so I'll do whatever it takes to see that he gets what the doctor says he needs. I'm like all of you: I don't really think he'll give in and say, 'Okay, I'll stay here and do whatever is best for me.' But I still have to try and make him see that this is the right thing for now. Then when he's on his feet, I'll go along with whatever he thinks is best."

I had never been one to give up on anything that meant something to me, and Kyle meant everything to me, so I knew he was worth it. Right now, I would trade everything if I could go back to a few weeks ago and have Kyle happy and well. I didn't get to do that. This was happening right now, so I had to deal with it, and I would. But I still said a prayer on the way to the hospital that he would come home and want to stay, that he would let me and the doctor take care of him for now.

Chapter 23

Lily and Toby wanted to make a trip to the upper world in a few days when the children got back so they could see Kyle and me and let us know about the unrest in the clan without Kyle there.

At the hospital, Kyle's family was there to see him and let him know that everything was all right back at home.

"Good, I'm glad to hear that," he told them. Even though he was getting better, we could all see that he was not well yet. As the day went on, the family could all see him getting more and more tired, so I gave him a goodbye kiss and so did the children. He was asleep before any one of us was at the door to leave. The children told him they would be back in a few days.

"Boy, mom, I see what you were saying about him not being himself right now," Carson said, and the other children just nodded their heads in agreement.

It was late when the children left to go back to the underworld and the only life that they had ever known. It was hard to see them go; I had tried to get them to stay at least until daylight. They wanted to get back, so I watched them walk away until I couldn't see them anymore. I felt alone for the first time since I could remember.

As I sat down in a chair, not unlike the one I was in on that night years ago when I was taken. I thought of how much I had changed and how much I missed the underworld. Now it felt like I was taking a vacation instead of living here again. Tucker and the puppy were playing in the yard as happy as they had been back at home with the clan.

It was not like that for me now. I went up the steps to the same door that I had once loved. Now it wasn't like that. I liked the place, but it would never really be home for me again. Because home was the underworld, and I missed it a lot more than even I thought I would.

Tucker was sleeping by my side, and the puppy was next to him when I woke up the next morning. All I wanted was to have a very strong cup of coffee before I got ready to go see Kyle. It was just breaking dawn when I got into the car and started off for the hospital. Even though Kyle wouldn't like the car, I did have him in mind when I got it. I had picked out a pretty blue one, and the inside was a light gray. Dumb as it might sound, I had thought that the light blue and grays would be calming to him. I felt like crying because I hated to think of talking to him about staying here. I knew very well how stubborn he could be. That was one of the things I love about him. If he thought he was right, he would stand his ground and would not budge an inch. But right now he had to see that I was right . . . somehow.

"What's going on?" I asked when I got to the hospital and saw doctors and people running around Kyle's room. The doctor took me aside and told me that Kyle had a setback, but he didn't think it was going to keep him down for long.

"What do you mean 'he had a setback'?" I was beside myself trying to get someone to tell me what the hell was going on with my husband, but everyone was busy trying to work on Kyle. I just stood there frozen in my footsteps as they ran in and out of Kyle's room. After a few minutes, someone came and talked to me and told me that Kyle had a stroke sometime in the middle of the night, but he should be all right in a few days.

"Kyle, you have to be all right. Can you hear me?" I said into his ear as I bent down over him. This time he only nodded his head. He was too weak to say anything and kept drifting in and out of consciousness.

I had to get out of that place for a few minutes because I couldn't handle this.

"What is going on here? He was fine yesterday, but today when I get here, you tell me he's had a stroke?" I was almost yelling at the doctor, but I didn't care who heard me right now. I wanted answers, and I wanted them right now. The doctor was trying to get me to sit down so he could talk to me, but I wasn't having any of it. He told me that it wasn't anything that they could foresee, but it wasn't all that uncommon either.

"I'm sorry, but I have to get back to my rounds now, but if there are any other changes I'll call you. Get some rest, and in a few more days, he should be able to go home just as soon as his tests show improvements."

I watched as the doctor walked away to do his rounds while my whole world was falling apart right here right now. I sank to the floor where I had been standing and started crying as people walked by me as if I wasn't there. Right now, I missed the underworld. If any one of the clan had seen me crying, the whole clan would have been there to offer to help in any way that they could. Whereas here in this world, no one even saw that I was crying, and even if they had, no one would care. They all had their own lives, and that was the only thing that mattered to them. This world could use some of the underworld qualities when it came to caring about others.

I cried until I had no more tears to cry, and then I got up and went into the room that held my whole world. Kyle was sleeping soundly, or at least it looked like he was. He had so many tubes hanging out of him right now that it made me want to cry again, but I would not give into that with him next to me. Because he might hear me so I would wait until I was alone for that. Right now, I had to be strong for him and our family. So I would be; I stayed in a chair next to him the whole night and the next day. I made sure he was sleeping soundly before I went home to shower and to rest for a few hours before going back to the hospital. Kyle was doing so well, now it seemed like we were at the beginning all over again. It was going to be a long road for him and even longer for me because somehow I had to make him stay here near the hospital and doctors.

Over the next few days, Kyle was back to himself again and wanting to leave the hospital.

"I can't stand it here anymore," he said. "I know I'll do much better when I'm out of here," he told me, but I wasn't buying any of it. I was the one who had seen him when he didn't even know I was in the room. It was only a few more days when the doctor told me I could take him home. Kyle was beside himself when he finally got to leave the damn place. The doctor shook Kyle's hand and told him that he was very lucky to still be alive and that he needed to take care of himself as well as come back in two weeks. If he was in any pain, then he was to come back immediately. Kyle thanked the doctor and said he would do what the doctor asked him to do. When they brought in a wheelchair for him, the fight was on because he didn't want to be pushed to the door.

"I can walk. I'm not getting in that damn thing," he told me with a hateful look on his face.

"Well, fine then, just get back into the damn bed because if you won't let them push you out of here then you have to stay here. It's up to you. What's it going to be?" I asked him with my arms crossed in front of me.

Kyle just got in the chair and gave me a look that said it all.

"Just get me the hell out of here now," he said with a huff.

I had already parked by the big doors, so he didn't have to walk, but a few steps to get into the car.

"What is this?" he asked as I opened up the car door for him to get in.

"Just get in the damn car and stop giving me so much trouble, will you?" I said as I pushed him in and slammed the door behind him.

"Look, I know that you're still not yourself, but we need to talk and right now is the best time while I have your undivided attention. I bought the house that I lived in when you and I started all this."

"How did you buy the house?"

"Well, I tried to tell you all that when you were in the hospital, but I guess you didn't hear me. Anyway, I bought the house with the money that I had in a few accounts that I opened before all this started, and also with some of the money that I found in the plane. Kyle, we have a lot of money now, so we don't have to worry about the doctor bills or any other bills that we might make while we're here."

Kyle was so exhausted, but he was trying to stay awake so he could understand everything that I was saying, but it was getting harder and harder to do. Kyle was trying to let me get whatever I had on my mind out before he said anything.

"I don't know how to start, so I'm just going to get to it. I know that you want to get back to the underworld, but right now I think we need to stay right here in the old house that I used to live in. I've talked to the doctors, and you have to go to the see them every week now. You are going to be on so much medicine for a long time that it would be almost impossible to keep going back and forth from the underworld."

Kyle knew that what I said made a lot of sense, but there was no way that he could even think of staying here full-time.

"Is it my turn yet?" he asked.

"Okay. Don't you even think of yelling at me or we will have a big problem."

"I'm not going to yell at you. Look, I know that I'm not ever going to be the way I was before all this. But I also know that I don't belong here, and I think you know that as well." I was not happy with what he had to say, but I wasn't surprised either because I knew him very well.

"Well, we can talk more about this when we get to the house," I told him. When I looked over at Kyle, he was asleep with his head resting on the window. What was I going to do with him? I knew that he wasn't well enough to go back to the clan. I also knew that the long walk would be too much for him. *It would kill him*, I thought.

It was dark when we got to the house, and I had to wake him up to get him out of the car and help him up the steps into the house then into bed. He was so weak that it hurt my heart to see him like this. Tucker got onto the bed and lay down beside of him as if he knew that this was not a good thing either. Kyle didn't even look up to see where I was going or to ask me for anything. He was asleep almost as soon as his head hit the pillow. Tucker was just as tired because he was asleep too.

I went to the kitchen to fix some coffee before I went outside to sit in the yard and think about what to do to make him see that we had to stay here for a while until he was back on his feet. It was really late when I went up to bed, and as I got in beside Kyle, I was asleep almost as soon as I put my head down. I was so exhausted. Being here with him in the bed with me felt so right, and that was all it took for me to get some much-needed sleep.

Kyle woke up long before I did and wanted something to drink. He started to get out of bed when he saw some water on a table by the bed for him. It made him smile because I was always thinking of him, right down to this glass of water for him. He got out of the bed as quietly as he could and found his way down to what he thought was the place where I made the daily meals; it was something to see.

He was not used to things like this. He had to admit it was nice to have water at your fingertips anytime you wanted it. The room had big windows to look out at the land; there was a big barn, and everywhere you looked there were trees and bushes. You could also see the mountains, and that made him homesick. But only for a minute because he knew he was in no shape to walk back home and sure wasn't in good enough shape to do what needed to be done there right now. And he sure didn't want any of the clan to see how weak he was right now, or he could lose his lordship, and he wasn't ready to give that up yet.

It was hard, but he had to go along with me this time and stay here for now and hope he would heal fast. He wanted to go home. On the other hand, as long as he was with me, he was at home. I was his whole world, and he couldn't do this without me by his side. Just then, he felt my arms go around him as I leaned against him.

"This place is something to see," he told me.

"Yes, it is, but I miss home too, and when we can, we will go there. I promise you that."

He turned to give me a kiss that said how much he really missed me. Then he said.

"I hate to say this, but we need to put this on hold for right now." He gave me one more kiss that told me what I was in store for when he was back to his self again.

"I can wait as long as I have to, so don't worry about anything other than getting better so I can have my way with you," I told him as he gave me a little pat on my little round butt that he so loved.

Over the next few days, Kyle was having a hard time with everything. He hated being here and he had to sleep a lot, so that was hard on him. I had my hands full with him, and I was at my wit's end.

Lily and Toby got to the house just before Kyle had gotten up to eat something and get a glass of water.

He also now loved my coffee, but the doctor had said he should drink decaffeinated, but I could not bring myself to give that to him, and besides, he didn't drink that much of it anyway.

"Look, I know I'm not myself right now and it's hard for you. I just don't see myself staying here for any longer than I have to," he said as he got up to walk around.

"Let me tell you what I think," I said. "I think that if you try to go home you won't make it very far, and you'll pass out and be right back here if they can get you here in time. I'm sure as hell not going to be the one to watch you kill yourself. So if you leave here right now, you leave without me." I could see the color leave his face, but he didn't say anything right then; he only sat back down and closed his eyes.

"I know that you're right, but it's so damn hard to give up the idea of going home. I miss it and I don't know if I can do this," he told me.

"It will get easier as each day goes by, I promise you. So please just give it some time, and you'll see." I had tears in my eyes as I told him this.

"I'll try for you, but I'm not making any promises," he told me as he wiped away my tears.

Over the next few days, we had some welcome company that made both of us feel a lot better. It was so good to have Lily and Toby to talk to for a few days, and it was good for Kyle to have a man to talk to as well.

I felt bad about some of the mean things that I had said to Kyle, but he made me so mad sometimes that it was hard not to say mean things.

"Betz, I know that this is just as hard on you as it is on Kyle. As your friend, I have to tell you that I don't think I could do what you have done here. With Kyle as sick as he is right now, I don't know how you do it."

"Well, I think we do what needs to be done. Somehow we get the strength to get it done. I'm going to miss not having you to talk to," I told Lily and then gave her a big hug.

"I'll miss you too. But I just know that it won't be long. Both of you will be home and things will be as they always have been," Lily said as she held onto me as if her life depended on it. She so loved the both of us that this was very hard on her and Toby as well as the rest of the clan.

I loved Kyle and wanted to help him, not upset him more. He was so hard to help sometimes. Kyle was not doing so well, it was hard for him; he was tired all the time, and the medicine wasn't helping him either. It made him want to sleep all the time, and maybe that was what he needed right now, but I didn't know how much more of this he could take.

Lily and Toby left to go back home, and now I felt alone again. All the children came to see us and stayed for a few days. It was good for Kyle; he missed them a lot and being with them again made him feel more like his old self again. We talked about everything that was going on at home, and just talking about the underworld made all of us feel better for now.

"I wish I was going back with you," Kyle told them as they got ready to leave to go back home.

"It won't be long, and you'll be back home," they told him as each one of them gave both of us a hug and started off for home.

"I hate to see them leave," he said as we walked back to the house.

"I know that. But you and I need to do what's right, and the best thing for us right now is to stay here close to the doctors and hospital for now."

He might not be able to make love to his woman right now, but he was going to at least put his big hand on that pretty round bottom of hers and give it a nice squeeze once in a while. Just to let me know what I was in store for when he was back to himself again.

I just leaned into him and said, "You are such a horny toad these days."

"Don't you ever forget it either," he told me with another pat on my bottom.

Chapter 24

"Sometimes, you're much wiser than I am," he said as he gave me a kiss.

The next few weeks went by fast, and Kyle was almost back to himself, and the doctor was happy with his improvement. I was happy to have my husband back again. He was up walking like he used to. He was beginning to look for more things to do around the yard, as well as doing some work out in the barn just to get out of the damn house. He had spent his whole life working hard, and it felt good to be doing anything other than sleeping all the time, which was the hardest on him. So for now he was happy to be outside and working with his hands again.

He was a hard worker, and it made him feel like he was back home to be able to work on some tools, even if they were not the ones he was used to working with. He had all the barn tools cleaned and put up like he always did with the ones back home.

"Well, I was wondering where you went to," I said as I gave him a glass of cold lemonade. The one thing that he really liked here was ice to put into a drink whenever you wanted it. That was something that he could get used to.

"You know what?" he said, as I sat down next to him to watch him work on some old rusty tools that I would have just thrown out if it had been me. Not Kyle, no, he had every one of them looking like the day they had been bought. That was one of the things I loved about this man; he knew how to take care of things. And he really enjoyed taking care of them.

"What's on your mind?" I asked him.

"I was thinking that this place isn't so bad after all. If it's all right with you, I'd like to come back here for part of the year and stay at our other home part of the year. I really have gotten to the point that I like this place too."

I wasn't sure that I heard him right so I had to ask him. "What did you just say?"

"You heard me the first time, and yes, I mean it," he told me and gave me a kiss to seal the deal.

"I am going to hold you to that," I said as I got up to go get dinner ready.

"Oh, say, could you fix me some of that thing you called 'pizza,' with lots of those green things on it?"

"Yes, I can, and those green things are called bell peppers, sir."

With that, I was off to the house to make him one of the best pizzas I had ever made. I had a new spring in my step as I walked into the kitchen to fix him a really good pizza with a big smile on my face.

Winter was on its way. Both of us decided to stay in the upper world home until winter was over with. He would be a lot stronger by the time spring came to make the trip back to the underworld home, and the doctor would have lots of time to make sure he was doing well before we left.

Over the winter, the children came back and forth and brought the grandchildren with them, and we all had a wonderful time together. Even the family was warming up to the upper world home now, and that was something that I never thought I would ever see.

I got Kyle to go with me to cut down a Christmas tree. We had a great day; I had made some hot cocoa and sandwiches to eat after we cut the tree down.

"How come you've never said anything to me about this Christmas stuff before now?" he asked me as we sat overlooking the land that was just behind the big red barn.

"I guess I just never thought of it before, because we had so many other things to get done all the time. I do really love to fix the home up for Christmas, and now that we're here, I can get the kids and grandkids some things to open at Christmas. They will love it, and then I'll fix up a dinner that you and everyone else will love."

"Well, if it makes you happy, then it's all right with me. What do you need me to do?"

"Now that you ask, there is something that you can do to help me," I said with a smile. "We need to go shopping for Christmas gifts."

Kyle really didn't know what the hell shopping was, but from the look on my face he was pretty sure he wasn't going to like it. He was right. He not only had to ride in the car thing to go to town, but he had to get out of the car and go into the biggest thing he had ever seen. I called it a shopping mall, and inside of it were all kinds of what was called stores, and I went into almost every one of them. By the time, we were done, Kyle needed a nap. He had never seen so many people in his life and never wanted to go back there again if he could help it. But I was so happy, and I got all kinds of things for the kids, and had all of it covered with bright stuff that was called Christmas wrapping paper. On the way home he couldn't stay awake for long. I had a smile on my face as I looked over at Kyle and saw him sleeping soundly as I drove back home. It was going to be a great Christmas, and now there would be a lot more of them.

Kyle had said that the clan could come to the upper world home a few at a time in the winter. Just to get a feel of what it was like to live here for a little while.

"As long as we can stay here and not go into that town, we'll be fine," all of them told Kyle.

"Believe me, I don't like going into the city any more than you," Kyle told them. "Though I have to say that the doctor saved my life and for that I'm grateful."

All the grandchildren loved to run and play in the barn and around the yard. It was a nice place to live, and I would be happy to be able to come back here part time to live out our lives.

"How is everything going at home?" Kyle asked Carson and Toby.

"Everything is fine. The clan is fine now that some of them have been here to see that you're getting stronger all the time and that you'll be coming back home soon," Carson said as he devoured another piece of pizza. As with Kyle, that seemed to be the clan's favorite thing in this world. My apple pie was a close second.

"Boy, I wish we could have this at home," Slade said.

"Well, maybe we can," I told them. "I'll need a few things from here to take back with us, or the children can take some of it home for us. And I'll show everyone how to make a pizza oven when we get there."

"Really?" all of them said with the look of awe on their faces.

"I just love to make my men happy," I said with a laugh.

"Hey, let's not forget us women," Raven said, and all of them started laughing.

All the memories that Kyle and I had been making here with some of the clan, and all of our family would be something that would make good stories for the grandchildren one day. So I was already starting to write a lot of it down before I forgot some of it. I wanted to have these stories for later.

Kyle was excited when the time started to get close to when he could go back to the underworld. I was really missing it too; so both of us were working hard to get everything ready to close up here. So when we left the house would be fine until we could get back here. This place was now a part-time home for all of us when we wanted to come to the upper world. When winter came, Kyle had told me as long as we could walk that far we could stay here and have Christmas with the family. So there would be lots of memories from both worlds.

Now that the clan saw how nice it was to have all of us together with gifts and a really big tree all lit up they wanted to try it back home in the underworld. I was glad I had been the one to be able to share this great holiday with all of them. I was also happy to show them how to make the tree lights out of candles for the underworld tree. With just a little work the women were making candles for lighting, it was just as pretty as the upper world tree was. All the young children loved to watch the whole clan put things under the tree right up to the day of Christmas. Now there were more things to write about there too. I didn't mind all the writing now because I was getting older, and it gave me more time to remember so many things that Kyle and I had done in our lives.

With the warm weather starting, Kyle and I got ready to go back home to the underworld for the summer. The children came to help get the upper world home closed up for the summer before we left. It was a long walk, but Kyle held up fine, and I was fine with the walk too, even though both of us were getting older now. We loved the new smells of the underworld because it didn't have any of the pollution that the upper world had. Everything had a fresh smell to it, and you just knew that the air was clean and sweet as it went into your lungs.

It had been a long time since we had seen the beauty of the long walk and the differences between the two worlds; both had beauty in their own way. As we got close to the underworld city, Kyle had all he could do to keep from running the rest of the way home.

"Betz, don't you love seeing the old city again?" he asked me.

I had to smile at him. He was so happy to be back here, and I now saw that I had missed the place almost as much as he had. It was just as much a part of me as it was a part of him, and as long as I was alive I would always want to come back to this home too. As we walked out into the big courtyard again for the first time in a while, I started to cry. It was so pretty with all the green trees and bushes, and all the pretty flowers were in bloom right now. It was as if everything was saying "welcome home" to both of us. The big waterfall was so appealing that I had all I could do to keep from running into the water right then.

Everyone came out to welcome us both back home, and they had made things to give us as gifts, it was so good to see that they missed us. Our cave was clean and the bedding was also clean and made up for us. Fresh flowers filled the room with a wonderful fragrance.

"Yes, it's good to be home," I said to Kyle as we got ready to get into bed for the night. He had a big day tomorrow as all the clan wanted to have a meeting.

Kyle was asleep before I got in beside him. Even though he was in good shape, he still got tired easily, and I seemed to be pretty tired myself. We slept pretty late the next day before getting up to go to the meeting, and I was going to go see how the children were doing in their classroom these days. After the meetings and visiting the classroom, we both felt like going for a dip in the hot springs. It had been a long time since we both felt like making love. With the hot springs and being back home and Kyle doing as good as he was things between us started getting even hotter than the water was.

In no time, Kyle had me on top of him, and he had his hands on both of my breasts and suckled them while I straddled him. We both let the drive of not being like this for a long time take its wings. Just because we were getting older didn't mean that we couldn't still make hot passionate love; some things really were better with age. Afterward, we both laid back and let the waters heal us both.

"This has been long overdue," Kyle told me as he kissed my full breasts.

"Yes," I answered him.

Then I pulled him back on top of me, and we let the heat do the rest for us. It was sweet and hot, and we both let the need to be together take flight.

Later on, in the main cave with everyone sitting around the big fire pit, Lily said, "I just want to say that all of us are happy to have you both back here with us. And we all think it's a good thing for you to stay there in the upper world home part of the time and here for the summers. We'll be looking forward to coming to the upper world home in the winters to see you and to know that you will be here in the summer."

"You know that I love you like a sister, and I can't think of anyone I want in my life more than you," Lily told me.

"I feel the same way about you," I answered.

"We have had a wonderful life, and a lot of it is because of you. Kyle has been a great clan lord. He might not have been anything like he is today if not for your love and assistance," she told me. "I always knew that he would be a good clan lord when we were back in our old clan, but to see what he has become now is mostly because of you. All of us know that even Kyle himself will tell you that."

"I love him, and always have, and he has made my life wonderful. We have a beautiful family, and this clan is great. So I think I'm the luckiest woman alive, and I also have you as my friend so what else could I ask for?" Lily was about to cry when I told her, "Oh no, you don't. We are not going there, so let's go find the kids and make a really big meal for everyone tonight."

"Back when everyone in Kyle's father's clan didn't want to have me around, you were the only one who made me feel like I meant something. You were so pretty, and I had never seen anyone like you before. You didn't look at me like I was a child because I'm small. It was nice to talk to someone as an equal, and you seemed to really want to hear what I had to say. I'll always love you for that," Lily told me.

Lily gave me a hug, and we went to try out the pizza oven that I had the men build for the clan while we were still in the upper world. I had the men build a stone oven to bake things in. It went over so well that the men even built one in the courtyard as well, that way we could fix meals out there even when there was snow on the ground. It was always nice and warm from the stone oven. It would become a good place to gather around. We would come to love gathering there to have clan meetings. Even in the snow it was nice and warm with the smell of good food cooking; it was welcoming, and the children would play in the snow then build their snowmen close by as the men talked.

There was also a big underground fire pit that we would use to put the large meats in and cook for a day, sometimes longer; it depended on the size of the game that we put into the ground. One thing was sure; it was always well cooked like that.

We would always have a big meal so both clans could get together, and do our trading and just visit. It made it a lot easier to talk out in the open with good food, and good company; what more could you hope for. It was a tradition that would go on long after Kyle and I were gone. Lily had been waiting for Kyle and me to get here before she tried to make the pizza. I had given her the recipe for it, so she was looking forward to making it now.

That night everyone loved the meal, and Lily was a big hit with everyone in the clan. After the cleanup, I was looking forward to going back to the hot springs again; when Kyle could he would meet me there later. It would be the place that we would spend a lot of our time when we were here as we got older. It seemed to help with all the aches and pains that came with old age. I was always so happy to get into the hot water, and just lay back and close my eyes. Sometimes it was hard to stay awake, but that was the one thing that I would never have to worry about. Kyle always had other things in mind when he got into the water with me. Ours was a love that you read about in the best love stories, and yes, it was very real. It never faded with time; it only got stronger as we grew older, and that is the kind of love all of us wish for and only a few of us ever find.

Chapter 25

The lovemaking was tender as we got older too, not so fast and intense with hot need as when we were young. Now it was warmer, soft, and sweet, I thought. The need was still the same, just not as overpowering to us. Life was good for us; the children and grandchildren were a sweet reward for a lifetime of loving someone. Kyle could not have seen that his future would be as great and fulfilling as it was today all those years ago when Kyle and Lily, and I, left his father's cave for the last time to find a life for just the three of us. Now, even he was astonished at what a wonderful life we had today.

As the days started getting shorter, I started getting things ready for the long trip back to the upper world home. I had Lily help me, so we had everything clean and ready for us when winter was over with. I always had mixed feelings about leaving both places; I loved them both. They were as different from each other as night and day, but both just as nice to go to and call home.

The whole clan wanted to come to the upper world this time for a day or two to see how it was in that world. They would leave a few men to take care of the underworld while the rest of the clan was gone. And the next time the other men would go to see the upper world. For some of the clan, it was just not good for them, and they would not come back to the upper world to stay. It was just too different, and they could not sleep there, and that was all right because they felt the need to be in the caves to feel safe. They would die where they loved to live.

For a lot of the clan, the upper world was new and exciting to explore. It was not so much different from their world, other than there was a big house to live in here and not a cave. The ones that came to the upper world liked staying in the big barn. They all loved that they could have ice and water at the touch of your fingers.

No one wanted to get into what I called a car, to go into that big loud thing I called a town. No, they would just like to stay in the barn while they were in the upper world.

Kyle was happy to have the clan see what it was like in the upper world. It would be hard for them at first to hear all the noise; it would take them a little while to get used to it, but in time it wouldn't bother them so much. There were too many of them to take into town at once, so Carson and I would take a few of them at a time to see what it was like in town as well. The barn was the place that we had fixed up with cots and things to make their stay as comfortable as we could. Kyle was pretty sure none of them would like the city part of the world he and I lived in. Kyle was right about that part, and some of them didn't want to come back and that was all right. Kyle and I both knew that might happen.

When the next time came for Kyle and me to leave the underworld for a few months, Kyle told the clan that he wanted to have one more meeting in the main cave before we left for the upper world. Everyone was to come to this meeting, even the women, and that was not like him, but everyone went as they were told to. I had no idea what Kyle was up to yet, but I would stand by him whatever he had to say to the clan.

"I'm glad to see that everyone has come to this meeting as this will be our last meeting with all of you as your clan lord and lady. Betz and I wanted to tell you our wishes as far as who we want to be the next clan lord."

Kyle stood up on a high rock with me beside him and asked the rest of the clan to stand too. As everyone stood there, Kyle took a moment to bow his head in prayer, and then asked Carson to come up to the big rock that was the standing place for the lord of the clan.

As we stood there for a few more minutes, Kyle could feel the rest for the clan's anxiety. He knew that he couldn't wait too long before he let everyone know that Carson would be their new clan lord.

He took Carson's hand and with a clear loud voice said, "I ask that everyone bless their new clan lord." He held up Carson's hand and said, "I give you your new clan lord."

Carson was carried by the men through the main cave. The whole clan started singing and dancing around.

With that, Kyle and I stepped down and went to stand beside the rest of the clan as they all welcomed their new clan lord. Carson had the clan carry his mate to the big rock to stand by his side as the new lady of the clan. There followed a party for the new leadership; everyone was happy to have Carson as the new clan lord and thought he would be the one Kyle would pick. None of them expected it this soon. Kyle was getting older, but he wasn't too old as far as they were concerned. Almost everyone in the clan thought that Kyle still had a lot of years left to lead the clan. But they knew that it was up to him to decide when he wanted to step down so they would accept what he wanted.

"I had no idea that you were going to do this at this time. I guess I thought you would wait a few more years before you stepped down as lord," I said to Kyle as we got ready for bed that night.

"Look, we both know that I'm not as young and sure as hell not in as good health as I used to be. I wanted to be able to do this while I was still able to do it the right way, not by default because of my health." Kyle was a big man with a very big heart, and the thought of not giving the lordship away with style and grace would have killed him.

So I was happy to see him be able to do it the way he wanted to do it with pride like the strong man that he would always be in my eyes. With all their children and grandchildren grown, it wasn't hard for them to come to the upper world to visit Kyle and me, Slade being the youngest. He was always happy to help Carson with anything that had to do with the clan. He wanted to be clan lord someday, and so he worked as hard as he could to get the trust of Carson and the rest of the clan. Even though it would be a long time before Carson would give up as clan lord.

The other clan had no idea about what they were doing in the upper world, and no one was going to tell them anytime soon as they had never wanted to go there anyway. No, this was only about Kyle's clan. What the other clan didn't know would not hurt them, so it would stay within Kyle's clan for life.

Willow and Slade's son Roy was a nice young man, and very close to his grandparents Kyle and me. He was more than happy go to the upper world with us so he could stay the winter sometimes. In time, he would be one of the clan that would stay there in his later life, but not for a long time.

"Well, I can't say I saw this coming," Kyle said to me one day as we were getting ready to go back to the underworld.

"What?" I asked.

"I never thought I would see one of our children want to stay with us in the upper world as much as Slade's son Roy seems to want to."

"Well, why not? I mean it's a nice place to live, and there are a lot of things to see and new things to experience that he would never get to in the underworld. He can have both worlds like we do, and maybe someday he'll want to go back home to stay, and if not, so be it. I know that for you this isn't the best world to live in, but for a lot of us this is the only world we have, and we do pretty well here. Even you like some of it, like water and ice at your fingers whenever you want it. So it's a good place to be and it might be the right place for him and his family someday."

"Maybe, but I still never thought I'd see it," he said.

The clan was a lot bigger now and with the other clan trading with them there was a lot of clans that the upper world had no idea existed.

That was something that was always hard to understand for me. How could we have been on the moon and all the other things we have done in today's world and not even know what was right under our noses? The underworld was just a few days' walk from my house with the big barn, and not that far from a major city in Oregon, and no one knew about the underworld. It made me smile to think of that, but it was also a blessing because if they did, it wouldn't be good because we always destroy what we don't understand. I knew that if the world knew, they would want to take away our lives as we knew them. There would not be the caves and wonderful things that the clans enjoy that made our world so great. They would want to take over everything that made that world wonderful.

It is a world that is like nothing else "in this world." It's not spoiled with cars and buildings. Whatever you do here, you have to work hard with your hands and body as well as your mind to get it done, because there is no one else to call to do it for you. Everything here is done by hand, but in the end that is part of the wonder of this world. You stand back and look at what you've done and say, "Wow, I really did this," and you feel proud. You don't have TV or radios to see how the rest of the world is doing.

If you want to know how someone is doing, then you have to go see them by walking there and sometimes that could take a long time to do. So you're in good shape. It is a hard life sometimes. It's a great life—so simple yet so wonderful.

I have no doubt that this is the way the good Lord meant for us to live. Only taking what we really need from the land to live, and helping one another   make life better for all of us—things that I wish were in the upper world. Their way of life was far too busy to even think about what anybody else is doing, and that is too bad because that's what it's all about: being the best you can be and not hurting anyone else to do that. Instead, you hold out your hand and help anyone who needs it. Somehow people in the upper world, for the most part, have forgotten how to do that and that's sad. But that does not necessarily mean everyone. That's what still gives me hope for both worlds; if the people of the underworld can live and care for others then maybe there is hope for all of us.

Now the rest of the story through Raven's eyes!

Chapter 26

Kyle would live to be a very old man even though he had a bad heart for the last years of his life. Many thought it was because he had kept himself in such good shape over the years, and some of them thought that it was because of the love of one woman who no matter what was always by his side, in everything that he did in his life, to love and help him. But whatever it was, he lived to be almost a hundred years old. He missed his birthday by a week. He died in his sleep in his own city, in the world that he loved so much. There in his own bed, beside the love of his life. That was a great way to go in everyone's eyes.

Yes, he made it back to the underworld one more time before he had to leave it for the last time. His life had been full and happy; he had what most of us could only wish we had but could never find.

Betz and Kyle, as well as the rest of the clan, had put in the clan's cemetery years ago. Betz had picked out a nice place for both of them in the cemetery under a large tree, and she had already put flowers by their plots. Betz wanted the cemetery to feel like a pretty courtyard and with lots of work it did. The clan had worked hard to put up what would be known from that time on as the clan cemetery, and it was a very pretty, peaceful resting place. Long ago, Betz had made a graveyard for all the pets as well that the clan had loved over the years; it was just behind the clan's. It was just as nice to look at as the one for the clan. Betz had put flowers and a few trees there so the dogs would have a place to rest when it was hot out; she took care of the trees for the dogs' resting place. There was a tall arbor that stood in front of the clan cemetery with the words "Rest in Peace All Who Enter."

It had broken Betz's heart to be the one to use the pet cemetery first with her best friend, Tucker. He had a wonderful life, and so she laid him to rest where he spent most of his life within the clan's city. She had put a little rock fence around it over the years and put a cross on his grave that said "Tucker, Rest in Peace, My Big Boy."

Betz was over one hundred and ten years old when she died. She was put to rest beside Kyle in the world that she had grown to love as much as he did. She wanted to be where she was in life, and that was beside the man she had loved her whole life.

Carson died of a fall that he took on one of the hunting trips that the clan still makes to this day, as part of their way of life in the underworld. He had broken his neck in the fall and died before anyone could even get to him. He was eighty-six years old and was also laid to rest by his parents.

Slade was now the lord of the clan and was getting old, but still going strong, like his father and brother before him. He is a strong and just leader who is loved by his clan.

Lily passed away a few years after Betz did; she always said that without her best friend she wouldn't last very long, and she was right. She was in her own bed with her family nearby when she took her last breath.

Toby went soon after her. He never got over losing her and even though he was a father as well as a grandfather he just didn't know how to go on without the only true love of his life. He died of a heart attack while walking to the cemetery to put flowers on Lily's grave. His family found him where he fell and died not far from her grave with the flowers still in his hand. He was laid to rest beside his Lily.

Sonny is still here, and so are most of the children other than Roy. He wanted to live in the upper world so when Kyle and Betz died, they left him the home that was the start of everything.

I'm really the only one left to write about my mother and father, as well as the rest of the clan. I try to keep up with all the things that my parents had built so long ago, and I try to write everything down just like my mother did for years with as much love and respect as they would have wanted me to give to this world.

I am so lucky to be able to live here in this world of wonder, and I don't take anything for granted. I know that it could all end tomorrow if someone were to find us. It would never be the same as it has been all these years, and that's why we are so careful not let anyone else know of our world here. Would you give this up, if you had such a wonderful place to live? No, I don't think so. You would want what we want: to live out our lives in this enchanted place, to keep it safe for the next generations. And that's the only thing that we are trying to do.

After I'm gone, I'm sure the children and then the grandchildren will keep writing about this enchanted place for as long as our way of life goes on.

"Raven, what are you doing? What's taking you so long?" Sonny asked.

"I'll be there in a minute," I told him as I put the pen and paper away until the next time.

Raven went out into the city's courtyard to help with the annual breaking ground for spring's new garden, something that her mother had started a long time ago and was still going strong every year. It was still one of her favorite things to do every year. I have lots of fond memories with my mother working in this same garden as I grew up playing in it, and now I have lots of fun memories with my children as well. That is part of the wonder of living here. The simple things in life like working in a garden with the ones you love.

Betz would love knowing that it still went on, after all these years. The clan's children were all still in the clan's school being taught just as she had started all those years ago. Yes, she would love to know that some things were still going on as if she were still here to help with everything. And who knows, maybe she is watching over all of us as we work in her garden. After all, that was what she loved to do for years. Oh, and the pizza oven is still just the same, and everyone still loves to have the whole clan around it, both in the winter, as well as the summer, to eat and do all the same things that Betz and Kyle had started all those years ago.

The courtyard was just as pretty as when Betz and Lily had put all that work into it for years. If anything, it was even lovelier now. There were more trees and so many flowers now of every kind. The waterfall is still the same and still one of the favorite places for the clan to go swimming and to stand under to clean. Yes, even though Tucker is gone, he still has a full line of his puppies, and they all had puppies down through the years. So the clan still had lots of pets for the children to play with and to this day not one of the clan would ever think of eating a dog again. Betz had made a very good point to the clan, and that was that dogs truly are man's best friend.

The clan men are still doing all the things that had meant so much to Kyle, to help keep the clan safe and happy in their cave city. So to this day they still have someone stand guard by the big rock on the other side of the cave that leads to their city. He would be proud of all of them for that because we don't take for granted that this place will stay safe on its own. We do as we always have done, and that is to take care of this world that we all love.

The clan men still train with Kyle's tools, and they always use them on all the hunts. One thing that still happens that he would be surprised about is that they all still go to the upper world every year to see Roy and his family. It is something everyone looks forward to doing to this day. They love just to get together and talk about the old times when Kyle and Betz were still with us, and, of course, have one very big pizza just like mom used to make for us.

The upper world home is pretty much the same as when Kyle and Betz had lived there, except Roy has built more bedrooms. Everyone can stay inside when they come to visit, and he still has the big barn, and it's pretty much the same, and all his grandfather's tools are still hanging where he left them. Every spring, Roy goes out there to give them all a good cleaning like he watched his grandfather do for years.

I asked him once why he still did that.

He just gave me one of his little smiles as he asked me, "Well, one day do you want to be the one to tell Kyle that we didn't take care of his tools for him when you get to see him again?"

With a laugh, I said, "Here, let me help you with those."

The upper world is great with all the big buildings and cars to get around in, but not for all us. We'll stay in our hidden world where there is still wonderful places to see that no one else has seen yet. At night, you can see a sky so full of stars that it feels like you can reach up and grab some of them. It is a peaceful place to live and raise a family. Mom knew this to be true as she loved both worlds, but when it came to her last days this is where she wanted to be.

There are no loud sounds to wake you up at night, just the sound of the world that I believe we were meant to have. With Just the wind, crickets, and the sound of running water to lull you to sleep every night. For me, that's the very best thing to make you sleep like a baby. Oh, I also like having the upper world to go to, and it is nice to see all that it has to offer, but it is not home to me, not like this is.

Raven knew that her days of going to the upper world were coming to an end though. She knew that she was getting too old to keep going for much longer now. That was all right too. Because like her mother before her, she would go for as long as she could, and then she would be laid to rest where the rest of her family was: in the lost city of her clan.

When it was their time, the rest of the clan would follow her and her family to the same place of rest as it had always been. In a world that no one could understand, but a world where everyone in the clan wanted to be. When it was time to go to their final resting place—that place was here, in the underworld of the clan of Kyle and Betz Larson.

It is a world that has given so much to everyone who came here and will take care of all those who will follow; the only price you have to pay is to take care of it.

That is all. Just keep it a secret from the rest of the world and also lend a helping hand to keep this lost city working, and you can live a life unlike anyone could ever dream of having, in all the big busy cities of the world, with too many people and everyone in a big hurry to get to nowhere.

Well, you can have that. But for me and my family, we'll stay here in this world with peace and quiet and just so much to love, that there are no words to describe it and give it justice.

Roy had a large family of his own now with three girls and four boys. Every one of them were happy to know that they had the lost city to go to and spend time with the clan and be able to come back to the upper world to live when they wanted to. They have the best of both worlds you could say. No one could blame them for wanting to hide it from a world that only wants to destroy things that it cannot understand.

So they keep it from everyone else. It is not something that any one of them ever wants to take a chance of losing. So it will stay safe for as long as any one of them are still alive. Then who could say what would happen?

Maybe someday, someone might find it by accident again. As was the case all those years ago when a plane found its way to a land that was unknown for years. Where one man made his way into a clan and helped them learn to speak English. Maybe someone will find this world as was all those years ago and just want to live with what the land has to give and be happy with this wonderful way of life here. Maybe the upper world will someday learn to live with what they are given, the way that it was meant to be and not destroy things that they don't understand. That is yet to be seen. Only time will be able to tell if that will ever happen.

For now the lost world and a city that has been forgotten by a world of people who don't remember how to enjoy life as it was meant to be. It has nothing to do with money or power. The best things in life are here, in this lost world. It's the little things we've forgotten to enjoy. Simple things like taking a dip in the hot springs with someone you love and only taking things from the land that we really need to take to live. Making a wonderful life from very little and feeling happy when the day is over because you had a good day. Just getting enough food to feed you and your people for a few months and going to bed at night and sleeping so peacefully. Because you know that you have done the best that you could do to help everyone have a good life here.

It is not for everyone, but for Kyle and Betz and their clan, this is the only way to live. So hopefully it will stay that way for years to come. Just a lost city in a lost land that no one knows is here . . . but it is.

Summary

Betz is a beautiful young girl with long, dark hair and cat-green eyes that are full of pain and is starting over in the pristine countryside of Southern Oregon. As she tries to get over a love gone wrong, her only companion is her little schnauzer dog, Tucker.

Little does she know her life is about to be flipped upside down when she is taken from a modern life and thrown into a yesterday world that no one even knows exist.

Will Betz be able to survive? Will she be able to make two entirely different worlds coexist? Betz will soon find herself in a cave with people who live like the cavemen did thousands of years ago. She'll have to adapt or die.

But even in this strange place, she will find that the only love she'll ever want does exist. However, it could mean the end of her life if she is to win the heart of the clan lord's son, Kyle.

Go on this epic journey with Betz and see if she'll survive or if fate will take everything away from her again.

CPSIA information can be obtained
at www.ICGtesting.com
Printed in the USA
BVHW030211020721
611046BV00005B/54

9 781503 591998